# Matching Mr. Montfort



## Brooke J Losee

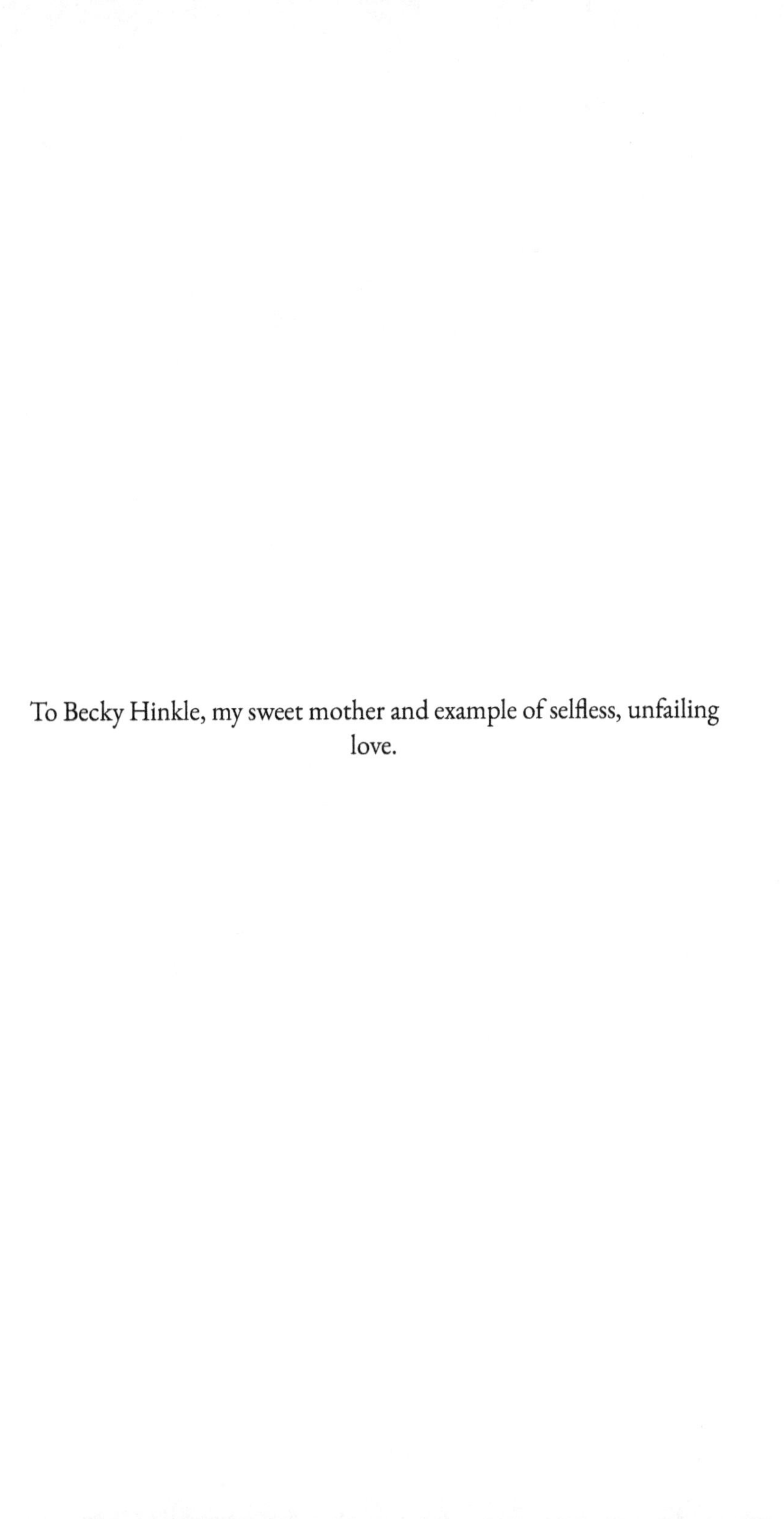

To Becky Hinkle, my sweet mother and example of selfless, unfailing love.

# *Chapter One*

## *England, 1817*

## GRACE

KENWICK CASTLE HAD SEEN its share of romance since the first Viscount Paxton bought the estate six generations ago, but at present, the stone walls were full of empty-headed nincompoops without a single romantic bone in their bodies.

I swept a strand of my brown hair out of my face and tucked my feet beneath me on a high-back chair in the grand drawing room, a book in hand, as I had most afternoons. My cousin and guardian, Rowe Apsley, had brought me here until the time came to make our journey to London for my first Season. The spot was familiar to me given I had spent a great deal of time at Kenwick with my cousins throughout my youth. The castle was like a second home, warm and welcoming.

Or, at least, it was on the rare occasion when my cousins were not making nuisances of themselves.

"Has he kissed her yet?" asked Rus, pulling my attention away from the page. He leaned forward out of his relaxed position on the settee next to me, a shock of auburn hair falling over his forehead, and rested his elbows on his knees. A wide smirk played over his lips and mischief danced in his green eyes. "You are so stoic when you read, Grace. I cannot make out anything that happens by watching you. It is most inconvenient."

"Inconvenient?"

"Yes. I am not entertained enough when your expression never changes."

"You could try reading it yourself. That might prove more entertaining."

Rus huffed a laugh. "A romance? Not likely."

I closed my novel with a snap and placed it on the table next to the chair, my irritation growing like the flames in the hearth as Rowe added another log for them to feast upon. My cousins were generally likable, but after a fortnight of enduring their taunts, my patience was at an end. "I am not your source of entertainment. Not now, and not when we go to London."

"Ah, but I will have plenty to occupy me in London. Here...well, there is so little to be had."

"And do tell me how you intend to spend the Season," I said. "Flirting with every debutant you see or avoiding them altogether?"

Russell, the oldest of the Apsley children at eight and twenty—beating his twin by mere minutes—laughed, relaxing into the settee with a smug grin, one leg crossed over the other. He enjoyed getting a rise out of me. It was all in good fun, and perhaps I would have found his teasing enjoyable were my nerves not already on end. But as it stood, I had lost too much sleep worrying about my future and was in no mood for humor.

"A bit of both, I'd wager," Rus answered, tugging at his cravat until it came loose completely. He draped the cloth over his knee. "And can you blame me? I'm the heir to a fortune and a title."

"An heir whose responsibility it is to marry and produce another heir," I quipped. "You might spend less time in meaningless flirtation and more of it looking for a companion willing to tolerate you."

Rus looked heavenward, his expression pinched in mock contemplation. "What a revelation! Rowe, did you hear your ward? She has given me an epiphany. I must set aside my rogue-ish ways and pursue a love match at once."

Rowe, who had resumed his seat in a chair opposite me, merely hummed in acknowledgment of his twin brother's theatrics, his eyes never wavering from the pages of his book. My guardian, while certainly less teasing and quieter than Rus, was no more inclined toward romance. A shame, really. They were both handsome gentlemen of means and in a position to provide for families of their own.

Not that I would ever openly pay Rus such a compliment. He needed no boost to his ego.

Rus heaved a dramatic sigh. "You must understand, cousin, we men do not run off to London intending to attach ourselves to the first woman who catches our fancy. It is different for us. We need not rush to make a match." He nodded toward where my book was resting on the table. "And we do not wear whimsical ideas of love and happiness on our sleeves like a goosecap."

"Just because I read romance novels does not mean I am a goosecap." I settled into my chair, folding my arms. I would not deny I enjoyed reading about heroes sweeping a woman into a dance or accompanying her on an adventure, but that did not make me nonsensical. There was nothing wrong with dreaming of something I would never experience. "I have no intention of seeking a match for myself this Season if you must know."

Or perhaps any Season. It was not as though I didn't wish for the type of romance I found so often within the pages of my books, but I had tossed the idea away before it could blossom...and wither. My odds of success were too low for such hopeful anticipation.

My statement drew Rowe's attention. His green eyes met mine, and he leaned forward abruptly, running a hand through his auburn hair. "What do you mean you've no intention of seeking a match?"

I shrugged. "Just that. I will enjoy the Season."

Rus, who seemed both surprised and pleased by this revelation, nodded. "I approve. Every woman should enjoy her first Season instead of chasing after some poor fellow and luring him into marriage shackles."

"Then it is good I am her guardian and not you," Rowe snapped. "To encourage such a thing is foolish. The sooner she has the protection of a husband, the better."

"And you are not enough protection for her until then?" One of Rus's brows lifted in challenge. The two of them were often like this: Rus seeking ways to press Rowe into an argument for the sake of an argument. The man was a tease, and no one was exempt. The two of them were opposites in every way but appearance. It was a blessed relief their personalities were so different, else no one would ever tell them apart.

"That is not what I meant, and you know it," said Rowe. "I promised her father I would see to his daughters' happiness, and I intend to do so."

He had succeeded where my sister, Amelia, was concerned. She'd married the Earl of Emerson after attending a house party last year and was currently enjoying a long honeymoon with him somewhere in York. Were I not so aware of how much Rowe cared about us, I might wonder if it was his goal to be rid of his wards as quickly as possible. But he was too kind and, frankly, too transparent for that. The man likely couldn't lie to save his own skin. He wanted to do right by my father—and by default, Amelia and me—plain and simple. It was a blessing, but that he would put off his affairs to see to mine also left me with a great deal of guilt.

And motivation.

"What makes you think Grace would not be happy on her own?" asked Rus. "Why must she marry?"

Rowe groaned. "I want what is best for her, and whether you care to admit it or not, it is in everyone's interest to marry. Both women *and* men. Heaven knows you need someone to keep you out of trouble."

"I do not see you rushing to the altar," Rus muttered.

"And I don't see me getting into trouble on a regular basis," Rowe countered. "I rest my case."

"Give it time. It shall happen. You will cause the most scandal of all of us simply out of irony."

"It hardly matters either way," I said, growing tired of their exchange. The two of them acted as if I did not sit here in front of them. "I will enjoy the Season and the company of any suitors that might come my way, though I am doubtful there will be any."

"What a silly thing to say."

The three of us turned toward the entry of the drawing room where Annette stood in a gown of deep green that set off her red hair to perfection. She was the eldest of the two Apsley daughters and the same age as me at twenty. Like her twin brothers, though, we could not be more different. Annette was as outspoken and untamable as her fiery hair.

Annette crossed the room and claimed a seat next to me. "You shall have plenty of suitors, Grace."

"I daresay you will distract them all." I leaned closer to her in a conspiratorial whisper. "And I won't care a whit if you do."

Annette glared back at me. "I do not want all the attention. Or any, for that matter."

Another incredulous groan rumbled from Rowe. "The two of you are a bad influence on one another. Neither wanting suitors? Have you both gone mad?"

"On the contrary," said Rus. "They are both more intelligent than I have previously given them credit."

Annette turned her glare on her brother. "How kind of you. I confess my lack of faith in your intelligence remains unchanged."

Rus pressed a hand to his heart, his face pinched in a façade of pain. "You wound me, dear sister, but pray tell, what do you want from the Season if not a husband?"

"Nothing," Annette responded. "I've no desire for a Season at all. I would prefer to be here, and you know my dowry is more than enough to sustain me for the rest of my life. Why should I give up any independence to be ordered about by a man who cares only for himself? But here I am, packing for London at Father's bequest."

"Ah, yes, lest we not forget *the agreement.*"

"Agreement?" My gaze shifted from Rus to Annette, who pinned her brother with a look sharper than any blade. "What does he speak of?"

"Nothing of consequence," said Annette, swatting away my question.

We had never been particularly close given my preference for spending time in the library over riding horses astride at breakneck speeds across the estate, but we should be allies, she and I. We were both entering society, and with Mother remaining at our country home to deal with her grief and Amelia off with her new husband, I hadn't anyone to confide in. I had hoped Annette would be willing to fill the role, but already, she kept things from me.

"Oh, it is *something,*" said Rus, his mischievous grin still in place. "Annette has promised Father she will entertain every suitor that comes her way with genuine enthusiasm. In short, she has agreed to give any man a chance to win her hand."

Well, that did not sound like someone who had no desire for the attention of suitors. My brows lifted in question, and Annette rolled her eyes. "It is a small price to pay. If I hold up my end of the deal and remain unwed through the end of the year, Father will not force me to attend another Season. He will give me access to my funds, too."

Ah. That made more sense. Annette was stubborn enough to play such a game...and win. With a dowry as significant as hers, she could afford it. I, on the other hand, would need a way to provide for myself as I advanced into spinsterhood. I refused to be a burden to Rowe any longer than necessary. He deserved to have a family of his own but would not seek a match for himself until his obligations to my father had been fulfilled. I had no desire to stand in the way of his future happiness, which meant I needed my own income.

I was not against marriage for myself. Truly, I wasn't. But my chances of finding a match were far lower than Annette's, and I would settle for nothing less than love. I could not understand my cousin's desire to throw the opportunity away as she intended to do. Had I possessed her beauty and two legs that worked to full potential, I would have welcomed the attention she was bound to experience, especially as the daughter of a viscount.

But I was not her, and a weak leg that left me broken would prohibit me in more ways than one. No, I was better off putting any hope of love to rest here and now.

"What of you, Grace?" Rus asked. "If you are not looking forward to marriage, then what about London appeals to you most?"

"I never said marriage did not appeal to me," I corrected. "Simply that I will not seek it for myself."

Rus's eyes narrowed. "Am I to understand you intend to seek it for someone else?"

I shrugged, all too aware Rowe was still studying me, and a hardy laugh escaped Rus. "That is precisely it! You wish to play matchmaker this Season."

I wouldn't deny it. I had heard of matchmakers finding success during the Season, and not just in assisting their clients. If I could prove myself good at pairing people off, I might find it financially rewarding, too. My goal this Season was to establish a name for myself. Help a few desperate souls find their love match. With any luck, word of my success would spread and clients would come to me. I had confidence in my abilities; I merely needed to prove them to everyone else.

I had helped my sister and Lord Emerson along, after all, and I was no stranger to romance novels. Did that not make me expertly qualified?

"Well," said Rus, "I commend your ambition, so long as you do not attempt to match me with anyone."

No soul deserved that.

"I would prefer not to have failure stain my record," I countered.

Rus laughed, unoffended by my terse comment, which proved my point. He was not ready to settle down, but someday, he would take marriage more seriously. Maybe then I could fathom pairing some poor woman with him. Surely I could find a match even for Rus?

Until then, I would create a list of successes. I would prove myself and help others find love. After all, if I could not have romance for myself, finding it for others was the next best thing.

# Chapter Two

## PHILLIP

THE VIEW OUTSIDE THE carriage window held my attention hostage as if the world beyond were a stage upon which a story I had never heard continued to unfold. My nose nearly pressed against the glass as I struggled to take it all in, my curiosity and excitement unleashed from their childhood slumber. I had never been to London.

Well, I had never been anywhere, really. Perhaps that was why I had found the long journey from my uncle's country estate in Berkshire so enjoyable. Not a minute lapsed when I did not see something new, whether it was the open landscape or the bustle of people in the many towns and villages we passed through. All of it drew my focus. I studied as much as I could, my mind in a constant state of analysis, committing every detail I could to memory.

A sharp pain ricocheted through my leg just above my knee, stealing my breath and making my muscles taut. I gritted my teeth and pulled away from the window. Uncle, who sat to my left, pierced me with a deep scowl as he tucked his pocket watch and the long, golden chain attached to it back into his coat. "Come away from the window and listen to me, boy."

I swallowed, pressing my hand against my stinging skin. Victor Perry often used his pocket watch to gain my attention, never mind that I had asked to sit on his left side to avoid the problem of not hearing him. Sometimes I wondered if he thought he could whip the malady out of me or if he believed my deficiencies were a matter of choice.

Either way, the chain of the pocket watch certainly worked to get what he wanted—my undivided attention.

"I have expectations," he began, sweeping a gloved hand through his dark hair. Gray peppered it now, somehow making him more intimidating than in my youth. "I did not bring you to Town to *play*."

I might have scoffed at the ridiculous implication were I not certain doing so would result in another whack from the pocket watch. "Yes, Uncle."

"And I expect you to act properly. Sensibly. You will not embarrass me."

"Yes, Uncle," I repeated, though I highly doubted I would succeed in that endeavor. Uncle was easily embarrassed. It was the reason he had kept me from Town all these years. Despite being his heir, I had rarely been introduced to any of his associates and accompanied him to parties or the like. He did not trust me not to humiliate him.

"Good." The man brushed the dust off his fine-tailored coat, his crooked nose—the result of an altercation with my father years ago—wrinkled in disdain. "As you might have guessed, I have something else for you to accomplish this Season."

"I must make a good impression on your associates," I said before he could continue. "It is important I establish a relationship of trust and they believe I can step into your shoes."

Shoes, in truth, I had no desire to wear. I had little choice in the matter, though. With nothing to my name, the only way to care for my mother was to do as Uncle asked. We needed this inheritance and the security it would provide.

"Do not put words in my mouth, boy," Uncle replied sternly. "Of course, that is all a given. What else have I raised you for but to continue my legacy?" He harrumphed and looked away from me. "Though I am hardly convinced you deserve it. What with the state your father left the two of you in. Poor intellect runs in the blood. Fortunate I came out so well. Hopefully, you fare better than him."

My jaw clenched.

Uncle had never hidden his animosity toward my father, his half-brother. I could barely remember the man, but even so, Mother had provided enough stories that I knew better than to believe Uncle's opinions or take them as my own.

One thing I could not argue against, however, was Father's poor decision-making when it came to our family estate, the one sitting in near-collapse at present. The walls, or what remained of them, and a small lot of land were all Mother and I had been willed after his death.

"What else would you have me accomplish?" I asked. The list was long enough now; I couldn't think what he could possibly add.

Uncle settled back into his seat and studied me for a moment. "You will find a wife by the end of the Season."

"What?" I sputtered. "What for?"

At this, Uncle chuckled slightly, though the humor dancing in his dark brown eyes was likely linked to his belief in my unintelligence rather than my shock. "What are wives for? Surely even you know what purpose they serve."

"Allow me to be more specific, then," I said, barely keeping the frustration from my tone. "Why do I need to find a wife so soon?"

"Simple. To ensure all I have built is not lost and further our connections."

An heir then. The subject had been strictly forbidden my entire life, a sore spot Uncle kept hidden. He'd married twice now for the precise purpose of siring a son. Both times, he had failed. His first marriage had ended without a child. The second had given him my cousin, Sabrina. Despite the difficulty of conceiving any offspring, he showed her no more love than he did me. We were both pawns, she and I. Nothing more.

"I want to make sure my legacy continues properly. Any children you have will be raised the way I see fit. I cannot ensure that if you wait to have them." Uncle withdrew a piece of folded foolscap from his pocket and shoved it toward me.

I opened it with furrowed brows and then glanced at him. "What is this?"

"I thought it quite obviously a list. Qualifications for your future bride."

Qualifications? My eyes roamed over the page. Titled and well-connected were listed at the very top. Of course, Uncle would believe those most important. But the qualifications did not stop there, continuing to include everything from beauty to sophistication, grace, and musical talent. And everything in between.

"I am not certain such a woman exists," I muttered. Though, truthfully, I wouldn't rightly know. I did not spend enough time among Society to have observed the talents of women. Sabrina was certainly well-trained as a lady. I had watched Uncle drill his expectations into her for years. But even she did not possess all of these qualities.

"No woman is so perfect," Uncle grumbled. "The list is a guideline. You will aim to find one who has as many as possible. Consider it a challenge." He held up his finger. "With the exception of titled or well-connected. Those are non-negotiable. I shall accept one, but both would be preferable. Do you understand?"

I nodded, a swirl of anxiety knotting my stomach. I did not know the first thing about courtship. Pleasing Uncle might prove difficult, and I could not afford to ignite the man's ire. He could disinherit me, and then I would be truly destitute. Fortunately, Sabrina and Mother were to join us in London in a week. At least I could gain insight from them this Season. Surely they could give me proper advice on wooing a woman?

And until they arrived, I would find the perfect candidate to satisfy Uncle's expectations.

LADY MILLICENT FARNSBE HAD not spared me so much as one glance tonight, which meant being seated next to her at the dinner table, given her title, had been a scheme orchestrated by Uncle. He likely believed the woman would meet several qualifications on the list he'd given me four days ago. She certainly held a title and connections being the daughter of an earl.

But Uncle's plan had one major flaw: Lady Millicent had been seated on my left side.

Not only that, but her voice carried a tone my ear simply could not decipher. Uncle's tone was similar. Unless I faced him directly, thus allowing me to watch his lips move, or he was positioned on my right side, his words were a mottled murmur and near indistinguishable. I hadn't any idea why some people were easier for me to understand, but it had been so my entire life and was something I had grown accustomed to. The solution was a simple one: always stand on the left side of those with whom I converse.

Except, when seated at a dinner party, I had little say in the matter. I would have a person on either side of me, no matter what.

"Phillip!" a voice hissed.

I turned sharply to my right, leaning forward slightly to see around Mrs. Wethers, the elderly spinster who was my actual dinner companion and who had not ceased talking since we sat down, to find Uncle glaring at me from farther down the table. At least at this distance, he could not whack me. His outburst caught the attention of two women opposite us, but they quickly lost interest when Uncle remained silent.

Once assured no one paid him any heed, he mouthed the words *pay attention to her*.

Of course, by *her*, he meant the earl's daughter and not the woman rambling on about every animal she had seen at the menagerie. Never mind that it was considered rude to pull Lady Millicent's attention from her companion or that I would prefer to discuss monkeys and the like rather than attempt to impress someone so intimidating.

I turned toward Lady Millicent with a deep breath, an apologetic smile already in place. "Forgive me, my lady. Did you say something?"

The woman faced me and glared. No, glared was not adequate for the fierce expression she wore. She had not said anything to me, which I knew, and I had a feeling the earl's daughter was not accustomed to being interrupted.

Regardless, I could not explain the situation to her, which meant I needed a different excuse to placate her pride. "I hope you will forgive me. This is my first trip to London, and I am afraid it has left my mind somewhat overwhelmed. To be in such gracious company as you and your father...well, it leaves me befuddled and inattentive."

Unfortunately, the explanation, while humble and partially true, did not erase her scowl. "One might question your place, Mr. Montfert, if you are so incapable of attentiveness or knowing which person at dinner is your companion. Town is not for everyone, and neither is the gracious company of the...ideal portion of society."

"Ideal portion? Perhaps so. How does one decide where to draw those lines? We are all people, no different than a pile of steamed peas." I nodded to the pile of green orbs on my plate. "They all look the same to me."

Her frown deepened. "I should say one starts by casting those aside who would compare people to peas. But if you insist on such a ridiculous metaphor, not all peas are the same. Some get smashed and broken, a blemish on Society. Those are the first to go."

I scooped up a spoonful and held it out in front of me. "And if none appear smashed or broken?"

She smiled, an evil sort of look hidden behind a set of perfectly straight teeth. "I suppose noting imperfections beyond the surface is a skill some of us are taught from birth."

"You must be right." I forced my smile to remain in place. Skill was not the word I would use for the self-importance she displayed, but what did I know? Either way, there were some imperfections even she could not see.

"Oh! Mr. Monfert, I must tell you of the strangest creature I saw. It had such unusual coloring—black, grey, and white. His eyes, though, looked as though he wore a mask like a bandit. Oddest little thing. Came right to the glass and startled me so!" Mrs. Wether's threw out her hand in exaggeration to fully explain the situation and bumped mine.

The one holding a spoonful of peas.

The green orbs flew from my utensil. My eyes tracked them through the air and widened when they bounced off Lady Millicent's neck and fell into...well, my eyes snapped away then.

Lady Millicent stood with a startled squeal. She fanned her bodice animatedly and seemed to march in place, screaming all the while as if an animal had been unleashed beneath her garments. I could hardly blame her. If something had rolled down my chest so unexpectedly, I might have done the same. The table erupted with chatter, and even Mrs. Wethers ceased talking until Lady Millicent calmed enough to allow her mother to escort her from the room to deal with the matter. Her glare once again rested on me the moment she returned, no doubt having discovered peas in her dress and not some ravaging beast, and my face heated.

Neither of us spoke another word to one another. An apology, I assumed, would not be accepted or wanted.

The remainder of the evening dragged on, and fortunately, I was not required to make much conversation over port, nor after with our early departure. Uncle and I expressed our gratitude for the invitation to the hostess and left the Earl of Branton's townhome, stepping into the cool air.

I knew better than to trust Uncle's silence as a representation of an evening well-spent. He would say nothing until we were tucked away in his carriage, away from prying ears. This was my third dinner party since we had arrived in London, and I had made no more headway tonight than I had at any of the others. In fact, I might claim to have lost more favor than I had won.

Uncle tapped his cane against the roof of the carriage, and the conveyance lurched forward. He glared at me from the opposite seat for a long minute, waves of shadows and light alternating over his deep scowl as we passed street lamps.

"Could you not engage the earl's daughter through a single course without making a spectacle?" he growled. "I have never seen a lady more angry over dinner, and I assume you were the cause of her distress."

There was no sense denying it. "Yes. Forgive me, Uncle."

"Forgive you? No, one mistake given your inexperience is somewhat understandable, but you've done nothing but embarrass me the entire week. I tire of it. I will not have my heir, broken though he may be, leaving black marks on all I have striven to build. Do you have any idea of the work it has required?"

I did, for Uncle had bemoaned his struggles repeatedly for years. He had risen from the lowly son of a miller to a wealthy gentleman of means. It had taken more than a decade and proper connections through two advantageous marriages to reach his current position.

My gaze dropped to my hands. One thing I could not deny was Uncle's determination. His ambition. He had brought himself out of poverty, a feat so few ever accomplished. He had even extended his success to include his half-brother a long time ago. That had been the beginning of the end of their relationship.

"I will do better," I said softly. "I know how I have failed these past few days. Time will help me to adjust. Experience will give way to confidence. I—"

The carriage jolted to a stop. I peered out the window, recognizing the affluent thoroughfare of St. James Street, and my brows knit with confusion. "This is not our townhouse."

Uncle scoffed. "How very astute of you, Phillip."

I waited patiently for him to continue, but my silence only seemed to fan his ire.

"White's," Uncle stated, one pudgy finger pointed out the window to where night darkened the Palladian façade of one of London's finest gentlemen's clubs. "It took some time, but I've secured your membership."

"M-my membership?"

"Do not be daft, Phillip. How do you expect to be accepted by Society without making a show at the proper venues? Anyone of consequence is a member of White's or Brook's." He straightened his coat. "On rare occasions, even both."

"But I've no political preference." A lie, but I happened to know my ideals did not always align with Uncle's. Voicing those differences was not worth the consequences, however. I had no political ambitions and little desire to converse with those who did.

Uncle leaned forward, gripping his cane with both hands, his eyes stern. "Your preferences do not matter. At present, the men who I wish to establish business connections with are Tories. Therefore, so are you."

The notion did not sit well with me, but I should not have been surprised by his demands. Everything was a game to Uncle—each move a crucial piece to his achieving his ultimate goal. His political loyalty swayed depending on whose good graces he needed to gain.

"Then I am a Tory," I said, dejection lacing my tone.

Uncle leaned back into the seat, satisfied with my acceptance. "Good, because tonight, I expect you to make some progress. If you cannot earn a woman's attention, perhaps you will fare better finding allies at the club."

He gestured to the door, and my jaw dropped. "You mean...*now*?"

"Now, Phillip. And do not come home until you've found some success."

"I'm to go on my own?" My throat constricted, and I swallowed hard. "But I hardly know anyone in London. How am I to—"

"Out, Phillip. Prove to me you are not worthless and I did not make a mistake in naming you my heir." One of his graying brows rose. "It is not too late for me to change my will."

A threat I had heard countless times before, though that made it no less daunting. There was nothing empty about it. If I did not come up to scratch, he would disinherit me without remorse.

I climbed clumsily out of the carriage, my heart pounding. I had never cared for socializing, but to do so by walking into a place I'd never been and surrounding myself with people I had never met...I might lose all six courses I'd consumed at dinner.

"And do not forget," he said in his cutting tone, "no one is to know about your *problem*."

The carriage door slammed closed, and without so much as another glance from Uncle, it rolled forward, leaving me alone on the cobblestone street. Leaving me and my *problem* to face London's elites on my own.

# Chapter Three

## PHILLIP

Beyond attending church services and visiting town when the need arose, I had never left Eldercrest Hall, Uncle's country estate, without him. He had insisted on accompanying me everywhere and had gone as far as hiring private tutors rather than sending me to Eton. When the time came for me to further my education at university, Uncle declared he could teach me everything I needed to know to take over the estate.

And I had not argued against him.

What was the point when I knew he would never heed my pleas? In any case, I was never certain I wished to attend school with my peers. My hearing difficulties often left me self-conscious, and most of the time, I preferred living the life of a recluse. It was easier, and I always had my mother to keep me company.

But I had no one next to me tonight as I stepped through the doors of White's. It was not lost on me that even Uncle's company, which I often resented, would have been preferred over the vulnerability I felt entering such an unfamiliar domain. I was a foreigner in a new land, and I had no notion whether the residents would prove friendly or hostile.

The interior of White's was lavishly decorated with all manner of fine furniture and wall hangings. From the spacious entry hall, I entered the larger morning room on my left, where soft chatter echoed from within. My stomach balled into a knot at the sight of half a dozen strangers, all occupying seats in one corner or another.

Near the large bow window, a man in a fine-tailored waistcoat sat at a long oak table in deep discussion with two other men, while the chairs nearer the hearth were taken up with individuals devouring the morning paper or books.

I decided upon an empty chair by one of the other windows where I could work up my courage for a moment before attempting to converse. It did me little good, as my choice for solitude seemed to draw the attention of everyone in the room. Their curious gazes settled on me, doing nothing to ease my nerves.

How was I to manage this? I knew no one here, and I had never been particularly well-versed in starting up conversations with non-acquaintances. Or even acquaintances, for that matter.

My body went stiff when a man with auburn hair sitting near the hearth put down his paper, stood, and crossed the room toward me. He took the vacant seat to my right, slumping into it with a heavy sigh.

Then he stared right at me.

I watched his unwavering gaze from the corner of my eye, uncertain how to proceed. How to end the awkwardness. Why had he sat next to me? Did he expect me to begin the conversation? Had rumor of my throwing peas down the daughter of an earl's dress already circulated among the elites?

I might be sick.

"You are new here," he stated.

With a quiet inhale, I faced him and nodded. "Yes. I am."

The man pursed his lips, his gaze trailing up and down my person. Was he judging me? Could he see my lack of experience merely by observation? It would not surprise me if he could. I could not tell peas apart, but apparently, it was a learned skill.

Seeming satisfied with his study, he offered me his hand. "Russell Apsley. A pleasure to meet you...?"

"Phillip Montfert." I took his hand.

"Montfert? I am unfamiliar with the name. From where do you hail?"

"Berkshire. My father was a landowner there, but I've lived with my uncle for nearly two decades. You may perhaps know him since he frequents London. A Victor Perry?"

"Ah," the man said. "Yes, I am acquainted with your uncle. I take it you are the chap meant to inherit?" He continued when my face morphed with surprise. "He has mentioned you in conversation. Mr. Perry is always attempting to convince my father to invest, you see."

"Shall I offer my apologies?" I asked before thinking better of it.

Mr. Apsley laughed heartily. "Not at all. Unless you intend to serenade me tonight with a lengthy speech about some new venture?"

No, but it was not far from the truth. Make friends, Uncle had said. He wanted me to be on good terms with members of the *ton* and gentry.

"Not a specific venture, but I have been assigned the task of mingling with the upper class and gaining their favor. You will do for now."

He laughed again, eyeing me curiously. "Honesty. A surprising characteristic for a man of business and quite refreshing."

I lifted my brows and shrugged. "I am not a man of business as of yet. Merely trying on the shoes for a later date in hopes they will one day fit."

"Mmm. I quite understand." He held up a hand and did a slow wave in front of himself as he spoke. "One day I shall be Viscount Paxton, and do you know how prepared I feel for such a role? Not at all. It can be a rather heavy burden."

"Agreed. An insurmountable expectation."

Mr. Apsley slapped my shoulder. "Precisely! Do you know what drove me to the club tonight? My father and I had a chat about my need to settle down soon." He scoffed. "I am hardly ready to shackle myself to a woman. I refuse to, in fact. This Season will not see me wed."

"It seems you and I have that in common. My Uncle has also asked me to wed this Season, and I must conform. He has threatened to disinherit me if I refuse."

My mouth snapped closed. I had been far too open, too forthcoming. The ease of our conversation had taken me by surprise, and with Mr. Apsley so unguarded himself, my troubles had poured out. Mr. Apsley needn't worry about being disinherited. The title and whatever fortune his family held would be his regardless. I did not possess the same luxury. Why should I share so much with someone who could not understand?

"I do not envy you, Montfert. It's a shame to be forced into such a prison. We are too young for that."

"Too young," I agreed, though my age was the least of my concerns. "I've not even experienced a London Season. This is my first trip to Town."

There I had done it again. How did he coax information out of me so easily?

Mr. Apsley reared back. "What? You mean...ever?"

"Indeed."

The man whistled, shaking his head in disbelief. "A terrible shame. I can no longer be saddened by my misfortunes—which, to be sure, are mere aggravations in comparison to your predicament. Tell me, if you've not been to London before, does that mean you've no inkling for a wifely candidate?"

"Not a one," I said with a chuckle. "I barely know anyone, let alone a lady who meets my uncle's requirements. He even gave me a list."

"Oof. There is a list, too? You are worse off than I feared, my friend."

His friend? A small smile tugged at my lips. I hadn't many friends, and I rarely conversed with people as easily as I did with Mr. Apsley. I had nearly forgotten my inexperience and my hearing impairment once our conversation began, a rarity.

Mr. Apsley bolted upright from his more relaxed position, his eyes wide. "I've had an incredible idea."

"Solved the world's problems, have you?"

He grinned, amusement crinkling the corner of his eyes. "You're rather funny, Montfert. I think I'll adopt you."

"Adopt me?" Confusion laced my tone. What in the heavens did he mean by that?

Mr. Apsley leaned closer to me. "I shall take you under my wing. You will have the most successful Season possible with my help—er, our help, rather."

"Our?"

He tapped a finger to his head. "The incredible idea. I happen to know of a matchmaker looking for clients. They can help you find a candidate who will meet your uncle's requirements, and I shall introduce you to Society and ensure you are invited to all the right parties so you might court the lucky lady."

"I..." What was I to say? This man was offering me the help I desperately needed. If the incident with Lady Millicent this evening had proven anything, it was that I could not do this on my own. I needed guidance.

"We will have a grand time of it," Mr. Apsley promised. "You can find the perfect woman to marry and keep your inheritance, and I will have the honor of helping you succeed."

"But why are you so willing to devote time to my cause?" I asked. "We have only just met."

Mr. Apsley pulled his lips to one side. "As I said, I like you, Montfert. Besides, if I'm busy assisting a friend, my parents are less likely to bother me about marriage." He shrugged. "And it sounds entertaining."

For him, it might well be entertaining, but still, the offer was appealing.

I lowered my voice. "And this matchmaker...can you guarantee they will be discreet about all of this?" The last thing I needed was for word to get out that I required assistance in finding a bride. Uncle would be furious to learn I had sought this sort of help, especially when it could blemish his name along with my own.

"Oh, yes," said Apsley with a firm nod. "I can personally guarantee they will not only be discreet but also find you a perfect match. This person comes highly recommended—past success, well-versed in the sort of romance women expect, and stubborn enough not to give up."

I hesitated to respond. Was this truly the best course? After all, I had only been in London for a few days. Surely that was not enough time to give up on finding a match without help?

But failing left me to count on Uncle's generosity and goodwill. I had faith in neither—not without doing everything the man demanded of me. No, I had far too much at risk to abandon this opportunity. I would swallow whatever pride I had left.

"Perhaps a matchmaker is precisely what I need," I said. "And I would gladly accept any help you are willing to give."

Mr. Apsley grinned, wide and triumphant. "An excellent decision. Leave it to me, Montfert. I'll arrange everything."

# Chapter Four

## GRACE

IN THE MANY TIMES I had been wholeheartedly annoyed with my cousin, I had never resorted to violence. Today, I would make an exception.

I clutched a copy of *Fourdyce's Sermons*, which served as amusing irony given I was about to pummel Rus over the head with it. I had backed him into one corner of the library at Apsley Court, the Apsley's townhouse in London, and although he held up his hands in a defensive effort to placate me, his smug grin testified of his lack of guilt.

And lack of fear, for that matter. Perhaps he knew I had no intention of actually harming him, but I was sorely tempted.

"I was only trying to help," he said. "Did you not mention your desire to play matchmaker? Here I delivered your first client without you so much as lifting a finger, and this is the thanks I get?" He gestured to the book I still gripped.

"We have not been in London more than a day, Rus! This is my first Season. Could you not give me time to settle in before acting so generously?" I used the term lightly. I was plenty capable of finding clients on my own. The entire point of establishing a name for myself was so I could obtain my independence.

Regardless, my leg ached from our travels and having a few days respite would have been appreciated.

"But you seemed so eager," he said with false innocence.

"Eager?" I lifted the book higher. "I *am* quite eager for something, now you mention it."

His brows furrowed, and the confidence in his voice wavered slightly. "You wouldn't."

"I hope she does," said Annette, who was watching us from the coffee brown settee near the hearth. "The only way you will ever actually listen to a sermon is if someone beats it into you."

"Those happen to be for females," Rus protested. "I needn't have any of those beaten into me."

"I would argue men would benefit as soundly from the instruction those pages contain. Besides"—Annette shrugged—"your shriek last night when you found a spider in your room was remarkably feminine."

Rus pointed at her. "I have it on good authority you were the one who put that spider on my pillow. Mark my words, Netty, I shall have my revenge for it."

Annete's lips lifted into a grin as her focus returned to her book. She certainly seemed unconcerned with her brother's threat, though I would not put it past Rus to have vengeance. But it would have to wait; we had a situation to discuss.

I tucked the book under my arm and swatted him to bring his attention back to me. "Who is this client? Are they trustworthy?"

"Trustworthy? I believe so."

I narrowed my eyes. "What do you mean, you believe so? How long have you known this person?"

Rus rubbed the back of his neck. "Almost a full day."

"A full—Rus! You brought me a client you, yourself, do not properly know? How much did you drink last night before thinking this was a good idea?"

He straightened his coat and lifted his chin. "None, as it were. We became quick friends, and the chap is desperate. He seems the sort of man willing to heed the advice of a...matchmaker."

"A woman," Annette interjected. "Just say it, Rus. It cannot be so painful."

"The idea is intolerable and has the potential for disaster. I should know. Every time I've heeded your advice, Netty, I ended up in trouble. Or worse—blamed for trouble I did not even cause."

"Makes up for all the times you've gotten away with it, then."

I snapped my fingers in front of Rus's face before he could retort. "Focus, Russell. I cannot meet with this gentleman without knowing more about him. When you say he is desperate, I need to know precisely what you mean. I am in the business of love matches, not scandal."

"I am certain he wishes for a love match, and if not, you may convince him he needs one. If anyone can find the poor chap a lady this Season, it is you."

"Flattery will not keep me from whacking you with this book."

Rus sighed, all humor gone from his expression. "Give the man a chance, Gracie. True, I do not know him well, but I do like him. He seems like a good person, and if all goes well, it may make a grand start to your matchmaking endeavors. Meet him before you decide against it."

My agitation deflated. "Very well, but you must go with me for the first meeting. I've no desire to be alone with him."

Rus nodded. "I will agree to that."

DESPITE RUS'S EASY AGREEMENT to accompany me, he had a fair number of complaints during our morning walk to Hyde Park. I reminded him this was all his doing, but even so, he attempted to place the blame on me, as troublesome cousins were often wont to do.

"Why must we go at this unholy hour?" Rus adjusted his cravat, tugging it away from his neck. The man had never been fond of them and typically ripped them off the moment he was home. "I would have preferred to sleep in."

"Would you also have preferred to arrive in the park at the fashionable hour? For all the debutantes to gawk at you?" I tapped a finger to my lips. "That must be why you are so put out. You've missed an opportunity."

Rus gave me a flat look. "You know full well I've no wish to be gawked at, especially by fresh debutantes. They are the worst crowd in London."

I highly doubted that, but for a bachelor with fortune and title, maybe it wasn't so far from the truth. Rus joked about his distaste for courtship, but I suspected there was a deeper reason for his reluctance. I hadn't any idea what it might be. Something from his past, perhaps?

Regardless, Rus was not likely to convey those particulars to me, a self-proclaimed matchmaker.

"You know it is better I meet this gentleman before the crowds arrive," I said. "You may take a nap when we return home."

"Yes, yes, I understand the reason, but that does not mean I have to like it."

"Where did you tell him to find us?" I asked as we entered the east side of the park. This early, there was not a parade of carriages gliding along down Rotten Row, nor any groups of gossips lurking to snatch up their next topic for discussion over tea. Still, this type of conversation was best held in private. If I came to trust Mr. Montfert—that was the name Rus had provided me after hours of prodding—then we might decide upon a better place to meet that would allow for less chance of prying ears. Until then, the park was a safe place, especially with my cousin at my side.

"Just north of The Serpentine. There is a nice copse of trees there to provide some privacy." Rus patted my hand, which rested on his arm. "You may not believe me, Gracie, but your reputation is important to me. It was never my intention to put you at risk."

"I know." My cousin might have been a bit absent-minded on occasion, but he meant well and cared for his family. Even for Annette, with whom he never seemed to cease arguing. Russell Apsley simply preferred to appear unbothered by anything and everyone. A façade I did not understand.

But that was a puzzle for another time.

Rus guided me into a little grove filled with shrubbery tall enough to obscure our view of the footpath. So surrounded by greenery, it nearly felt like being back at Kenwick Castle, where the gardens spread over vast acres and paths meandered through hedges and flora.

"This place is lovely," I said in a reverent tone.

"I suppose it is. I confess I haven't given much thought to the scenery while here before."

I turned to face him, narrowing my eyes. "For what purpose did you come here before?"

The rakish grin that spread over Rus's face said I likely did not wish to know, and he offered no details to satiate my curiosity.

"I think I'll have my nap now." Rus crossed the little clearing and slunk down against the tree with the thickest trunk. He slid his hat forward so it blocked the sunlight from reaching his eyes.

"A nap? Here?" I placed my hands on my hips and glared at him. Not that it did any good. He could not see me with his hat in such a position.

"You said I could take one," came Rus's muffled voice. If I wasn't mistaken, his words had carried over a yawn.

"I did not say you could take one *now*. Mr. Montfert shall be here any moment."

Rus shrugged. "So scream if he attempts anything improper. I am a light sleeper."

"That is hardly true. A herd of elephants would not wake you, Rus. Besides, you must make introductions." I waited for him to respond but was met with silence. "Rus!"

Whether he was simply ignoring me or unwittingly proving my point, I could not say, but it hardly mattered, for another figure entered the clearing. He possessed chestnut hair that poked out from beneath a brown hat, and his coat, one of the finest I'd seen, reflected the state of his finances. His cravat was starch white and perfectly knotted. By all appearances, Mr. Montfert could at least afford to pay me as my first client.

That, decidedly, did little to settle my nerves.

His gaze roamed the clearing until he found me, and then with a slight frown, he approached. "Forgive my intrusion, but I am to meet...someone here."

"Yes. You are to meet me."

He drew back, and his gaze wandered down my body and back up again. "I was not expecting a woman."

My brows raised. What had Rus told the man? "Did my cousin leave that particular detail out? Never mind. A more important question is does my sex matter?"

He removed his hat and ran a gloved hand through his hair. His eyes, the same blue-gray as the sky, held a weariness I hadn't expected. Despite that, I could admit he was a handsome man, and should his personality prove reasonable, finding him a match would not be challenging.

"It does not matter, per se, but...is it proper for us to meet? Alone."

Ah. He feared for my reputation. Or for his own, should we be discovered. I could alleviate his concerns on this front, at least.

I gestured to Rus. "I assure you, I will take precautions in that regard. Next time we meet I will bring a better chaperone."

"Mr. Apsley," the man said, his lips rising in a slow smile that reached his eyes. Gracious, but he was handsome. "I hadn't even noticed him there."

"As I said, I will bring a better chaperone next time as this one is broken." I stepped forward, extending my hand toward him. That was how men of business greeted one another, was it not? "Since he is not conscious enough to make introductions, I suppose we are left to our own devices."

He stared at my hand a moment before taking it. "It would appear so. I am Phillip Montfert."

"Grace Scott."

Mr. Montfert released my hand and bowed slightly. "A pleasure to meet you, Miss Scott."

I wasn't entirely sure I agreed. Not that the man was anything but polite; merely that the circumstances of our acquaintance were complicated. I had intended to arrive in London and formulate a plan, not take on clients straight away. I felt ill-prepared, thrown into the deep without knowledge of how to swim.

I sucked in a breath. "Well, Mr. Montfert, how shall we begin? I fear I know little about your...situation. Rus only mentioned you were desperate to find a match this Season."

His ears turned pink, and he rotated his hat, his fingers sliding along its brim. "Yes. My uncle—I am to inherit all of his holdings, you see—has demanded it of me. I am not very experienced with society, as this is my first trip to London. It is all a bit overwhelming. I need the help."

His willingness to admit as much softened me toward him, but still, I hesitated. Getting things right for this first client was crucial. I could not make a business of matchmaking by launching with a failure.

"What sort of match are you hoping for, Mr. Montfert?"

"What sort?" he repeated with mild confusion.

"Are you hoping for companionable friendship, something more, or is marriage merely a business transaction for you? Your answer, you see, has a bearing on whether I can help you." Or wanted to. Perhaps I had allowed my romantic notions to cloud my vision, but I wished to see people happily settled. If I could not find love for myself, then doing it for others would suffice.

A line formed between Mr. Montfert's brows as he seemed to consider the question. He took several moments to respond, and I appreciated him giving it careful thought.

"I think companionable friendship"—my heart sank before he continued—"but my preference would be for more."

"More?" Did I dare hope?

His face had tinted again. "My parents were quite fond of one another. I had always hoped that if I did marry..." His gaze dropped to the ground, and he shifted on his feet. "Perhaps I am asking too much."

"No!" I rushed forward and placed a hand on his arm. "You are not asking too much. I confess I had hoped you wished for a love match."

He stared at where my hand rested on his sleeve for a moment before meeting my gaze. His lips pulled into a small smile. "You are willing to help me then?"

I smiled back at him. "I am, and we shall start straight away. Tell me, what sort of things are you looking for in a wife?"

He retrieved a piece of foolscap from inside his pocket. "My uncle has high expectations. You'll find qualities listed here. At least one of the first two must be met. The rest are preferred, but not essential." He winced. "My uncle's words; not mine."

"This will certainly give me a place to start," I said, accepting the paper from him. "I'll need some time to go through it and consider possible ladies that meet them. In full disclosure, this is my first Season, and I am not well-acquainted with every member of the *ton*."

"That is quite fine, Miss Scott. You are likely better acquainted with them than I am. May I trust you will reach out once you've had time to ponder the list?"

"I shall."

"Good. Your cousin has my direction, and you may send a note under his name to avoid any risk of scandal." He paused. "And I thank you for doing this. You have my word I will compensate you for your time. If you have a price in mind—"

"We may discuss that when we next meet." I had not even remembered to ask for compensation, and my shoulders sank with relief. Mr. Montfert was handsome, but I could add respectful and honest to that list as well. "I will send you word as soon as I am able."

A snore rumbled from Rus's throat. Mr. Montfert and I stared at him, then laughed. My new client stepped forward, scooped up my hand, and placed a short kiss on my glove. The action released a horde of butterflies in my stomach.

That was not very business-like.

But it was gallant. I would add it to his list of qualities, too. The man's prospects were increasing by the minute.

"Until next time, Miss Scott." He bowed and left me to wake my snoring cousin on my own.

# Chapter Five

## GRACE

ATTENDING ONE'S FIRST DINNER party in London was an exciting but terrifying affair. My fingers played with the tips of my gloves as another wave of nerves washed over me. I had looked forward to my debut since before Papa's death, but my fantasies had not been at all like this. In those visions, both my parents and sister had stood at my side, and we had eagerly shared the experiences Town had to offer.

I had neither of my parents, with Papa gone and Mama still mourning his death, nor did I have Amelia, who remained in York with her husband. Their absence left me anxious, but at least I had Rowe to guide me through it all.

He sat opposite me in my family's coach—his coach, now that he had inherited everything. Father had left us in good hands under Rowe's protection. My cousin was as good and stalwart as any man could be.

"Are you ready?" he asked softly as though he had read my thoughts.

"Yes, though I am nervous. Silly, really. It is not as though I have never attended a dinner party."

"Would it make you feel better to know I am always struck with a bout of nerves before a party? Or a ball. No matter how many I attend, the sensation follows me." Rowe chuckled, shaking his head slightly. "I would much prefer to remain home over socializing."

I sent him a guilty smile. "Were it not for me, you could remain home."

Rowe met my gaze. "Do not misunderstand, Grace. I am happy to accompany you. It is both my duty and my honor. And besides, my mother would never allow me to turn reclusive. Not until I have married, at the very least."

"She does seem intent on seeing her children happily settled. Rus mentioned your father has urged him to marry soon. I imagine much of it is at your mother's encouragement. And, of course, there is Annette's *agreement*."

We both laughed. Rowe sighed, though it was done with an odd sort of contentment. Or perhaps resignation. "Mother has marital goals, to be sure. Her focus has not yet landed so heavily on me, but I shan't escape it forever. But let us not worry about my affairs tonight. It is you who should study your prospects."

I scoffed. My prospects? I had none of those, nor did I expect to gain any.

"Do not make light of the idea, Grace. I will not force you toward marriage, but you should have an open mind. Who is to say you will not meet a man tonight and fall madly in love with him?"

"Very well, I shall keep an open mind." But not for myself. No, I had read over Mr. Montfert's list—which I found was rather ridiculous—and while finding a woman with title, wealth, and all the qualities the paper requested was impossible, I had to start somewhere. Surely one of the women in attendance tonight would meet some of them.

Not that I would tell Rowe any of this. He remained unaware of my meeting with Mr. Montfert, largely because I feared his disapproval. Rowe was not the sort to demand and restrict, but when it came to my reputation, his protectiveness may well bring my matchmaking plans to a halt.

The coach stopped in front of a white building with dozens of windows. The front entrance was framed with two columns and covered by a roof that extended out to the pavement. Rowe alighted first and then handed me down. I ran my hands down my lavender gown, smoothing out any wrinkles caused by the journey, and stared up at the building's façade, my stomach twisting.

"Ready?" Rowe offered me his arm, and I gladly accepted his support, though we did not move from our place on the pavement. We waited until Rus, Annette, and Lord and Lady Paxton had alighted from their coach and joined us before pressing forward.

"Smile," Lady Paxton whispered to her daughter. "It will not do for you to enter the house scowling, darling."

"I have nothing to smile about," Annette grumbled before doing as her mother asked.

It was no secret she had little desire to be here. Or in London at all, really. She and Rowe were similar in their love for the countryside, though how they enjoyed their time there could not have been more different. Rowe practically lived in the library, while Annette was far too adventurous to remain indoors. Even in the winter she rarely kept within the walls of Kenwick Castle unless forced by either her parents' orders or snow.

If Annette were to marry, she would need a husband who understood that sense of adventure. One who would not attempt to douse her fiery nature. Would there be such a man present tonight?

A spark of giddiness rushed through me. Perhaps studying the men in attendance was not the worst idea. I could search for a match for both my cousin and my client. That would provide more than enough distraction from my nerves.

We entered the house and removed our coats before moving to a large drawing room fitted with deep blue wallpaper patterned with elegant floral swashes. Several paintings adorned the walls, and in addition to oriental vases and fine furniture, the room held an air of superiority. Apsley Court was quite similar in its grandeur, but still, I stood in awe of it all.

"Lovely, is it not?" asked Lady Paxton with a gentle smile.

My cheeks heated for having been caught gaping. "It is very lovely. I am always so impressed when entering a new place for the first time, regardless of the decor. Or perhaps because of it. The choices in such things can say so much about the people living there."

Lady Paxton's smile grew, and the skin at the corner of her eyes crinkled. The woman was beautiful, her auburn hair the same shade as the twins', and she carried herself with such grace and kindness. Though I was not one of her children, she had always made me feel as if I were, and I appreciated that more than I could express.

Especially in my mother's absence.

"I agree," said Lady Paxton, "but we should never allow presumptions grown from studying the decor to shadow what we gain in conversation. You will find our host and hostess, though very wealthy, are quite amiable. Come, I will introduce you both to them."

Lady Paxton waved Annette and I forward to where Lord Paxton was already engaged in conversation with the host. The man wore a fine, deep red waistcoat, and his graying hair was styled with pomade that glistened beneath the candlelight. Wrinkles lined his jovial expression, and the woman who stood next to him—his wife, a dark-haired beauty with matching dark eyes—wore a smile that painted her amusement with the men's conversation.

To the woman's left stood another man—one far younger, though he possessed similar dark hair and eyes. I could only assume he was related to them. A son, perhaps, and a rather dashing one at that.

"Forgive my intrusion," said Lady Paxton, dipping into a curtsy to the woman while the older men continued their discussion. "My husband has abandoned us in his eagerness to speak with Mr. Paget. You would think the two of them have not already spent hours together since arriving in London."

Mrs. Paget chuckled. "There is nothing to forgive. Had you waited for them to finish, you would likely not have spoken with me at all. They are something, the two of them."

"Indeed." Lady Paxton gestured to Annette and me. "May I introduce you to my daughter, Miss Annette Apsley, and my niece, Miss Grace Scott."

"It is very nice to meet the both of you. This is my son, Lieutenant Edward Paget. He is recently returned from The West Indies."

The lieutenant bowed, and when he straightened, his gaze bounced from me to Annette, where it lingered for several moments before he spoke. "A pleasure to make your acquaintance."

The elder Mr. Paget laughed heartily, shaking his head with vigor.

His son grimaced. "They are discussing the policies revolving around the slave trade. Despite recent laws, there is still much happening in the colonies. My father is not convinced a motion for emancipation would pass in The Commons. Unlike your father, Miss Apsley, a genuine supporter of the movement."

Mrs. Paget glared at her son. "Edward, that is not an appropriate topic to discuss with ladies. Keep your politics out of my drawing room while I have guests. I cannot stop your father, but I will not have it from you as well."

"My apologies," said Lieutenant Paget, though he hardly seemed affected by the chastisement. He waited until his mother and Lady Paxton were deeply engaged in their own discussion before speaking again. "Tell me, as I have been without London society for some time now, what is it ladies of quality prefer to discuss?"

"As this is our first Season, we are as hopeless as you, sir." Annette smiled sweetly, but I recognized the challenge in her eyes. She was testing him. What sort of test and what she hoped to gain from his answer, I could not say.

"I cannot imagine anyone as lovely as the two of you could ever be described as hopeless in any endeavor." He said two of you, but his attention focused solely on Annette. I fought a grin. Whether she wanted it or not, my cousin had captured his attention.

"Quite untrue," said Annette. "There are a multitude of topics for which I find myself hopeless, abolition being one of them. I now know my father's stance, and your father's, but I wonder on which side you have planted your opinion?"

The lieutenant's lips twitched. "My mother recently forbade me from discussing such things in her drawing room."

"Am I to understand you agree with her assessment that women should not discuss the very politics that affect our country, or are you merely so disinterested in a person's right to freedom, so far removed from the issue in your finery and extravagance, to have no opinion at all?"

Oh dear.

"If those are truly my only options, then I fear an answer will offend you either way." Amusement danced in his eyes, and part of me wished to warn him of the fire he was stoking. Annette's passion for championing her freedom would not respond well to someone who supported any sort of enslavement.

Not that the lieutenant had offered his opinion. He danced around the topic, I suspected, simply to frustrate my cousin. Why he would wish to do so when they had only just met, I hadn't any idea.

Either way, my concern proved unnecessary. Annette maintained her composure, hiding the fury I was certain welled within her. Once again, she fabricated a smile. "Then I believe it best I find conversation elsewhere to avoid offense from you, sir. Have a pleasant evening." She offered a curt nod before turning away from him.

Not wanting to be left alone in conversation with the lieutenant, I followed, but not before I caught his grin. Lieutenant Paget was certainly unoffended by my cousin's abrupt departure. If anything, he seemed to take victory in it.

"Incorrigible man," Annette muttered when I had caught up to her. "One would think spending time in the colonies would offer him a better perspective."

"Do you think he witnessed things firsthand?" I asked.

"Undoubtedly. And to not be moved by it?" She shook her head, and I chose not to remind her the man had not verified his stance on the subject. The matter was best laid to rest for now.

Dinner passed quickly, my attention divided between engaging my companion—a kind gentleman by the name of Mr. Willoughby who was likely fifteen years my senior—and studying the others in attendance.

Several young ladies had been invited, all lovely in appearance and clearly raised with the expected poise of upper society.

I had, rather foolishly, hoped picking a candidate for Mr. Montfert would come easily. I had not considered how instrumental seeing two people interact was to the art of matchmaking.

But I had promised to find him a prospective bride, and I would do my best to determine who among the group might be suited for the role.

After leaving the men to their port, I circled the drawing room in hopes of talking to each of the eligible women. They were all amiable, though some more than others, but I found the conversations did little to assist me in my cause. How was I to know who would best suit a man I hardly knew? Even knowing a little something of his personality would have made this much easier.

Miss Angston was proficient on the pianoforte, while Miss Lancaster could sing quite beautifully, both of which I learned as the women performed after the men arrived. Then there was Lady Evelyn, a dark-haired beauty that seemed to draw the attention of every bachelor present, barring Rowe and Mr. Willoughby, into conversation with such elegance I wondered if her voice was not a siren's song.

My client's bride need not have all of the qualities on the list, but so many of the women of the room qualified in one way or another, I hadn't any idea how to narrow down Mr. Montfert's options.

I chided myself for not asking him more questions about himself during our meeting and took a seat on the nearest sofa to rest my leg. It had ached the moment I woke this morning, no doubt the result of traveling and my walk to Hyde yesterday. I had been too excited to meet with my first client to consider the ramifications.

"You appear rather put out," a quiet voice said.

I turned toward the chair on my left to see a woman with dark brown hair and blue eyes watching me. I had not spoken to her yet, but Lady Paxton had introduced us before dinner. Miss Rigby did not come from a titled family, but by all appearances, they were quite wealthy. However, I had learned nothing of her personality during our meal, as Miss Rigby spoke very little to her dinner companion.

In fact, she had spoken little to *anyone* tonight.

Perhaps I had learned something, then. She was shy, though she did not seem unkind—always offering a ready smile and conversation when engaged.

"A...friend of mine has found himself in a predicament, and I'm afraid my mind has yet to help him find a solution." I smiled, hoping the vague answer would both satisfy her and open the door to more conversation.

"It is kind of you to put so much thought into helping him," she replied.

"What are friends for if not to help us, entertain us—perhaps create mischief with us." At least, that is how Amelia and I were. We were sisters, but we'd always been the best of friends. I confided in her, and not having her with me now was more painful than I had thought it would be.

"I suppose so," said Miss Rigby, her brows slightly furrowed as if considering my statement.

I struggled to find an excuse to continue our conversation, and after some time, Miss Rigby picked up the book resting on one of the side tables. She began reading from the beginning, and I wondered if it truly interested her or if she simply preferred anything over socializing.

Would Mr. Montfert prefer a quiet wife?

The thought was worth considering. There was nothing for it; I needed to meet with the man again and find out what he wanted in a wife beyond the things his uncle's ridiculous list demanded.

# Chapter Six

## PHILLIP

After a little more than a week in London, I already wished to return home. The bustle of the city and expectations of society weighed on me, a heavy burden that could leave one entirely exhausted. All the same, expectations kept me in Town, as I had no hope of convincing Uncle to allow me to leave.

We had attended five dinner parties since arriving, and despite meeting numerous eligible young women of the the *ton*, I was no closer to finding a wife.

Much to Uncle's irritation.

I headed for the breakfast room, my shoulders tight with the anticipation of seeing him. Last night had not gone well at all, and Uncle had yet to berate me for unintentionally offending our host—a man Uncle had hoped to bring in on a new business proposition—by inquiring if he needed assistance in fixing his wig.

Or, what I had thought was a wig. It turned out his hair simply grew very lopsided.

Rather than allow me to apologize, Uncle had discreetly pulled me aside and instructed me to leave due to an urgent matter. I had obeyed without question while he mended any damage my mistake had caused.

He did not seek me out upon returning home, but I was not foolish enough to believe I had escaped his ire. My chastisement would likely be worse given how much time he had fumed without releasing it.

To my relief, the breakfast room was free of raging uncles, however I did not find it empty. My cousin, Sabrina, sat at the table, elegantly poised with her dark hair neatly styled and a dainty tray of food before her.

She met my gaze and smiled slightly, giving me a nod of acknowledgement. "Good morning, Phillip. Forgive me if I do not stand, but my body is thoroughly exhausted from our journey to London. I feel as though my legs will hardly hold me until I've properly eaten."

I dismissed her concern with a wave and bowed in greeting. "I am glad to see you made it in one piece. How did my mother handle the trip?"

"She handled it perfectly well." The answer came not from Sabrina, but a familiar voice just behind me. I turned to see Mother standing in the entry, smiling as though she had not seen me in months.

I took her in, every familiar feature from her gray-streaked hair to her tired blue eyes, and the tension coiling within me released. Mother opened her arms, and I eagerly went to her, wrapping the woman in an embrace. She and I had never been parted for so long.

"How are you?" I asked, then placed a kiss on her cheek. "It must have been rather late when you arrived."

"It was," she replied, wrapping a hand around my arm. "The carriage broke an axle, and we were required to stop for repairs. But do not concern yourself with me. I want to hear all about your time in London so far."

I winced, and Sabrina chuckled from her place at the table. "I do not believe he wishes to share with us."

"There are moments I would rather forget," I said, guiding Mother to the sideboard. "Many moments."

Sabrina chuckled again. "That is to be expected from anyone visiting London for the first time."

Her words caught me off guard. Sabrina and I had never been particularly close. Indeed, I was uncertain she was close with anyone. The woman reminded me of her father in many ways—careful in her associations and guarded to the point no one ever saw her true self. Admittedly, since moving back in with us at Eldercrest Hall, something about her had been different. She was...kinder? Perhaps that was not the most accurate word, but I found her attitude toward me was far less judgmental and arrogant.

What had changed? Though neither she nor my uncle spoke of the house party they both attended last spring, I suspected something had happened there.

"I doubt you ever embarrassed yourself during your first Season," I said, helping Mother into her chair. "You are too graceful and poised to make a fool of yourself."

Sabrina grinned at the compliment, but her expression remained soft, free of the arrogance that normally filled it. "It merely takes practice, Phillip. You will get on just fine with more experience. London will make you a proper dandy over the next few months."

"A dandy? I think not." I took my seat once I had plated my breakfast. We spoke of the events in the upcoming weeks. Mother listened with rapt attention as I detailed my experience thus far, and while sharing some of the less enjoyable parts still heated my face, neither she nor Sabrina chided me for the failures.

Teased, perhaps, but not chided.

"Well, I, for one, am glad I will have good company this Season," said Sabrina. "London can be quite dull. It sounds like you need a bit of guidance, Phillip, and I am more than ready to assist you."

I waited for her to elaborate. Sabrina was too much like her father to offer assistance without some sort of payment or benefit. When she said nothing more, I asked, "You will not be too busy searching for a new match?"

"Not at all. I've no interest in remarrying."

I lifted a brow. "You've no interest?"

She shook her head, and although both her tone and expression suggestion she meant it, I found it difficult to believe. Sabrina had always been determined, and part of that determination was to match herself with the highest title and fortune she could find.

Of course, she had married a duke and still held the title of duchess. She could hardly get much higher, but based on the rumors circulating London, her standing with the ducal family was tenuous. Now that she had returned to Town, I wondered if the gossip would intensify.

And how she would respond to it.

"Then I do not know how good of company I shall be." I speared a piece of ham and held the meat before my mouth. "Uncle has asked that I spend the Season searching for a wife, which will keep me preoccupied."

It would, based on how unsuccessful I had been thus far.

"He wishes you to marry?" Sabrina asked, her dark brows furrowing. "Then you have my sympathies. No doubt he offered you a list of qualities he expects in your spouse."

I nearly choked on the ham and required a long drink to clear my throat. "He has. Did he provide you with something similar during your debut?"

She pinned me with a look. Yes. Of course he had. Uncle expected things of me, not unlike the way he expected things of his daughter. If we had one thing in common, it was that we were little more than pawns he could move about the board.

Sabrina hummed for a moment. "I should think we could help each other. You can keep my suitors at bay, and I will introduce you to all my female acquaintances. Well, perhaps not all of them. Only those I know my father would be satisfied to connect his name with. Or your name, as it were."

"I would appreciate that." Heaven knew I needed all the help I could get. My matchmaker had yet to send me any sort of correspondence. It had been two entire days. I should not expect anything so soon, but I grew more anxious the longer I waited. What if she could not find me a match at all? What if I truly was hopeless?

Rather than settling on those questions, my mind chose to focus on one word—she. My matchmaker was a woman. I took no issue with it, of course, but when Mr. Apsley had suggested the idea, for some reason I had assumed the person helping me would be a gentleman, one experienced in the art of courtship after having found his own success.

Instead, I had found myself in a secluded clearing with perhaps the loveliest creature of my acquaintance. I wondered how I had possessed any ability to speak at all after spotting her, for she had stolen my breath and left a thick haze over my thoughts.

Ridiculous, really. Such a response could only be the result of my inexperience among Society. Miss Scott was no anomaly. Surely there were dozens of women in London who claimed that sort of beauty?

Warmth spread over my hand, and I lifted my gaze to meet Mother's worried eyes. "Whatever qualities your uncle has asked for in your future wife, do not forget it is your heart that should make the final decision."

I smiled at her, though it felt strained. I would very much like my heart to be involved. Father had been far from perfect, but even as a young child, I had known the love between my parents. I wanted it for myself, but expectations—especially those that came from Uncle—did not always leave room for the things I wanted.

In fact, it was a rare phenomenon.

Following breakfast, I gathered my things and took the first flight of stairs from my chamber, noting the departure of Mrs. Ellis, a matron with heavy investments in Uncle's business ventures, before Uncle called me into his study. My heart pounded, and I chided myself for ever thinking I might escape him a little longer by leaving the house.

He ordered me to sit, and I obeyed while he closed the door, making the study feel more like a prison than anything. Uncle took a seat at his desk, his eyes full of harnessed fury, ready to be unleashed. I swallowed and tugged at my cravat. "I know I have disappointed you."

"Disappointed? *Disappointed?*" He slammed his fist on the desk, and I flinched. At least I was far enough away that his pocket watch could not be used for punishment.

"You cannot know of my disappointment, boy. I had made good progress with Lord Bently, and you nearly ruined it all with your offensive comments."

"It was not my intention—"

"I do not care what your intentions were! So help me if you ever humiliate me so deeply again, I will have my solicitor draw up a new will with haste. You may take your mother and return to that pile of rubbage of a house your father left you."

My jaw clenched. That pile of rubbage was not suitable for anyone to live in. "Forgive me, Uncle. I will do better."

He scoffed, shaking his head, then his stony glare swept over me. "And where, might I ask, are you going this morning?"

"Bond Street. Russell Apsley has invited me to join him at Angelo's at noon. He intends to teach me to fence." Why, I hadn't the slightest idea. The man had promised to help me enter Society, not stab at other men with a foil.

Uncle's expression smoothed, the anger draining away to surprise. "He invited you?"

"Yes," I answered through gritted teeth. "We met the other night at White's. I am capable of fostering relationships with other humans."

Perhaps not of the female variety, but that was neither here nor there at the moment.

"This is good." Uncle rubbed his hand over his chin thoughtfully. "This is very good. Well done, Phillip."

I gaped at him. The man had never, as far back as my memory recalled, offered me any kind of praise. I hardly knew what to do with it. "T-thank you, Uncle."

"Well, off with you then. This friendship of yours with Mr. Apsley might prove very lucrative. I have been attempting to lure his father into my ventures for some time. Do not ruin this opportunity to get close to the viscount like you do everything else. Or the future viscount, for that matter."

Ah. There it was. The insult I had been waiting for. The expectation. The scheming. Uncle was incapable of having a conversation which did not include those things. At least, with me.

I stood and bowed. "I will do my best to please you, Uncle."

"You are quite bad at this," said Apsley.

I did not need the reminder, and the comment fueled me to make another attempt. Apsley blocked my advance, then swiftly spun out of my reach, chuckling.

"Mind your—" His words became garbled as he circled to my left side, and before I could turn to defend against him, his foil jabbed into my fencing jacket. My shoulders sank with disappointment, my chest heaving with our exercise over the past hour.

Apsley slapped my shoulder then pointed to the benches near the wall of our private room. The man removed his jacket, and I followed suit before we sat down to catch our breaths.

"I am hopeless at this sport," I said.

"Not hopeless. You need more practice, to be sure, but no one would expect you to walk out of here a master on your first day."

Uncle would have. He expected perfection in everything. There were few gentlemanly pastimes I excelled in, much of which came down to my hearing difficulties. I could ride fairly well and had decent aim with a pistol, but hunting was out of the question, and dancing...well, one could not properly dance when they struggled to keep time with the music.

"Shall we plan to meet twice a week?" Apsley asked. "Or is that too frequent?"

I shook my head. "Twice a week will do. I cannot see myself getting any better at this, but the exercise is exhilarating if nothing else."

"Indeed, I find I do best when I'm frustrated. Assign my opponent the face of someone who has recently annoyed me. Like my sister. It is nearly always Netty, in fact."

"You imagine stabbing your sister?"

"If you had one, you might understand," he countered defensively. "I would like to see you live in a household with four women and not wish to jab their eyes out on occasion." He shuddered. "Figuratively, of course."

"Of course, but they cannot all be so bad?"

Sabrina had her moments, but for the most part, she left me alone. I had not experienced the sort of nagging he described.

"I suppose not. Mother is tolerable when she is not hounding me about marriage. Netty...well, Netty is terrible, but Bridget is mostly pleasant, though I admit I do not spend much time with her. She is still in the schoolroom, you see."

"And what of Miss Scott?"

Apsley shrugged. "She is agreeable when not threatening to beat me with sermons."

I opened my mouth to question him on this particular revelation, but he continued before I could. "That reminds me, Grace asked me to pass a note to you."

My heart stuttered. "She did?"

I tried to reign in my nerves while he dug around in his pocket. The moment he had retrieved the paper, I snatched it from his hand and unfolded it, making him chuckle. My eyes skimmed the short letter so quickly I had to read it a second time to fully comprehend the words. "She wants to meet with me again tomorrow."

Apsley held up his hands. "I needn't know the details. Grace has informed me my services as chaperone are no longer required."

"No longer required or no longer wanted? She did mention you were a poor chaperone."

Apsley crossed his arms over his chest. "Very well, she told me I was not allowed to come, but that is fine by me. I have no desire to be present during your meetings as you discuss love and marriage and"—he stuck out his tongue and made a gagging sound that drew out my laughter.

"Careful," I said with a grin. "Or she might think to find you a match, too."

He nudged my shoulder, wearing a playful smirk. "Hardly. Gracie knows I've no desire for marriage at present. She thinks me a lost cause, I believe."

"A lost cause." I heaved a heavy sigh. "A few more meetings with me, and I might claim the same label."

# Chapter Seven

## PHILLIP

Arriving early in the secluded clearing within Hyde Park had not eased my nerves. Morning dew covered the grass, and more than once, my boots had slipped due to my constant pacing, nearly landing me on the damp ground. What a fool I would look should Miss Scott arrive to see my body sprawled out, my clothing covered in dirt and wet spots.

I shuddered. Speaking to a beautiful woman was difficult enough without the shadow of that sort of embarrassment.

I drew in a deep breath and forced my feet to cease moving. This impending meeting had kept me awake long into the night, my thoughts muddled with worry and anticipation. What if Miss Scott returned to declare me a lost cause, as she had her cousin? The man was a future viscount, for heaven's sake. Surely finding him a match would not be so difficult? Apsley was charming, wealthy, handsome, titled—the list was extensive. I would inherit, so long as I obeyed Uncle's demands, but I had little else to claim.

*You are broken. Worthless. A disgrace.* Uncle's words permeated my thoughts, but I shoved them aside. I'd learned a long time ago not to give them credence. I suffered from a hearing deficiency, but the malady made me none of those things. It had taken years for me to find my confidence, and certainly no thanks to Uncle's constant beratement.

I ran a gloved hand through my hair, likely leaving it in disarray. Uncle would not be happy if I returned home with an unkempt appearance, but I hadn't any idea how to keep my nerves from manifesting in a physical way. A few out-of-place strands of hair seemed better than a soiled coat and breeches that would inevitably result from pacing.

Voices sounded on the other side of the trees, and my heart attempted to leap out of my chest. It was too early in the morning for it to be anyone but Miss Scott. The fashionable time to parade about the park was not for at least another three hours.

The voices drew closer, and the rattle of the rocky ground gave way to silence, which meant they had left the main path to follow the grassy one to the clearing. I suddenly felt as if my limbs had grown an extra two feet, and I made several attempts to put them in a natural position. Behind my back, clasped in front of me—why did it all seem so awkward? I may as well place them on my head and dance like a buffoon.

I shook my head. When had I become so ridiculous?

The rustle of skirts drew my attention to the opening between the trees, where not one, but two women entered carrying what looked like large blankets. Their bonnets shielded their faces, but still, I knew for certain one belonged to Miss Scott. Her brown curls dangled against her cheeks, peeking out from the side of the light pink bonnet, and there was the familiar curve of her hips...

Not that I had intentionally paid attention to that specifically when we first met. I was a man of detail and had a knack for remembering shapes and colors. Perhaps it was my body's way of making up for deficits in other areas, but the gift had served me well at times.

I clasped my hands behind my back in a tight grip to keep them from moving anymore, but doing so did nothing to help the perspiration forming on my hands. At least neither of the women would notice with my gloves.

They both approached and curtsied, and I returned the expected greeting. "Good morning, Miss Scott."

"Good morning, Mr. Montfert. May I introduce you to my cousin, Miss Annette Apsley."

Ah. So this was the infamous Netty that Apsley had spoken of so fondly. Her appearance certainly fit with his description of her character. She had fiery red hair and bright blue eyes that promised mischief.

"A pleasure," I said. "Are you to be our new chaperone, Miss Apsley?"

The woman's eyes narrowed on me. "I am. What sort of cousin would I be if I allowed Grace to converse with some strange man alone in the park? I needed to meet you for myself."

My clasped hands tightened. "I hope after today I no longer seem like a strange man."

I had my doubts. By all accounts, I *was* strange. With little experience in Society and a request for her cousin to find me a match, this woman had every right to harbor some concerns.

"We shall see," said Miss Apsley. Her brows lifted as she backed away from me. "I'll be watching. From over there."

She continued her retreat backward until she reached the opposite side of the clearing. She unfolded the blanket and spread it over the grass before taking a seat and opening the book that had been wrapped inside the material.

"We noticed how wet the ground was before leaving this morning," said Miss Scott. "Since there are no benches available off the path, I thought it might be best if we had something to sit on to avoid getting wet."

"A brilliant idea. I only wish I had thought of it." I gave her a smile, which she returned, and together we spread her blanket over the ground between two trees. A book had also been hidden within the folds of Miss Scott's blanket, though it appeared to be a diary rather than a novel.

Miss Scott sat down and leaned against the trunk, bringing her knees to her chest. She opened the book and removed a pencil that had been stuck within the diary's pages, revealing blank paper. "I thought today we might talk about you."

My stomach clenched. "About me?"

She nodded. "I realized it will be difficult for me to find you a match while knowing so little about you. Your Uncle's list is rather specific, but"—she tapped the pencil against the paper— "those are the things *he* wants in your bride. Not the things you want."

"Oh, well, I confess I have given it little thought."

Her brows lifted, a hint of exasperation in her voice. "You've given little thought to what you want in a wife?"

"You must understand, Miss Scott. I have always known my uncle would have a great deal to say about who I married. Honestly, I am surprised he is giving me a choice in the matter at all. I half expected him to arrange something. So, no, I had not given it much thought. Not because I did not wish to, but because I saw little point in wasting my time." I paused. "Or perhaps in raising my hopes for something that would never be."

Her expression softened. "And if you fail to find someone, he likely *will* pick for you. Is that why you asked for help?"

"That is part of it. In truth, I am very unpracticed when it comes to socializing. I had scarcely left my uncle's estate before coming to London. A handful of dinner parties with our closest neighbors is all I can claim by way of experience, but even those will do me no good here. My neighbors are all old and wrinkly."

She hid a chuckle behind her hand. "Oh dear, that does seem unhelpful, though it also means you have a fresh canvas to paint on. I remember seeing London for the first time as a little girl. It was a wonderful experience and one I have never forgotten. So many times, I have wished I could go back and feel the same excitement again. There is nothing quite like a new experience, and it is a shame we are only given each opportunity once."

She nodded toward her cousin, who I noticed was watching us rather than reading.

"Take reading for example," said Miss Scott. "I can dive into the pages of my favorite book again and again, but it will never be the same as the first time I did so. Each pass brings with it something I had not noticed before, and there is comfort in the familiar. Still, sometimes I wish I could forget and experience it anew."

"I can understand the sentiment," I said. "There are many books I wish I could read for the first time again."

"You enjoy reading?"

"I do. As you can imagine, leaving my uncle's estate so infrequently left me to explore the library more often than not. I spent a great deal of time there."

Miss Scott tapped her pencil again. "And do you have any particular favorites? Reading material can say much about a person."

I chuckled. "I'm afraid that will be of little help to you. I read everything. Favorites? I suppose I have them, but they have a tendency to change based on the time of year or my mood. Beyond that, I am not inclined toward one genre over another. Nor fiction over technical studies. It all has its place."

"Even romance novels?" she challenged.

I shrugged, though the way my face heated likely gave me away. I had read my share of romance novels. Our library only held so many books, and apparently at least one of Uncle's wives had enjoyed them. I would not confess aloud I had enjoyed them, too, however.

"You are wrong." Miss Scott's lips lifted into a lopsided grin, and she turned the pages of her book back to the front. "That does tell me something about you."

She scribbled a few words, and when I leaned toward her to see what she had written, she turned it at an angle to prevent me. "This is for my eyes only, Mr. Montfert."

"That is highly unfair, especially if it is about me."

"I never said it was about you."

I folded my arms. "So it is not?"

Her lips pinched as she fought a smile.

"I thought so. I do not know how I feel about you taking notes on me, Miss Scott. It is unnerving."

She flipped the pages forward again. "You will have to grow accustomed to it then, for I plan to ask you a great many questions and take notes."

And so she did.

We spent an hour that way, and while her questions were meant to get to know me better, I found myself asking her just as many. What began as an exercise that felt raw and vulnerable, quickly turned comfortable as we sat in the shade beneath the trees. The gentle way she spoke, without judgment of my answers, eased my nerves, and I enjoyed the way the light shimmering through the branches above highlighted the amusement in her eyes whenever she thought a response was entertaining.

"Now that I know something about you," she said, tucking her feet beneath her, "I want to know what you would look for in a wife. I know you haven't given it much thought, but I think it's time we change that."

"But my uncle—"

"There is no reason we cannot satisfy both of you. Your wants are just as important as his." She bit her lip. "More so, in my opinion."

How I wished I could agree with her. Under perfect circumstances, I might have chosen a wife based on feelings alone, but I did not have perfect circumstances. I had a tyrannical uncle, a mother who relied on me, and nothing to my name. Not yet, anyway.

I ran a hand through my hair. "I do not even know where to begin."

"Well, does a particular hair color catch your eye?"

Hair color? Had I ever paid attention to that save for the purpose of recognition? No, I had not, and considering it now, I had no answer. Sabrina's hair was dark, and even I could admit my cousin possessed a certain beauty, but was it my preference? What of golden hair? Or fiery red, like Miss Apsley's?

I glanced at the woman. She was reading now, and strands of hair rested against her cheeks. Beautiful, but nothing specifically about her coloring or features moved me in any way. Was I so indifferent?

My focus returned to Miss Scott, and I took in the shade of her hair, the color of chocolate, just like her eyes. Something stirred in my chest, and I took it to mean I preferred something between the two ends of the spectrum. "Brown. I believe I prefer brunettes."

Miss Scott smiled, and that stirring in my chest started again. "See, Mr. Montfert. You do have preferences. You need only allow yourself to ponder them." She scribbled the information into her book.

"I suppose you are right, but it still feels odd to point out such preferences. Especially to another…"

"Woman?" she finished with a grin. "Yes, I imagine it must seem strange. Perhaps we can skip the more physical aspects for now. What of her personality? Attraction is important, of course, but would you prefer a wife who is, say, bold and outspoken? Or one with a more quiet demeanor?"

A valid question and one that would help in her endeavor to find a good match for me. Shame I hadn't an answer. "Well, I…"

I rubbed a hand over my face with a soft, frustrated growl. It was no wonder I was having such a difficult time searching for a wife on my own. I had no idea what type of woman I was attracted to, only a list that stated what I *should* be attracted to.

"I am not one who enjoys being the center of attention nor likes attending every event London has to offer. So, perhaps a wife who can socialize with the skill and grace I lack, but who is also content with staying home to enjoy quiet evenings. I do not mind outspokenness. I haven't a desire for a wife who fears speaking her mind, but I think it is important that a person also knows how to listen." I shook my head. "I cannot imagine any of that was at all helpful. You've given me two very different options, and I have requested my future bride be both."

"Hoping for balance is nothing to be ashamed of," she said with a light chuckle. "I think it is something we all hope for in a companion."

"Even matchmakers?" I asked, cocking one brow. In truth, I knew little about Miss Scott. She could very well be engaged or courting. The detail did not matter to me, as far as her qualifications were concerned, for I had already seen her dedication to assisting me. Still, I could not help but wonder if her heart belonged to someone.

"Especially matchmakers." She shifted on the blanket as if to stand, and I shot to my feet to help her. She thanked me, and together, we folded the blanket, tucking her book within.

"I have a few prospects in mind," she said. "I cannot claim to know them well, but it would be worth making introductions. Do you plan to attend the Morrison's ball Friday next?"

"I do not believe we have received an invitation," I said.

She hummed. "Perhaps Rus can see to it. He can charm an invitation out of anyone."

That hardly surprised me. "If it is your recommendation, I will be there...assuming your cousin does, in fact, procure me an invitation."

"Good. In the meantime, I will work on a list of potential brides. It would not hurt for us to meet again before the ball as well. The more I can know of your preferences, the better our chance of success."

It was a logical request, but something in the way it stirred my anticipation felt like more than logic. I set the notion aside. "I am free most mornings. You need only inform me of your schedule."

She nodded. "Then we shall plan on that. We may even meet later in the day so I can make introductions here, luck permitting. Any chance to see you interact with the women will prove beneficial."

"More observations for your book," I said, nodding to where it lay hidden in the folds of her blanket. "Had I not been the one to ask for your help, I might think such attention to me has ulterior motives."

The corners of her eyes crinkled. "I did not take you for a flirt, Mr. Montfert, but it is good to know you are capable. I will add it to my list."

Her list? Was that what existed near the front of her book? A list of my qualities?

Miss Apsley, who had noticed us preparing to depart, crossed the clearing with her neatly folded blanket draped over her arm. We bid each other farewell, but as Miss Scott took her first step to leave, her leg gave out beneath her. I caught her about the waist, and her hand grasped the fabric of my coat, bringing her close.

Close enough for me to catch the floral scent of her perfume and feel her warm breath skitter across my neck. How fortunate that her blanket was smashed between us, else she might have noted the fierce pounding of my heart.

That did not need to be added to her list.

I held her steady until she regained balance. "Are you well?"

"Yes. I am stricken with a weak leg, I'm afraid, but you needn't worry about me. I can manage. Thank you for the assistance." She said it all with such confidence. A simple fact to be stated without concern of how I might respond.

I nodded, releasing her, and the two women continued on. I intended to wait until they had left the clearing before departing, just as an added precaution, which left me to watch Miss Scott limp away at a slow pace, though nothing in her countenance reflected the struggle as the two women chatted and smiled.

I wondered at her nonchalance—how indifferent she was to me learning of her ailment.

And I wondered what had caused the malady in the first place.

# Chapter Eight

## GRACE

THE WALK TO BERKELEY Square from Apsley Court was not particularly long, but the excess exercise I had received over the last week had taken its toll. I had not met with my client again yet, hoping time would dull the ache, and it had to a good degree. As such, I intended to meet with Mr. Montfert tomorrow, so long as I did not aggravate my leg overly much today.

At home, it was easy to forget the malady that had ailed me since childhood, as there I could take time to rest when needed and did not spend my days walking miles to and from shops, parks, and the like. But this was my first Season, and I intended to experience it to the fullest. If that meant ignoring the pain shooting through my limb, then so be it.

"Shall we get ices at Gunter's?" Annette asked. "It is warm enough today to warrant a cold treat, I think."

"I'm not opposed," Rowe answered. "I must stop at Dangerfield's afterward. I'm in need of more material on—"

"Sheep herding," I interjected teasingly. He was always reading about the subject.

Rowe gave me an annoyed look, but there was a smile in his green eyes. The man had worked hard since inheriting my father's holdings, educating himself with the kind of commitment Father would have been proud of. I often wondered why Rowe had not been made aware of the will, so he might have been better prepared, but the only person with the answer had passed on. Even my mother had not anticipated it, though none of us had ever begrudged Rowe for inheriting.

He was the perfect person to take on the task of maintaining the estate, and I trusted he would always care for my family.

My jaw clenched. If things went according to plan, Rowe would not need to look after me for the rest of his life. I had no doubt I would end up a spinster, but I would find a way to provide for myself. Mr. Montfert and I had not agreed upon a sum, and I would bring up the topic at our next meeting. Now that we had established a good rapport, I saw no reason not to, and he had mentioned his intention to pay me for the help.

Hopefully, he would not be the last.

"You are turning into quite the bore with your incessant reading," Annette said to Rowe. "But then, you always did prefer the company of books to people."

"I shan't deny it. Perhaps that is why I get in less trouble than many of the people I know." He grinned at her. "There is nothing troublesome about reading a book in a library."

"Rus might disagree. He manages to find trouble anywhere—including libraries."

Rowe's brows furrowed, but before he could ask what his sister meant, my gaze caught on the familiar faces of Miss Rigby and her mother. I grabbed Annette's arm, dragging her forward. "Come! Let us invite Miss Rigby to join us."

Annette came willingly but scowled. "I hardly know her."

"Neither do I, which is why I want to catch up and extend the invitation." I continued when Annette blinked at me in confusion, lowering my voice so Rowe would not overhear. "She's one of the candidates I've chosen for Mr. Montfert. I wish to get to know her better."

My cousin's expression smoothed into understanding. "I see."

We drew closer, but the fast pace became harder to maintain, each step sending sharp tendrils of pain into my leg. Fortunately, Miss Rigby and her mother had the same idea as we did and entered Gunter's.

"Good morning, Mrs. Rigby, Miss Rigby," I greeted with breathy words once we had entered. "How are you today?"

"Fine," Mrs. Rigby answered with a forced smile, then turned her attention back to the room with an assessing gaze.

I would not be deterred. "Would the two of you care to join us?"

The matron ignored me, but Miss Rigby smiled. "I would like that. Mother, I am going to sit with Miss Scott."

Her mother turned toward us with a scowl, but it quickly faded as she took note of Rowe standing next to me. "Mr. Apsley, how good it is to see you."

Rowe, who had been staring at Miss Rigby, seemed to shake himself from a trance and smiled, dipping his head slightly. "A pleasure."

His eyes darted back to the younger woman.

Odd. Rowe was never so easily distracted, but he was not the only one. Annette glared at someone across the room. I followed her gaze until mine fell on Lieutenant Paget, who stood conversing with half a dozen women, a roguish grin on his lips.

"Annette?" I whispered.

She turned toward me. "I wish to leave."

"We just arrived, and besides, I have invited Miss Rigby and her mother to sit with us," I said through gritted teeth. "Surely you can survive long enough to have an ice?"

Annette huffed, muttering under her breath. "Debatable."

"Perhaps we should find a table," Rowe suggested, clearly confused by his sister's sudden change of demeanor. "There is one free just there, in the corner."

Once we were all seated, I chatted with Miss Rigby while we waited for our ices. Prompting the girl into conversation was a chore, though she seemed pleasant and kind when she did engage. She responded with intelligence, offering her opinion on topics when I asked, but never drove the conversation herself. I did not allow her reluctance to bother me, for I was now more certain than ever it was born out of shyness rather than snobbery. All points in her favor.

She also enjoyed reading. And had brown hair.

Could she be Mr. Montfert's perfect match?

I wasn't sure I'd fully convinced myself, but seeing them together at the ball—an event I asked Miss Rigby if she planned to attend—would clarify the matter. I took a bite of my cherry ice, musing over how I might make the introduction.

Annette sighed next to me, and I turned to face her, realizing for the first time she was not enjoying an ice of her own.

"Did you not want one?" I asked, nodding toward mine. "It was your idea to come, and I know you like the chocolate."

"No, thank you."

I rolled my eyes. Sometimes my cousin could be quite dramatic. No doubt her abstinence had something to do with the lieutenant. Some strange point of rebellion.

Rebellion of what, I did not know, but it was certainly not worth losing an ice over.

I glanced over at the man and found him staring at us despite the numerous women vying for his attention. Annette followed my gaze, and once she realized his focus was on her, she stuck up her chin.

"Do not look at him," she ordered under her breath. "He will think we care that he is here."

"But you do care," I said.

"No. Well, yes, but only because I do not wish to be anywhere *he* is."

"You've had one conversation with the man. How can you dislike him so much after one conversation?"

Annette shifted in her chair to face me, and I was glad Rowe was conversing with Mrs. Rigby and her daughter. They did not need to overhear this discussion.

"He tried to call on me two days ago," said Annette. "The nerve of the man after being so...so...offensive."

"Technically, he never answered your question at the dinner party, so I fail to see how—"

"And"—she held up her finger, continuing to talk over me—"you know I have an agreement with my parents. I must accept any suitor, which means if he calls, I cannot deny him. I was fortunate to have been out with Mother the day he came."

In the man's defense, he was not the only suitor Annette had complained about since we arrived in Town. Two others had called on her, including Lord Hartley, who wore vibrant yellow waistcoats and a purple coat. While Annette played the part of gracious hostess perfectly, the moment they left, she ripped apart their characters like a knife to canvas.

Annette stiffened and sucked in a breath. "No. He is coming this way. Hide me."

"Hide you?" I asked with a chuckle. "How do you expect me to do that? Besides, he has been staring at you for the last quarter hour. It is not as though he hasn't seen that you're here."

The lieutenant approached and bowed politely in greeting. The women who had not left his side since our arrival followed him, and for the first time, I noticed a bit of weariness in his expression. Perhaps he did not enjoy their attention as much as he let on.

"Might I join you?" he asked after all pleasantries had been exchanged.

Annette gripped the edge of her chair when Rowe offered him the only vacant seat—the one next to her. The man sat down with a nod of thanks, and the group of women that had surrounded him took the dismissal with frowns as they dispersed.

"How are you today, Miss Apsley?" he asked.

Annette lifted her chin but did not spare him a glance. "Well, I thank you."

"Cold?"

She faced him, confusion knitting her brows. "I said *well*, sir."

"I heard you. I assumed you were cold since you are the only one in this entire establishment who has chosen not to enjoy an ice today."

Annette smiled, a façade of politeness I was certain the man could see through. "I find I cannot enjoy them in an atmosphere that is tainted."

The lieutenant propped his head up with one elbow on the table, leaning toward her with a smirk. "Tainted how, Miss Apsley?"

I assumed since the man had called on my cousin that there was some genuine interest on his part, but if he continued to taunt her this way, he would ruin any chance he had. Still, I admired his gumption. If nothing else, he was not put off by Annette's barely concealed disdain.

"I would not wish to cause offense." Annette smiled prettily and fluttered her lashes.

"Then it is good I am not a man easily offended." He batted his lashes back at her.

Annette rolled her eyes. "How unfortunate for me."

I covered my mouth to prevent the laughter building inside me from escaping. I hadn't any idea what sort of game the lieutenant was playing, but he was clearly enjoying himself. Perhaps he was a tad incorrigible, but I could not help but be amused by the situation. Because of her agreement with her parents to accept the attention of any suitor this Season, she could not simply dismiss the man, no matter how much she disliked him.

"Are you at home to callers on Friday, Miss Apsley?"

Annette's jaw clenched, and she ground out her response. "Yes, sir."

"Good. I'll be sure to return to Gunter's then so as to not unintentionally taint your experience." He stood with a wide grin then bowed before leaving our group. Annette gaped after him, seeming some mixture of appalled and shocked.

My laughter broke free.

"Yes, yes, laugh," Annette said. "You would not find so much humor in it if you were in my position."

"You must give the man credit; he tricked you well."

"Oh, shush." Annette whacked my arm playfully, her lips twitching. "I will give him no such credit, and I cannot decide whether to despise him more or feel relieved that he has no intention of calling on me again."

"I would not bet on the latter," I said. "The man might still show up on Friday. He takes pleasure in teasing you."

"Heaven knows why."

I gave her a pointed look, and she shook her head vehemently. "I know what you are thinking, Grace, and I beg you toss those notions away this minute. I shall count myself lucky if I never see him again."

Something told me Annette would not be so fortunate.

HAVING BID MRS. RIGBY and her daughter goodbye at Gunter's, Annette and I walked arm in arm through Berkeley Square with Rowe following behind us. We still needed to stop at Dangerfield's so Rowe could purchase a book or two, and while the siblings conversed on our walk, my mind pondered over my conversation with Miss Rigby.

I liked the woman a great deal and wondered if Mr. Montfert would find her equally as pleasant. Even if he did, would Miss Rigby take to him? He was handsome and set to inherit a fortune, but there was more to romance than those things. A love match, after all, involved two hearts; not just one.

Annette nudged me with her elbow, pulling me from my musings. "Ahead of us," she whispered.

My gaze landed on Mr. Montfert as he left Dangerfield's, and before I could think better of it, I called to him. At this distance, he did not hear me, so I called again, louder this time.

Still, he did not turn around. Before I could make a third attempt, he started walking and joined a woman leaving the shop next door. My feet halted. I recognized that head of dark hair and elegant figure.

Sabrina Stafford, the Duchess of Rochester. The woman who had nearly ruined my sister and her chance at happiness.

Sabrina took Mr. Montfert's arm, and he smiled down at her. Something twirled in my stomach, and the sensation remained even as the two of them walked farther away from us down the street.

"Grace?" Rowe placed a gentle hand on my shoulder, his voice soft with concern. "Are you well? How do you know Mr. Montfert?"

"He is an acquaintance." Much as I trusted Rowe, he would not approve of me playing matchmaker for financial gain. I continued when his brows drew closer. "I am surprised, is all. I was under the impression that he has an interest in a friend of mine. Perhaps I was mistaken. Do you know him?"

Rowe shook his head. "Not well, really. I met him while out with Rus a few days ago. The two of them have become fencing partners, it seems. As for your concern about his interest in your friend, I would not discredit it so soon. He and the Duchess are cousins, and I doubt there is more to their relationship. Her father has named Montfert his heir, according to my brother, and demanded he marry or face disinheritance. Mr. Perry's expectations are high, as I'm sure you can imagine."

I could imagine it. No wonder Mr. Montfert had been desperate enough to hire me. In a way, it made me more eager to help him.

But the nephew of Mr. Perry? I did not know how to feel about helping a man so close to the woman who had hurt my sister. Amelia had been trapped under Sabrina's thumb for over a year before any of us became aware of the situation. Somehow, Sabrina had learned of Amelia's illegitimacy and used the information as blackmail, and Mr. Perry was no better.

While Sabrina had promised to never reveal the truth once Amelia became engaged to her now husband, Lord Emerson, I was uncertain I trusted her to keep her word. When we first met, I had idolized the Duchess for her kindness and elegance. But that kindness was a front. She wore her mask well and fooled many.

Did Mr. Montfert wear a similar disguise? And what would I do if I discovered he did?

# Chapter Nine

## PHILLIP

THE AIR HAD GROWN warm by the time Sabrina and I returned to the house, and I eagerly shed my coat and gloves.

"Thank you, cousin," said Sabrina. "It was important that I visited the shops today."

"Why is that?" I asked, handing my things over to the butler.

"I happened to know this particular silk is selling at a much higher price near Piccadilly. I told the shopkeeper I could give him insider information if he would sell it to me at a discount, which he agreed to do. The information would have reached him without my help eventually, but I saw no reason not to take advantage of being the conveyor of it."

"I see." Forcing a smile to my lips was difficult. In many ways, Sabrina mirrored her father, especially in the way they had mastered the art of manipulation.

Sabrina tucked the parcel she had obtained from the haberdashery against her and headed directly for the stairs. I had not intended to go out today at all, but she had made me a deal I could not refuse—a promise to introduce me to any of her eligible acquaintances we met along the way.

Miss Scott was working hard to find me a wife, but I would take any assistance I could get. My future, and Mother's, was riding on my ability to please Uncle. Agreeing to accompany my cousin was a small price to pay.

Though why she wished for my escort, I hadn't any idea.

I followed Sabrina up the stairs, taking them quickly until I had caught up with her. "Why did you request my escort? As a widow, Society would not frown upon you being out and about without one."

We reached the landing, and Sabrina glanced at Uncle's study before responding in a hushed voice. "Because I do not wish to be hounded by men who think I am searching for a new husband."

"So I am a deterrent?" I supposed it could work. We were cousins, but that did not mean people would not assume a courtship between us. It was not an uncommon occurrence.

"Of a sort, though the reason I need the company will likely shift soon."

My brows furrowed. "What do you mean?"

She drew in a deep breath and nodded to the end of the corridor to the small parlor there. I followed her into the room. It boasted light blue wallpaper and darker-hued furniture, but the overall effect of the coloring was to give the space a cooler feel, despite the warmth outside.

Sabrina took a seat in one of the high-back chairs, and I claimed the one opposite. Her explanation required a degree of privacy, it seemed. We had never been particularly close, but her actions concerned me. Sabrina had never been one to hide or shy away from conversation. She wore her confidence well.

But the woman sitting across from me did not display that familiar confidence. She toyed with her gloved fingers as if hesitant to continue.

"There are rumors circulating about me," she said at last. "I suspected they would come out eventually, but even so, I do not feel prepared to face them."

"What sort of rumors? If there is anything I can do—"

Sabrina leaned forward and placed a hand on my arm. "You were always too good for this family, Phillip." She slumped back into the chair, her forehead wrinkled. "There is nothing you can do, but I would rather not visit the shops or attend parties alone. It is easier to ignore things when I have someone at my side, and you know once my father hears the gossip, he will not step foot in the same room as me in public."

"They are as bad as that?" I asked.

She stared at me for a moment, as if trying to decide how much to disclose. "I suppose you will hear them for yourself soon enough. I would rather you have the truth from me, especially if you are to be my escort.

"After my...after the late duke died, Father encouraged me to remarry. I am sure you know this and can guess at his reasons. I was never anything more to him than what he could gain through my connections. He did not like the idea of me—and by extension, himself—losing ties with the ducal family, and so, he insisted I attempt to ensnare the duke's heir.

"What neither of us realized at the time is that such a marriage would never be legal and my efforts were both pointless and ended up severing any connection I had with the family. The new duke was engaged at the time, and after refusing my attention on multiple occasions, I was banished to the dower house.

"After that, I decided it was better to leave the estate, and I returned home."

I remembered the day Sabrina had arrived at Eldercrest. I had not seen her since the wedding and had been shocked by her harried appearance. She always carried herself with such poise, and the change reminded me that, beneath her guarded exterior, was a person with feelings and fears.

My uncle had not been so sympathetic to her plight, agreeing to allow her back into his home upon the condition that she remarry. Sabrina had gone to a house party not long after, I suspected, for the purpose of gaining another husband.

The details of the event had never fully been shared with me, but Sabrina had returned unengaged, and her relationship with my uncle had grown far more tenuous. The two of them were often at odds, but there was a new sense of determination in Sabrina that I had not seen before. More than once, I had overheard her and my uncle discussing marriage, and each time his demands were met with a refusal. I envied her bravery. I had never stood up to the man, but my cousin had found the strength to do so after years of strict obedience.

"My marriage negotiations did not favor me in the slightest," she continued, her tone quieter. "I am at my father's mercy, and while I refuse to obey his demands, it is quite likely he will disown me should these rumors spread. Perhaps if I do not pay heed to them, Society will be taken by some other scandal and lose interest."

"From where do you think the rumors came? Did the new duke—"

"No. At least, I do not think they came from him. He had no intention of allowing the information to reach London. He wanted to protect his wife from any sort of scandal." She shrugged with a grimace. "But gossip spreads between households. Only so much can be done to prevent it. Powerful as a duke might be, even he cannot control wagging tongues below stairs."

"I'm sorry," I said. "Uncle will not take the news well."

"He will not, but I care not for his opinion. Quite frankly, I want nothing to do with the man who sired me. I've come to realize he cares nothing for me, and I do not want to become him. His manipulations have hurt far too many people. *I* have hurt too many people on his behalf."

I bit my lip, uncertain I should speak my mind. We had never had the kind of relationship friends shared—the kind that offered comfort and criticism. But she had confided in me, and surely that meant she might be more open to my advice? She sounded genuinely repentant of her past actions and, if nothing else, wished to be better than her father.

"Sabrina..." I hedged.

She glanced up at me, and her lips lifted in a gentle smile. "You have something you wish to say. Something, I think, you believe I might find offensive."

I chuckled. "How could you tell?"

"Call it a gift for reading people." She paused, her smile fading. "Tell me, Phillip. I shan't take offense, and I would wager it is something I need to hear."

I nodded, already feeling guilt pool in my stomach. "You wish to be nothing like your father, but the man is manipulative, Sabrina. I have seen those same manipulative tendencies in you, even today." I gestured to the parcel she still held. "The silk, for instance. Even your offer to help me in exchange for my escort about town. They are harmless manipulations, to be sure, but manipulations nonetheless. I suspect you were not aware of them. They came to you naturally."

She blinked back tears. "I never considered... You are right. I have spent so much of my life tricking and blackmailing to get what I want—to meet Father's expectations—that it has become ingrained in me. I do it without thinking. I am so sorry."

I leaned forward, took her hand, and gave it a light squeeze. "But you want to do better, and that is the first step. You've recognized the habit. Now, you need only focus on squashing it."

She smiled tentatively. "I wish it were so easy, but you are right. I am going to fix this." She released my hand and stood, dashing away the lone tear that had escaped. "Thank you for being honest with me, Phillip."

With that, she left the room. I silently wished her luck in the endeavor, for some things could never be fixed. I should know.

Never, in the last two decades since I had come to live with my uncle, had I ever felt comfortable during one of our meetings. Even at the age of eight, when he had taken guardianship, the man had intimidated me. He and my father were as dissimilar as brothers could be. Where the man who sired me tended toward a relaxed temperament, Uncle was fueled by unyielding determination. My father had been slow to anger and preferred to spend his time with his family. Our home had been one of safety and love.

Living with Uncle was akin to walking on ground made of glass, where each step was fraught with danger and a simple crack resulted in punishment. While I owed the man my gratitude for saving me and Mother from a life of destitution, I quickly came to understand it came at a cost. Our relationship would never resemble what I had lost.

He would not replace my father in any sense.

Even now, as I sat in the study with him, his stare bore into me with unveiled expectation. I had been assigned the role of heir, and if I wanted to keep it, I must do as I was told. That had always been the way with Uncle. He wielded my lack of fortune like a weapon, one that easily corrected disobedience and kept me in line.

That had been a difficult lesson for an eight-year-old to learn, but that boy had been locked away in a box without a key for two decades now. With my future in Uncle's hands, I had no other choice.

"You've been out with Apsley several times this week." Uncle's gruff voice made the statement feel like an accusation.

"I have. He has become a good friend."

Uncle pursed his lips, nodding slowly. "I admit, when I told you to become acquainted with members of the *ton*, I did not think you would find success so quickly. This bodes well."

I ignored the insult in his words. "I am doing my best to please you."

Uncle sat back in his chair and steepled his fingers. "That remains to be seen. Have you found a woman worthy of courting yet?"

The muscles in my jaw tightened. Worthy of courting? I wanted to scoff. His list made it quite clear the sort of person he deemed *worthy*—a creature that simply did not exist. Still, I would keep the opinion to myself.

"I have a few I am considering," I said, a half-truth. "However, I would like a bit more time to assess their qualities. If I find any of them meet many of the attributes on your list, I will offer her name for your approval before moving forward."

Uncle studied me for a moment, and for the first time in my life, I felt an inkling of approval. Rarely did we have a conversation where he did not berate me for one mistake or another or remind me my dysfunctional hearing labeled me a broken man and not fully fit for Society. Perhaps I had finally earned his respect, or at least a small portion of it.

"The Season will close before we know it," he said. "I trust you will make haste with your assessments?"

"Yes. There is a ball next week, and I intend to learn more then. Apsley requested an invitation on my behalf. It came just this morning."

"Good. Good. That will give you an opportunity to watch these women among your peers, too. It is of great importance that your wife be capable of mingling with the upper class. Are any of them titled?"

"I..." Lud. Miss Scott had not revealed much about the women, including their names. I hadn't any idea if they held titles or simply came from wealthy families. Surely it was some mix of the two? I had made it clear to her how important those things were to Uncle. "I am uncertain, but it is my top priority to find out."

Uncle narrowed his eyes. "See that you do. I have a meeting I cannot miss, so I trust you can manage one ball without me. Until then, we have ledgers to look over."

He slid a stack of them toward me, and my brows lifted. I had been tutored extensively on estate management, but Uncle had never allowed me firsthand experience. "You wish me to help?"

"If you are to take over my holdings one day, then you must learn the ins and outs of my business dealings. We will start with these." He tapped a finger against the ledger in front of him, one made of leather with a deep red tint. "Once you've proven yourself...well, we can move on to other things."

"What does that ledger contain?"

"Nothing you need to worry about at present." He nodded toward my stack. "Verify those are properly balanced. Once you've finished, you will bring your findings to me. I will know if you miss anything."

His words could not be more clear. This was a test and one I needed to pass.

# Chapter Ten

## PHILLIP

I greeted Thursday morning with nervous anticipation. After fencing practice yesterday afternoon, Apsley had given me another note from Miss Scott, asking to meet this morning in Hyde. I was eager to see her and discuss my options further, and waiting for word from her had been torturous.

She requested we meet before the fashionable hour, though less early than before so we might discuss a few matters in private before parading about the park in hopes of her making introductions with some of the women on her list. There was no guarantee they would be there, of course, but still, I found myself anxious.

Knowing Uncle had business matters to attend to all morning, I descended the stairs without notifying him of my intentions. As I reached the bottom, the butler opened the door to let in an elderly woman with small peacock plumes rising from her bonnet, her expression wrinkled under the force of a wide smile.

She met my gaze, and somehow, that smile grew. "Oh, Mr. Montfert! What a pleasure to see you."

"Good morning, Mrs. Ellis. How are you today?"

"Well. Very well, indeed. I was just telling Mr. Ellis how lovely it is. Fine weather we are having. Sun for days, with not a cloud in the sky. You intend to go out and enjoy the warmth, do you not?"

"I do." My smile grew strained. Not because I disliked conversing with Mrs. Ellis, but because I was not sure how to navigate her forgetfulness. I had met her upon first arriving in London, as she often met with Uncle to discuss investments. Mr. Ellis had been one of Uncle's clients for years...until his passing three months ago. Mrs. Ellis, however, seemed to forget her widowed status from time to time, showing up in bright colors unbefitting of someone in mourning, but she never missed a meeting with my uncle or forgot my name. It was curious how the mind could pick and choose what it remembered.

Regardless, the last thing I wanted to do was remind her of the grief of losing her husband.

"I best be off to enjoy the sunshine," I said. "Have a good day, Mrs. Ellis."

She nodded, and I stepped past her. The butler handed me my coat and hat, which I slipped on as I left the house. Mrs. Ellis was not wrong. With the sun shining overhead, it was a lovely day, making my jaunt to Hyde pleasurable.

When I arrived in the clearing, Miss Scott and Miss Apsley were already there, the latter sitting against a tree reading. I exchanged greetings with them both and then took a place on the ground to Miss Scott's left. The spot was tight, nestled between her and a tree, and she looked a question at me when I brushed her shoulder and shimmied into the space, stretching my legs out in front of me.

It must seem strange for me to choose that position when there was more open space to her right, but I would not risk being unable to hear her, nor did I have any desire to explain myself. Uncle demanded I keep my hearing struggles a secret, but admittedly, I had no wish for anyone else to treat me as he did. To judge me.

I cleared my throat. "What shall we discuss today?"

Her curiosity evaporated, at least for the time being, and she retrieved her notebook from her reticule. "More about you, naturally."

I gave her a wry look. "Of course."

She passed me a teasing grin. "You needn't sound so excited about it, Mr. Montfert."

"If I thought myself more interesting, perhaps I would be more excited. I am coming to learn that *I* am not my favorite topic of discussion."

She studied me for a moment, as if attempting to discern the truthfulness of my words, and then opened her notebook. She tapped her pencil to the page. "We can agree you are not vain, then. Some people adore speaking of themselves. I do have a question for you first."

She bit down on her lip as if hesitant. I nudged her with my shoulder and smiled, hoping the gesture would put her at ease. "Whatever it is, you may ask."

"Well, I do not know how much Rus told you about my intentions, and since you have offered to pay me—"

"I will. You may name your price, Miss Scott. I desperately need the help, and you have put so much work into making this list already. You cannot know how much I appreciate the effort."

She nodded. "I have been giving it some thought but cannot seem to settle on what would be fair to us both. You are my first client, sir, and while I can promise to do what I can, there is no guarantee this will work."

"I understand." I lifted my hands to placate her concerns. "My payment is not contingent upon that."

"Very well, but let us not decide on the value of my services until we have determined their success. I would be far more comfortable with that." She bit her lip again, and my eyes settled on them. I studied the color, which was a deeper shade of pink now, and the shape of them. How they curved with perfect symmetry.

I tore my gaze away. "That is fair. Now may I ask you a question?" I continued when she offered a hesitant nod. "Why are you so keen on becoming a matchmaker?"

"Ah." She smiled, her attention straight ahead. "It's simple, really. I expect to become a spinster, which suits me fine, but I do not wish to be a burden on my family. My cousin, Rowe, was named my guardian and inherited all of my father's holdings upon his death. I trust Rowe to take care of me, but he should not have to. And so, I seek financial independence. Matchmaking is a solution."

I opened my mouth but could not find the words to question her. A spinster? My mind could not account for her decision. It was as if she had resigned herself to it, which made little sense to me. Miss Scott was not old enough to be considered on the shelf—she, herself, had admitted this was her first Season—and furthermore, her beauty alone could draw a man of wealth or title.

"But enough about me," she pressed on when I kept silent. "I've learned a little more about your circumstances. My cousin may have mentioned that you stand to lose your inheritance if you do not wed."

I winced. "A threat from my uncle, and one he has utilized before."

"You've no choice," she said with quiet sympathy.

I tilted my head from side to side. "We always have a choice in our decisions; it is the consequences we have no say in. I could choose to disobey him, but..." I drew in a deep breath. There was no reason to hide the whole of it from her. "My father left me with nothing, Miss Scott. Without this inheritance, I am destitute but for the meager pin money I have stashed away over the years. That fact would not be so bothersome if my mother were not also relying on me. For her sake, I do as my uncle wishes."

"Then let us find you a wife." She placed her hand on my arm, and a string of chills raced over my skin, a counter to the warmth of her fingers permeating through my coat.

Miss Scott asked me questions, so many that I lost track of the time. She forced me to think more about my own wants and desires for the future than I ever had, while also keeping me at ease. Something about her calmed my soul—made me forget, for a time, the challenge I faced. With her, my lack of social experience seemed…irrelevant.

"I've made you a list of possible matches," she said, extending her notebook toward me. I read the names listed there, none of which were familiar, and smiled at how she had crossed out several, some with more effort than others.

"You have been busy." I pointed to one of the marked-out names. "What made you decide against this one?"

"She is not ready to settle down, in my opinion. Miss Baker is far too flirtatious for you."

"Too flirtatious?" I reared back in jest. "I can be flirtatious."

Miss Scott chuckled. "I know you can, but I did not think you would want a wife who enjoys flirting with every man of her acquaintance."

"Hmm, no, I would not. What about this one?"

"Why are you more interested in the ones I've decided against than the ones I think have potential." Amusement sparkled in her brown eyes, catching the few sunbeams that managed to enter the clearing between the trees, and she shook her head.

I shrugged. "It is nerves, I think. Speaking of women who would not suit me is easier than considering those who might. I tend to embarrass myself when I get nervous and find the best way to avoid it is to avoid situations that set me on edge."

"Which includes talking to ladies," she guessed.

"Indeed, unless they happen to have wrinkles. I can generally manage those well enough."

"You say that until one old enough to be your grandmother sets her eyes on you," she warned. "You are too handsome not to attract eligible ladies of all ages."

I barked out a laugh. "Too handsome? I am not paying you to forge pretty compliments for me, Miss Scott."

"It requires little effort when it is true. But tell me, what is it that makes you so nervous? Do you handle it better when you have met the lady before?"

My mind was still struggling to process her response. Miss Scott thought me handsome? Genuinely? The idea sent warmth radiating through my chest. "I...yes, I suppose it helps if I have met them. Or seen them before, even. Familiarity to any degree is useful."

She tapped her pencil, this time not against her notebook, but her lips. My gaze fixed on them, and that odd stirring I had felt during our last meeting returned.

"Oh! I have an idea." She tossed the notebook aside and rose. I clambered after her. Miss Scott walked to the other side of the clearing, her chin lifted as she stared up into the trees. Then, her assessing gaze wandered over the many branches until she seemed satisfied and reached for the lowest one.

"What are you doing? I asked.

"Climbing this tree," she grunted out the words, pulling herself up and digging her half boots into the bark until she reached the branch. Standing on it, she looked down at me in slight exasperation. "You must climb with me."

"What?"

"Climb with me. It is not difficult."

"I...but why? And should you be doing such a thing with your leg?" Never mind the impropriety of it all. Ladies did not climb trees, did they? Or gentleman, for that matter. I was fairly certain Uncle would be appalled, should he learn of it.

Miss Scott grinned and continued her climb. "I do not make a habit of letting my leg interfere with something I want, Mr. Montfert."

"And right now you want to climb a tree?" I asked skeptically.

"No, I want *you* to climb the tree. I am merely leading you." She paused and gestured for me to approach the trunk. "Quickly. From up here, we might spot your potential brides. This way, you will have seen them before, thus easing your nerves."

I looked from her to the lowest branch, then back again, watching her as she tested each step and adjusted when they seemed unsteady. This was not settling my nerves in at all.

"You might as well do it," said Miss Apsley, who sat not far from where I stood, her eyes trained on her book. "When Grace is determined about something, she rarely backs down. In this instance, she will stay in that tree until you join her."

My jaw clenched. I could not rightly let her remain in the tree all day, now could I? After another moment of consideration, I shrugged out of my coat and tossed it and my hat onto the ground. I reached for the branch and hoisted myself up. From above, Miss Scott tossed instructions at me as we both climbed.

"Watch out for this branch," she said, pointing at one. "It is a bit suspicious. I do not think it will hold your weight. Oh, and that one there has an army of ants crawling across it, so avoid it if you can. And do not look up when you are directly beneath me. I shan't like you peering up my skirts."

My face heated with her last instruction, thoroughly distracting me the remainder of my climb as I tried, with great effort, to avoid looking up her skirts by accident. It seemed my eyes were drawn in that direction against my will now that she had put the notion in my head.

Most ungentlemanly.

Once we had climbed as high as the thinning branches would allow, I looked out over the park. We were still well-hidden between the leaves, but through the bare spaces, I had a view of the people walking the paths toward The Serpentine.

I glanced at Miss Scott, taking in her content expression. Her smile. The way the shallow breeze teased her chocolate brown hair and the sun coated her cheeks and nose in an ethereal glow. How did a woman with a weak leg find peace in a tree?

How did she look so beautiful doing it?

"Are you well?" I asked.

She looked at me, seeming to take my meaning. "My leg is fine, though I might regret this tomorrow." She shrugged as if this was not an unusual occurrence. "My impulsiveness sometimes gets the better of me, but I find moments like this worth a little pain."

Her gaze returned to the park, and she began to point out women of her acquaintance, but my eyes remained on her. Moments like this, she had said. She meant the view of the park, or perhaps the exhilaration of climbing, but this moment stemmed from neither of those things for me as I looked at her. Miss Scott was brave and impulsive, charming and witty. She was kind and sympathetic.

She was altogether lovely.

My matchmaker had pushed me to consider the qualities I wanted in a wife—to dig deep within myself and contemplate my own desires, not just Uncle's. And here, clinging to the branches above Hyde Park, I realized I did have a list.

One I feared was a reflection of the woman next to me in the tree.

# Chapter Eleven

## GRACE

THE APSLEY TOWNHOUSE WAS alive with visitors Friday afternoon, and while none of them were there for me specifically, I took great amusement in watching my cousin fend off suitors. As promised, Annette entertained each of them with the politeness and sophistication one would expect from the daughter of a viscount. She wore a smile and poured tea, her voice amiable and her expression pleasant.

Inside, I doubted she felt any such sentiment. Annette saw the institution of marriage as a shackleing, freedom-stealing design hardly worth the benefits Society claimed she would reap. With a substantial dowry, I supposed she could afford to think that way. Even without marriage, she would want for nothing.

Well, perhaps that was not entirely true. I was not convinced Annette would not experience some regret in choosing to spend her life alone. She may claim to have no interest in romance, but I suspected much of it was a front propagated by fear. Despite being raised in a home with loving parents and a father who rarely begrudged her of freedoms, Annette worried she would not find the same in a spouse.

In fairness, she had a right to worry, as so many men of the *ton* held strict expectations on the role of women.

"Miss Apsley, might I request your first dance at the Morrison's ball next week?" Mr. Conners asked. The man had taken a liking to Cook's lemon tarts, and at present, his upper lip was home to the remnants of them. Despite his inability to eat without making a mess, he did seem kind, if not a little overly jubilant.

Annette tilted her head, offering him a tiny pout. "I fear my first dance has been claimed."

Mr. Conners scooted to the edge of the cushion. "What about the second?"

"No," Mr. Laurance interjected before Annette could respond. "I've claimed the second already."

"And I the third," Lord Monksfield added.

Mr. Conners' shoulders sagged, his face wrinkling with disappointment. Lady Paxton passed her daughter a look, and Annette drew in a deep breath meant to give her patience. "I am certain there is a free spot on my card, Mr. Conners. Would it be fair for me to add your name? Then you might find me at the ball to learn which dance is yours."

The man grinned in response, all evidence of dejection gone. "That would be capital, Miss Apsley. I look forward to it."

"As do I," Annette ground out, her smile still in place.

Much as I had always dreamed of being courted, I did not envy her right now. The men visiting were fine. I could think of nothing off-putting about them. Still, I could not see myself marrying any of them, nor could I see a suitable match for Annette. It was one thing to receive attention from a gentleman a woman liked, but to have it thrust upon her with no way to deny him? That seemed tortuous.

But Annette was determined to have her parents forget the idea of her marrying, and for that reason alone, she put up with the parade of suitors.

"What of you, Miss Scott?" Mr. Willoughby, who sat next to me and was certainly possessed of a more quiet demeanor, asked. "Have you a partner for the first dance?"

I shook my head. It was kind of him to ask, especially when it was clear the men were not here for me. "I am afraid I cannot dance due to my leg, sir, but I appreciate you inquiring."

"I see. Well, I hope I shall see you there nonetheless."

"You shall, of course. My cousin may even have another spot on her dance card if you wish to fill it."

His smile dimmed a little. "I would be honored."

Once the men had gone, Annette slumped into the settee with a groan. "What have I done to deserve this?"

"Grown into a beautiful woman with connections to the peerage, for starters," I said before taking the last sip of my tea. "I did tell you men would be beating down the door to call on you."

Annette glared at me. "It is highly unfair and rude of them to ignore you so completely. Although, Mr. Willoughby seemed quite set in his attention."

I scoffed. "Do not tell a fudge, Annette. Those men were here for you alone. Mr. Willoughby was simply being polite. That is all."

Annette pursed her lips. "He asked you to dance, did he not?"

"He did, but as I have no intention of dancing at all this Season, I was forced to turn him down."

"You truly do not intend to dance?" asked Lady Paxton, her brows furrowed.

I shifted on the sofa. My aunt knew of my ailment and how often it affected me. Indeed, I suspected Rowe had spoken to her about it before we came to London, since she was serving as my matronly sponsor in a way. Still, I hated admitting my weak leg would keep me from something I might otherwise enjoy. I did not allow it to hold me back if I could help it.

But dancing had proven too painful on more than one occasion. I had learned that avoiding the activity altogether was better than the limb failing me on the dancefloor.

And was far less embarrassing.

"I think it is for the best," I said. "But do not worry for me. I will enjoy myself regardless."

Besides, I had plenty to occupy me during the ball. I had not introduced Mr. Montfert to any women in the park—though we did observe two of them from the tree—and he would meet a few for the first time tonight. All of my attention would go to observing their interactions.

I hadn't time for dancing, in truth.

I ignored the prodding disappointment in my chest.

Annette sighed. "I never thought I would be jealous of your leg, Grace. What I wouldn't give to have an excuse not to dance."

"But then you would have a painful limp to deal with," I reminded.

Annette grimaced. "You're right. It was rather thoughtless of me to say something like that. Forgive me."

I swatted her comment away. "I took no offense, and I can understand your reluctance. You have had an inordinate amount of callers and requests today."

Annette sat up, pointing at me. "You see, Mother. I am not the only one who thinks so. A few dinner parties can not possibly account for this many men coming to call on me. Something is amiss."

"You have made an impression; I cannot imagine what more you think it could be," said Lady Paxton with patience.

"I did not make *that* grand of an impression." Annette crossed her arms. "At least the whole of it is done for today. I do not think I could handle one more—"

The butler cleared his throat from the entrance of the drawing room. "Lieutenant Paget is here, my lady."

Annette groaned, and her mother shot her a frown of disapproval.

"See him in," said Lady Paxton, then waited for the butler to disappear before whispering the rest. "Sit up, Annette. You are to receive all suitors with cordiality. That was our agreement."

"Calling hours are nearly done," Annette mumbled under her breath. "It is beyond rude for him to come now. Why should I act cordially?"

We all stood when the lieutenant entered the room. Lieutenant Paget bowed, but his eyes remained solely on Annette, his grin a token of triumph over having caused her clear displeasure. The man enjoyed playing with fire, it seemed.

Before pleasantries could be exchanged, the butler reappeared. "I beg your pardon, my lady, but a Mr. Montfert has arrived to see Miss Scott."

Lady Paxton's brows furrowed. Given she had never met the man, I could understand her confusion.

"He is a friend of mine," I said to alleviate her hesitancy.

My aunt gave me a curious look before asking the butler to retrieve our visitor. Mr. Montfert entered, and his gaze sought me out immediately. Our eyes connected, and a warm smile stretched over his handsome face, releasing a fluttering sensation in my stomach. None of our other visitors today had created this strange anxiousness in me, but then, none of them had come for me, either.

Since neither my aunt nor the lieutenant had ever met Mr. Montfert, I made introductions. We all took our seats, the lieutenant next to my cousin and Mr. Monfert next to me. For the second time since our first meeting, he chose the smallest space at my side, forcing me to scoot over the cushion to make room. It was odd, but I dared not question him about it here.

Lady Paxton seemed all too content alone in her armchair where she could watch us. I would have to clarify a few things with her, else she get the wrong impression about my client.

What was he doing here, anyway? I wanted to ask, desperately, but such a question would stoke Lady Paxton's curiosity. I loved my aunt, but the fewer people who knew of my matchmaking business, the better. Had Annette not overheard Rus telling me about finding my first client, I may not have even confided in her.

Although, she had made for a far better chaperone than Rus.

"How are you, Miss Apsley?" the lieutenant asked.

"Not cold." She gave him a significant look, one full of accusation. "I thought, sir, you intended to spend time at Gunter's today."

"And miss your calling hours again? How utterly devastating that would be. Besides, I would not wish to taint anyone's air simply by breathing."

"You are tainting—" Annette's mouth snapped closed, and she quickly glanced at her mother. "How considerate of you. To breathe here. Instead."

He fought his amusement. "I could think of no better place. After all, you are so accepting when it comes to my breathing."

"Accepting by no choice of my own. Your condition is a rather regrettable burden upon mankind."

"Annette!" her mother chided.

The lieutenant held up a hand. "Not to worry, Lady Paxton. I am quite certain your daughter did not mean to infer she would prefer me not to breathe at all."

Based on the way Annette was glaring at him, it was obvious she would, in fact, prefer that. But the lieutenant seemed all too aware of this, grinning from ear to ear while she simmered in a fury she could not unleash.

A soft nudge to my side drew my attention, and Mr. Montfert leaned closer to me, his voice low. "That man has a death wish, I think."

I covered my mouth to hide my giggle. "Indeed. I would warn him of the danger, but he infuriates her on purpose. It is a game to him."

Mr. Montfert tilted his head, eycing the two studiously. A strand of his hair tickled my cheek with the increased proximity, and my heart tripped into an unusual rhythm.

"Perhaps," he whispered. "But the game may not be what you think it is." He pulled away, his eyes searching my face. "Or maybe you do realize that, given your talents."

My talents? He could only mean my matchmaking abilities.

"It is too early to tell," I whispered back. "There is attraction, to be sure, but whether anything can come of it, or should come of it, is yet to be seen. A love match requires more than tease and charm."

He nodded, his expression pensive. As if he was truly giving my response thought. "Should we intervene then, or is it your stance to give them space to work things out themselves?"

I blinked at him. He had not asked if I, the matchmaker, should intervene, but if *we* should. It all felt very...conspiratorial. Phillip Montfert was meant to be my client; not my partner in crime.

Not that finding Annette a love match was a crime, though she would likely call it that. Regardless, I had promised her I would not make her one of my clients this Season. It was difficult to find someone a match who did not want one. She had enough pressure from her parents, and I had no intention of adding to it.

I shook my head. "We let them be. I have one match to contend with at present, and it deserves my full attention."

He smiled, full and appreciative, and the weight of it quickened my pulse.

Lady Paxton steered the conversation to shallow topics about the weather and upcoming events, and soon, the visit came to an end. Both men bid us farewell, and I found myself so distracted by the disappointment of their departure I did not realize until later, when my head fell upon my pillow, that I had forgotten my question.

Why had Phillip Montfert come to call on me in the first place?

# Chapter Twelve

## GRACE

IN THE DAYS LEADING up to the ball, I had no more calls from Phillip Montfert. Annette faced half a dozen suitors, and the constant barrage of men was beginning to wear on her. Simple observation made it clear she had no interest in any of them, but because of the conditions of her agreement with her parents, she could not turn them down each time they asked to ride or promenade. I often wondered if she regretted making the deal at all, but anytime Lord or Lady Paxton brought up the idea of marriage, Annette's passionate determination returned anew.

She would not wed this Season, of that, I felt confident.

Standing in the drawing room, I smoothed my gloved hands over the fabric of my pink ballgown. It was the first time I had worn it, and my feelings were rather muddled about it. I had argued heartily against Lord Paxton—who had generously offered to pay for my Season—purchasing something so extravagant when I knew the Season would not end in a betrothal for me, but the man had insisted on not one ballgown, but three.

Rowe entered the room, dressed in a fine black suit that set off his green eyes, his auburn hair perfectly styled. He smiled upon seeing me, a genuine one that made me almost reconsider living on my own. I hated being a burden to him, but I did love my cousin and truly appreciated the care he had taken to provide for me, Amelia, and my mother. Papa would have been proud of his nephew.

"You look lovely," said Rowe, coming to stand in front of me.

"And you look dashing. Perhaps you will catch someone's eye tonight." I waggled my brows.

Rowe chuckled, a light pink tinting his cheeks. "I think not. My focus will be on you. It is your first ball."

"Yes, but that does not mean I wish for you to hover. Lady Paxton will ensure no harm befalls me. It is not as though I intend to run off to the gardens for a secret rendezvous."

"Of course not. I trust you to act as a proper young lady ought. It is my sister who most concerns me. You and I both know Annette has never been one for heeding the rules of propriety."

"You are wrong, though. She may not adhere to guidelines while at Kenwick, but she has been nothing but proper since we arrived in London. Perfectly so."

Rowe laughed, shaking his head. "You are right. Her agreement with my parents has likely ensured her behavior remains above reproach."

"Indeed, but even still, I do not think you have cause to worry. Annette has no interest in suitors. I cannot imagine she would run off to the gardens with a gentleman or cause any scandal with one. To do so would ruin any chance she has at dying a happy, free spinster."

"Do not allow my parents to hear you say that. They might think to cause a scandal simply to see me wed." Annette entered the room, her wavy red hair pinned elegantly with white flowers adorning it. Her ball gown was also white, but a green sash encircled her waist. She was beautiful, and it was little wonder she had so many callers.

"Mother and Father would never force you to marry unless your reputation were in jeopardy," said Rowe, pinning his sister with a serious look. "And you know they would never cause a scandal. They want you to be happy."

"Yes, I know," Annette admitted. "I simply cannot understand the push for me to marry so soon. Why can I not have one Season to enjoy myself?"

"Likely because they know, if given the chance, you would spend every Season simply enjoying yourself," I said.

Annette grinned, proving the accuracy of my statement.

Russell joined us a few minutes later, and before Annette could find something to tease him about, he announced Lord and Lady Paxton would not be joining us. "Father is feeling unwell," said Rus, his tone more somber than I had heard in weeks. "Mother has elected to wait with him until the doctor arrives."

"The doctor?" Annette's brows furrowed. "He is so unwell as that? Perhaps we all ought to—"

Rus placed a hand on his sister's shoulder, his expression filled with a sympathy he so rarely wore, especially when speaking to her. "All will be fine, Netty. It is likely a cold. Neither of them wish for the two of you to miss your first London ball."

"But…what if I need guidance?" Annette bit her lip, for the first time appearing unsure of herself. I understood her worry. Not having my mother here with me had been difficult, but Lady Paxton had filled the role in the ways I needed. Her absence tonight would be felt keenly by both of us.

Rus pulled his sister into an embrace, one Annette surprisingly returned. He whispered words of comfort in her ear, and I smiled despite my nerves. For all Russell's teasing and air of nonchalance, he cared deeply for his family. These moments, while rare, were undeniable evidence.

Rus pulled away. "Shall we be off, then?"

Annette gave him a grateful smile and nodded. The four of us settled into the coach and rode to the Morrison's townhome in silence, though it was not the bothersome, unnerving sort. Instead, excitement filled me. I was eager to introduce Mr. Montfert to the women on my list and see whether they would suit. It was as though I sat on the precipice of success.

Perhaps I was overconfident. I had only met with the man three times, which hardly suggested I knew him well enough to feel who would match him well. Still, the romantic in me conjured scenes of them waltzing, even ending the night with a stolen kiss.

Something wriggled in my stomach—an odd sensation that disappeared once I had banished the last image from my mind.

Rus handed Annette down from the carriage, then me, and each of us took one of the twins' arms. Hundreds of candles lit the ball room, their flickering flames reflected off the glass chandeliers. The crowd had already grown so thick I could not make out the pattern of the chalk adorning the floor. Gentleman in finery, ladies in opulent gowns dressed with the latest fashionable trimmings, and liveried footman—the entire scene was a painting from my brightest fantasies.

Annette, however, did not seem to share in my elation, for she was already fighting a scowl. I nudged her with my elbow. "Smile, Annette. I will remind you since your mother is not here to do so."

My cousin rolled her eyes, but my words did bring a smile to her lips. "I feel exhausted already. My dance card is nearly full, Grace. How am I going to survive the night?"

"It's full already?" Rus asked. He sounded surprised, but he also wore a mischievous grin.

Annette noticed and narrowed her eyes. "It is, thanks to my many callers this week, which you would know if you were ever around to bear some of the burden."

Rus tilted his head with an expression of false befuddlement. "It is rather curious I knew precisely which days you would receive the most callers, is it not? Almost as if I had orchestrated that very thing."

Annette's jaw dropped. "*You?* You are the reason I have had men constantly bombarding me with their attention?"

Rus smirked. "I did tell you I would have revenge for that spider. A pity you cannot deny any callers I send your way."

Well, it seemed Rus had left his caring elder brother persona back at the house.

Annette started forward, but Rowe held her back, whispering. "Let's not make a scene. If you still wish to throttle him once we return home, I will be happy to assist you."

"Traitor," Rus grumbled.

"You're the traitor for sicking half of London's bachelors on your sister," Annette spat. "Especially the one man in Town I absolutely cannot stand. Really, Russell? You had to send Lieutenant Paget to vex me?"

This time, Rus's expression reflected genuine confusion. "I am not acquainted with Lieutenant Paget. I know his father is close friends with our own, but it was my understanding his son was still off serving in The Navy."

Interesting. So, the lieutenant had come on his own. I had suspected as much, though that likely aggravated Annette more than it comforted her.

"He returned a few weeks ago," I said when no one offered Rus any clarity.

"Ah. Well, had I known, I would have added him to my list, but alas, I can take no credit for his calls. Perhaps you have a true admirer, Netty." Rus grinned. "Although I would not discount the other men. I asked them to each call on you once, and according to Mother, several of them have returned. That was not my doing."

"You are the worst sort of brother," Annette ground out.

"As I aim to be." Rus straightened his coat. "I am off to the card room. Behave yourselves. Do not do anything I would do." He patted Rowe on the chest as he passed by. "That includes you."

Rowe scoffed.

Music began to play, and Annette's first partner appeared to claim her dance. I stayed at Rowe's side, searching the room for my client and the women I intended for him to meet. I found Miss Rigby near the refreshment tables, quietly sipping lemonade next to her mother, who was observing the room with her nose wrinkled in disgust.

"Would you care to join me in greeting Miss Rigby?" I asked Rowe.

My cousin glanced across the room at them, then shook his head. "I think it best I remain here."

"Whatever for?"

"I happened upon Mrs. Rigby and her daughter while out a few days ago. It would seem there was some...confusion on Mrs. Rigby's part about my identity. She believed me to be Rus that day at Gunter's, which led her to welcome my conversation, but when I corrected her assumption while out, she did not take it well."

I closed my eyes. "She thought you were the heir and hoped you would call on her daughter. Which is why she was happy to see you."

Rowe smiled wryly. "Do not feel badly for me, Grace. I have dealt with such things my entire life. I am only sad my limited acquaintance with Miss Rigby is likely at an end."

"Why should that be?" I asked. "You are still a gentleman."

"I am the spare. It would seem her family has higher expectations for their daughter. Silly, really. It was not as though I had intentions toward her." Rowe shrugged as if indifferent, but I could see the disappointment in his eyes. I had sensed his attraction to Miss Rigby that day at Gunter's, but was it possible there was more to his interest?

Guilt pricked at my chest. I did not know how to feel about possibly matching my client with a woman my cousin fancied.

Not that Rowe would admit to as much. Perhaps it was best not to worry over it. Rowe insinuated Mrs. Rigby disapproved of him for lack of title, anyway.

My eyes widened. Did that mean she would also disapprove of Mr. Montfert? Surely she would if the family expected their daughter to marry for title. Rowe had a fair income, just as Mr. Montfert did, and still he had been rejected.

Well, not rejected, *per se*. Rowe had not attempted courtship. But if Mrs. Rigby would not even allow an acquaintance with her daughter, what did that say of Mr. Montfert's odds?

The entire situation made my head spin, and I commanded myself to remain calm. There was no harm in making introductions tonight.

I would not have answers unless I proceeded with my plan, and even if things did not work out with Miss Rigby, there were other options.

"I think I will go," I said. "Miss Rigby is kind, and I would like to remain friends with her. I understand if you would prefer to remain here."

Rowe smiled softly. "Go on, then. I promise not to hover, but you will forgive me if I keep an eye on you. I am anxious for you to have a splendid evening. Should you need me, I will be right here."

I placed a hand on his arm and squeezed. "Thank you, Rowe."

Leaving my cousin standing on his own, I crossed the room. Miss Rigby welcomed me with a warm smile, but her mother ignored my presence completely. That suited me fine, for it would be far easier to have a conversation without her listening.

"Miss Rigby, there is someone attending tonight that would like an introduction to you," I said, keeping my voice low as I searched the crowd for any sign of Mr. Montfert. He was fairly tall, and spotting him would not be difficult, assuming he had arrived.

"Me?" asked Miss Rigby, her voice equally low. "I cannot imagine why."

"What man would not wish to meet you? You are lovely, kind"—I struggled to name more qualities. I was certain she possessed them, but I did not know her well enough— "anyway, he is a friend and has expressed specific interest in meeting you. Would you be open to making his acquaintance?"

Miss Rigby bit her lip, stealing a glance at her mother, who had taken up a conversation with someone she deemed more important. "An introduction would suit me, Miss Scott, but I should warn you my mother is very particular."

I nodded. "I understand. The man I speak of is not here yet. Would you tell me more about yourself until then? I think we could be good friends."

She smiled shyly. "What is it you wish to know?"

Our conversation nearly turned into an interrogation as I pried for information. Miss Rigby took all of it in stride, and she seemed happy not to stand by her mother in silence. Before leaving the townhouse, I had reviewed my list of Mr. Montfert's characteristics, his likes and dislikes. It pleased me greatly to learn that Miss Rigby shared several of his interests, most notably a love for reading.

She also checked off some of the requirements from his uncle's list, claiming talents for singing and playing the harp. I had decided that satisfying Mr. Perry's demands, to some extent, was unavoidable, loathe as I was to do so. The man had almost broken my sister's heart, encouraging his daughter to steal Amelia's now husband by any means necessary. Fortunately, Sabrina had refused in the end.

Sabrina had tormented Amelia for months before finally apologizing and giving up her chase of the earl. I still did not know whether we could trust her and, admittedly, Mr. Montfert's connection to the woman made me uneasy. But he had done nothing to suggest he was anything like his cousin or uncle, and I would withhold unwarranted judgement.

"There," I said, subtly pointing across the room to where Mr. Montfert and his cousin had entered. "That is the man who wishes to meet you."

I watched as Miss Rigby took him in. "He is handsome. What can you tell me of him?"

Very little, for at that moment, Mr. Montfert caught my gaze and his lips lifted into a smile. My breath caught, and my pulse raced as he and Sabrina made their way toward us. Mr. Montfert was dressed in a pale blue waistcoat, black coat, and a perfectly knotted, starch-white cravat. His wavy hair had been styled, but a single strand draped over his forehead, begging to be brushed aside. He walked with a confidence suited to his tall figure, determination in his step.

No, handsome was not nearly an adequate enough description.

# Chapter Thirteen

## PHILLIP

Sabrina may not have been the most comforting person to accompany me to the Morrison's ball, but it hardly mattered. The moment my eyes fell on Miss Scott, my nerves calmed. There was something reassuring about her presence, an ease about her smile that filled the room with a steady warmth. Perhaps it was because I had so few friends, but my soul seemed to cling to her, and I found I trusted this woman completely despite our few interactions. I could not imagine receiving matchmaking help from anyone else.

Which was why I had asked Apsley about Miss Scott's calling hours last week.

After our meeting in the park, I had thought of little else but the women Miss Scott believed could make me a good match, and each day, my anxiety over the matter increased. I had so much riding on things going well, and realizing my lack of experience when it came to calling on women had dragged me into a state of panic.

How did a gentleman go about visiting a woman he had an interest in? What did they speak of? Should I make my intentions clear from the beginning, or did timing play a key role?

Those sorts of questions plagued me until I could stand it no longer. I needed answers to calm my troubled mind, and Miss Scott would have them. I trusted her to advise me, to prepare me. And so, I had gone to Apsley Court to beg for her opinions and encroach upon her time.

Except, I had left with more questions than answers. With Miss Apsley entertaining suitors and Lady Paxton's presence, I could hardly ask for the type of advice that required a private conversation. However, sitting next to Miss Scott had brought me to a state of equanimity. I had relaxed into our conversation and forgot most of my troubles. How did simply being near her affect me so?

And why did I feel a buzz within my chest each time she touched me or whispered in my ear?

Or smiled at me the way she was now.

My feet carried me toward her as if tethered and pulled. I crossed the room without thought, eager to greet her. She stood next to a tall woman with brown hair, braided in a sort of spiral and pinned to her head. Tiny white beads were strung throughout, making the lady quite lovely, if in an understated way.

My stomach knotted. Was this one of the women Miss Scott had spoken of?

It suddenly took effort to keep moving forward, my eagerness displaced with uneasy anticipation. What if I was about to meet my wife for the first time? Did that not warrant my nervousness?

Whether it did or didn't, I stopped in front of the ladies and, after releasing Sabrina's arm, dipped into a shaky bow. "Good evening, Miss Scott." I gestured to my cousin. "May I introduce—"

"We've met," Sabrina interrupted, shooting me a curious look. I suppose I had led her straight here without explanation. That justified her confusion.

"You've met?" I asked, her words finally sinking in. "When?"

Sabrina bit her lip, and her gaze dropped to the floor.

"We met last year," Miss Scott answered after a moment. "At a house party. But Her Grace and my sister were...friends before that."

Based on the tension spilling from both women, something had happened at that house party. Uncle had never offered me any details, and I knew Sabrina had returned home unengaged, despite Uncle's plans. I would have to ask my cousin more on the matter later.

Sabrina cleared her throat. "I do hope Amelia is well?"

Miss Scott nodded. "Yes. She is traveling with her husband in York."

A soft smile spread over Sabrina's lips. "That is good to hear. I wish her nothing but the best."

Sabrina's tone held a gentle plea, one I could make no sense of. Still, it was there, and Miss Scott's expression softened as she seemed to notice it as well.

"Thank you."

With a nod, Sabrina gestured to the woman next to Miss Scott. "Forgive me. I fear I have interrupted introductions."

"Oh. Yes." Miss Scott shook her head, a light blush filling her cheeks. "This is Miss Harriet Rigby. Miss Rigby, I present to you Her Grace, the Duchess of Rochester, and Mr. Phillip Montfert."

I did not miss the way Sabrina winced at the pronouncement of her title. Whatever triumph she had once felt in claiming something so prestigious had faded.

"A pleasure to meet you, Miss Rigby. I do hope you will excuse me, but I've just spotted a friend of mine." Sabrina met my gaze, silently offering me permission to remain. I doubted there was a friend. I had promised to stay by her side at events as much as I was able, but my cousin possessed uncanny intuition. As if she knew I needed this time without her presence.

"Let me know should you need anything," I said before she walked away. I did worry about her being alone. Would the gossips find her here tonight? Was it not my duty to protect her from them?

A wave of frustration washed over me. It was impossible for me to do everything I needed to do. Uncle's demands were clear, but if anyone understood the pressure I was under, it was Sabrina. I had to trust she could handle the evening on her own for a time.

The orchestra teased the room with a few notes as they prepared for the dancing. My attention fell to Miss Scott, and she nodded subtly to Miss Rigby. Yes, this lady was one my matchmaker meant for me to meet.

"Has your first set been claimed, Miss Rigby?" I asked.

The woman's cheeks flushed, and she shook her head without giving a verbal response.

I offered her my arm, and she took it with a hesitant smile. The music began, and I led her to the end of the line, my heart pounding the entire way.

There. We were dancing. What was I supposed to do now? Should I attempt conversation? Flattery? No, I did not have the focus to do that and keep time to the music. Concentrating on my footwork was more than enough, and the one time I did look at Miss Rigby, I stepped on the tips of her slippers.

Then apologized profusely, which led to my timing being off for the remainder of the dance. By the time the second began, Miss Rigby requested a turn about the room and refreshment rather than remaining on the floor. I happily obliged.

"You are a lovely dancer," I said, offering her a glass of ratafia.

"That is kind of you to say." Silence settled between us. The woman was attractive, and she seemed sweet, albeit quiet. I was not opposed to quiet. The problem rested entirely on my shoulders, for I hadn't any idea how to strike up a conversation with her. Or any woman, for that matter.

I had done poorly at that very thing since coming to London. Time and again I proved my conversational skills were lacking. I did not know how to navigate society in a way that would please Uncle. I had never begrudged his decision to keep me isolated—for I preferred to remain home over attending balls and parties. Only now did I truly understand the sort of deficit that reclusiveness had created.

"How is your family, Miss Rigby?" That was always a safe topic, was it not?

"They are well. Do you know them?"

"Well...no. Do you have any siblings?"

She nodded, at last breaking away from her shyness to at least engage. "An older sister. What about you? Do you have any siblings?"

"I haven't the pleasure, but I have lived with my uncle and cousin since I was eight." I glanced across the room to where Sabrina sat alone, her chin dipped and a dejected look on her face. A pang ripped through my heart. How could I focus on Miss Rigby knowing I had abandoned my cousin?

"Cousins can be a wonderful substitute for siblings," Miss Rigby continued, oblivious to my inner turmoil. "I was never particularly close to my sister—she is ten years my senior—but I have cousins who always treated me well."

"That is a blessing. To have someone who treats you well." I glanced past her to Sabrina again, expecting another prod of guilt. Instead, I found Miss Scott sitting in the chair next to her. The two of them were deep in conversation, a lightness to their expressions that had been absent during introductions. Whatever tension existed between them had been set aside, at least for now.

I smiled, appreciation expanding within my chest. Miss Scott had noticed Sabrina sitting alone and joined her, a small act of kindness that likely meant more to my cousin than she would ever admit, especially with rumors threatening her social standing.

"Miss Scott is a sweet woman."

I started a little, despite Miss Rigby's quiet voice. She stared up at me, an inquisitive look in her eyes that I did not know how to read. I swallowed. "Yes, she has been a good friend to me."

A good friend? No, I was her client. That was all.

"How long have the two of you known each other?" asked Miss Rigby.

"Not long. We met after I arrived for the Season. Two weeks at most."

Miss Rigby cocked her head to the side. "Really? How interesting."

I wanted to ask her what about my statement she found so intriguing, but she wrapped a hand around my arm and, with the gentlest nudge, tugged me forward. "I think I would like to sit down now. Would you mind returning me to my mother?"

I nodded. Miss Rigby was doing the leading at present, and although the music still played for the final song of the set, I did not mind ending our time together a little early. I deposited Miss Rigby at her mother's side, enduring what I could only call a sharp glare from the matron, before excusing myself and taking the short walk to where Miss Scott and Sabrina sat.

I plopped down in the chair next to the left of my cousin and released an unintentionally heavy sigh.

"Come now, Phillip, it could not have been so bad." Sabrina grinned at me "Miss Rigby seemed pleasant."

"She is," I said quickly, catching Miss Scott's gaze. "Quite pleasant."

It was true. I could see nothing inherently wrong with the woman. She had a sweet disposition and carried herself well. But...

I needed to speak to Miss Scott. Alone.

I stared over the dancefloor as if that would provide a solution. Asking Miss Scott to dance would offer us more privacy, but it would not allow an opportunity for discussion. Between the loud music and my inability to simultaneously converse and focus on the steps, it was a poor idea.

My eyes caught on a familiar head of red hair. Miss Apsley was dancing, and her partner happened to be the same man who had been there the day I visited Apsley Court.

And the lady appeared positively disgusted with her fortune.

I chuckled, sliding from my seat and swiftly moving past Sabrina to sit in the vacant chair next to Miss Scott. I angled my body toward her, our knees brushing. Improper, perhaps, but necessary. I would never hear her otherwise.

Miss Scott's brows furrowed, but she made no attempt to move away from me even as I leaned closer. "Your cousin has yet to have a change of heart where the lieutenant is concerned."

I nodded toward the dancefloor, and a short burst of laughter escaped Miss Scott. She covered her mouth with her hand, something I'd noticed she often did to temper her amusement.

"Oh, dear. That glare is nearly enough to set the poor man on fire," said Miss Scott.

"Somehow, I think he might enjoy taunting her even as a pile of ashes."

Miss Scott covered her mouth again, and my lips twitched.

"Indeed, he would." She drew in a breath to regain her composure. "Annette has no wish to marry, so I imagine his persistence—regardless of his intent—frustrates her more than anything. It does not help that her brother has graciously sent her suitors all week."

"Ah. I see how that might put her in a foul mood."

"It is even worse than you can imagine. Annette cannot—" Her mouth snapped closed, and she studied me as if wondering whether I was worthy of her confidence. We had shared much conversation during our last meeting in Hyde. Two hours of sitting on the grass, asking one another personal questions, had quickly dismantled the wall between strangers.

I trusted her, and I wanted her to trust me as well. It was odd to feel so invested in earning Miss Scott's respect, her confidence, when I so recently met her.

"Would you care to take a turn about the room with me?" I asked.

"You ought to put your attention on someone else. I have an entire list, if you will recall?" She pointed to a woman in a cream gown with golden hair. "That is Miss Morrison, the daughter of our host. She is a talented painter. And just there"—her finger aimed at the other side of the room—is Miss Angston. She is more proficient on the pianoforte than anyone I have heard. She is polite and well-connected. Her family is related to the Duke of Halford, though somewhat distantly. And Lady Evelyn is rather kind, albeit far more outspoken than Miss Rigby. She also has darker hair—"

I lifted a hand with a chuckle. "I will dance with as many as you suggest, time permitting, Miss Scott. Where shall I begin?"

She regaled me with more of each lady's characteristics until the next set began. I danced first with Miss Angston, who seemed to grow agitated with my lack of skill, though she remained polite even after I had stepped on her toes. Lady Evelyn laughed when my boot snared the hem of her gown, not in a way to intentionally embarrass me, but the intensity of the sound drew eyes to us nonetheless. Following my dance with Miss Morrison, I escorted her to the refreshment tables only to spill ratafia on my waistcoat.

At least I had not tossed peas down anyone's dress this time.

I slumped back into my seat next to Miss Scott after nodding in acknowledgment to the man sitting in the other chair next to her. Sabrina had finally taken the floor with a gentleman, leaving the spot vacant.

"How is your leg today, Miss Scott?" the man asked.

"Oh, it is no worse than usual. The pain comes and goes, as it always does."

I tilted my head to listen in on their conversation better.

"Has it ailed you for a long time?" the man asked.

"Since I was quite young, yes. I was taken up with a fever for weeks at age five, and while I clearly recovered, the illness had a lingering effect on my leg. Doctors claim there is little to be done for it, and so, I manage as best I can."

"Admirable, indeed, Miss Scott. Admirable, indeed."

My stomach clenched with his praise. I agreed with the man; that she could face life with such enthusiasm despite her pain was something worthy of accolade. What was more, Miss Scott did not shy away from telling others about her difficulties. To me, that was more brave than anything. Still, I was not particularly fond of listening to this man's compliments. His tone alone was enough to suggest his interest in her, though Miss Scott seemed oblivious to it herself.

"Oh, look, the set has finished," she said. "Tell me, Mr. Willoughby, have you had the opportunity to dance with my cousin?"

The man hesitated, then smiled. "Not yet. Shall I see if her card is full?"

"I am certain she would welcome it," answered Miss Scott.

He left us with a nod, his expression barely concealing his disappointment. As soon as he was out of earshot, Miss Scott turned toward me, a hungry eagerness in her eyes. "How did it go?"

I rubbed the back of my neck. "Somewhere between well and terrible."

Miss Scott's brows puckered, and her shoulders slumped. "Surely it did not all go poorly?"

"Only due to me being a buffoon. I stepped on toes more than once and added ratafia to my wardrobe." I gestured to where a stain darkened my waistcoat.

Miss Scott covered her mouth, but I still heard the delightful sound of her chuckle and noted a smile peeking out beneath her gloves. Her reaction should have added to my embarrassment; instead, I regretted that she covered it so well.

"What of Miss Rigby?" she asked. "I admit, she is the one I was most excited for you to meet."

" I fear I failed to coax her into much conversation. I am not ready to give up, however. She is lovely and seems very amiable."

The line between her brows deepened. "Lovely and amiable. Is that all?"

"Well...yes. Should there be something more? It was half an hour, Miss Scott. Hardly enough time to come to any sort of firm conclusion."

"I suppose that is fair." She sighed, her lips pursed in a way that drew my attention to them. "You will forgive me. Sometimes I get carried away with my romantic notions."

"That is not such a bad thing for a matchmaker. A prerequisite for the job, I should think."

My words brought out her smile again, this time exposed without her glove, and its appearance inflated a bubble in my chest.

"I've danced with the women on your list who are present," I continued. "Might we take a turn about the room now? It is easier to discuss things when we are away from prying ears."

She nodded and accepted my hand. I assisted her from the chair and guided her fingers to my arm. Once we were a safe distance from the crowd, I said, "So, you were hoping I would experience love at first sight?"

"It would have pleased me greatly, I'll admit," she said with a chuckle. "A storybook ending right before my eyes."

"Hmm, not quite an ending, but a beginning, perhaps. Although, generally one does not find happiness at the beginning of a romance novel."

"That is all true. Let us hope, then, there is still happiness to be found between you and a lady here."

I smiled, but it felt forced, as if the idea of marrying any of those women did not hold the kind of hope or excitement it should. I would not let the uncertainty discourage me. When I came to know them better, the rest would fall into place.

"You will tell me more about Miss Rigby, will you not?" I asked. "Or at least the reason you believe we would make a good match."

Miss Scott nodded. "Yes, but not tonight. I wanted to observe your interactions first. You have time yet to try another dance with her, and others, for that matter. Who knows, you may find someone without my help."

"I highly doubt that, but if you believe I should dance, then I shall. I already know who I will ask next."

"Oh?" One of her dark brows raised in question. She remained entirely oblivious to my intent until I steered her toward the line forming in the middle of the room.

Miss Scott's feet came to an abrupt halt. "Oh, no, I cannot dance Mr. Montfert."

"Neither can I. We will make a good pair."

She shook her head. "Really, I cannot. I…" Her shoulders fell, and she studied me again. I would not prod her to confess anything she didn't wish to, but my curiosity begged to understand.

"If you do not want to dance with me—"

"That is not it at all, I assure you." She bit her lip and then pulled me toward the edge of the room away from the crowd. There was something in her avoidance of my gaze, a vulnerability I hadn't seen from her. When she finally spoke, her voice became a hushed whisper, requiring me to lean close to hear over the music.

"It is my leg. I have found activities such as dancing are too much."

"But not climbing trees," I teased gently.

She shook her head, her cheeks tinting a rosy shade. "That is different. There have been a number of times at assemblies where my leg has given out on me in the middle of a dance. I think it is the movement. A slower dance I could handle, but certainly not a reel. As you know, a lady cannot turn down a gentleman for one dance only to take part in the next. It is simpler to refrain entirely. I try not to allow my disability to prevent me from participating in activities, but there are some things I simply must avoid. Dancing is one of them. Besides, I have no wish to cause a scene and spoil the fun for everyone else."

"You've no need to feel embarrassed, Miss Scott."

"It is not embarrassment—well, perhaps it is to an extent. The difficulty frustrates me more than anything. I hate having to admit that I cannot do something simply because my body prohibits it."

I could believe that. In all the time I had spent with her, not once had she complained. Were it not for witnessing her limp, I might never have even suspected she struggled. But more than that, I found her frustration relatable.

"So," she said, "please do not take my refusal to dance as a personal offense. Besides, you needn't waste your time with me when you have a wife to find."

"No time with you is a waste," I replied before thinking better of it. Not that it wasn't true. Simply that…well, the comment might be misconstrued as flirtation. I cleared my throat. "Regardless, I still wish to dance with you."

"But I told you—"

"Would you *like* to dance? If I could promise it would not cause you pain, would you wish to?"

A slight smile lifted her lips, and she narrowed her eyes. "What are you scheming, Mr. Montfert?"

"Do you trust me?" I extended my hand to her.

Miss Scott's dainty fingers fell into mine, and despite both of us wearing gloves, warmth spread over my hand and up my arm like fire flooding my veins. Miss Scott deserved to dance, and I would see to it that she did.

# Chapter Fourteen

## GRACE

I KNEW HOW TO dance. The steps were ingrained in me just as they were in most members of the upper class. Amelia and I had a dance instructor growing up, but it became clear within those first few lessons that the activity was not one my body could endure. Instead, I had watched from the sidelines while she practiced.

Memorizing. Imagining. Longing.

Those were all I could do, even now, and I hated myself for it. How many novels had I read where the heroine was swept away to dance with a charming hero? I wanted that for myself.

Out of sheer stubbornness, I had often practiced alone in my room, and each time, my leg suffered. *I* had suffered. Allowing my disability to keep me from doing anything had never been my way. I climbed trees, went for long walks, and rode horses—all of which caused me pain. But I did them because I had no intention of missing out on life in any way.

Dancing, it seemed, was where my body drew the line.

Which was why my heart pounded so fiercely as Mr. Montfert led me gently by the hand. I was generally not embarrassed by my malady, but were I to fall on the dance floor in front of everyone, I had no doubt my cheeks would turn red as beets.

But he had said this dance would not cause me pain. He had asked me to trust him.

And I did.

Mr. Montfert led me past the line of people gathering for the next set and into an alcove somewhat hidden from the rest of the room. It wasn't entirely improper, but Mr. Montfert was too much of a gentleman to compromise me in any way, and besides, as I glanced beyond the dancers, I could see Rowe watching me with a concerned expression.

I sent him a smile, hoping to provide reassurance. It did not erase the worry lines creasing his brow, but he stayed put.

"There," said Mr. Montfert, depositing me in the center of the alcove. "You will stand here."

"Stand? I thought we were going to dance?"

"We are," he reassured. "Do you know the steps—that is, do you know where to position your hands when we come together?"

I nodded, still utterly confused. Mr. Montfert smiled. "Good. Your feet may remain still. I will handle the footwork."

I opened my mouth to question him, but the music began, and so did our dance. Mr. Monfert moved as he would were we in a line with everyone else, but I remained still. It required a great deal of extra steps on his part, and his attempt to keep time while doing them brought us both to laughter. He danced around me, and when it came time for us to circle together, he instructed me to lift on my feet while he held my hands and spun me in place.

To anyone watching, it must have looked ridiculous and nothing like a formal dance. But I loved every second of it. I was dancing. At my first ball.

Each time we came together, I performed the expected hand gestures, grinning so wide my face began to hurt. Mr. Montfert's expression matched my own, and there was a light of amusement in his blue eyes that drew me in. How it must have wounded his pride to appear so foolish, and yet, nothing about his features suggested he cared what anyone thought. He simply enjoyed our dance, despite its oddity, and so did I.

By the time the set ended, he was breathing heavily, and a bit of perspiration had formed on his brow. He offered his arm to me. "You danced."

I took it with a wide grin. "I danced, and I cannot express my gratitude." The last words came out choked with unexpected emotion. I had planned to avoid dancing at every event this Season. Mr. Montfert had ensured I experienced it at least once, and I hadn't any idea how to thank him properly for it.

His hand fell over mine, and he gave it a gentle squeeze, his expression soft. "You needn't thank me at all, Miss Scott. Dancing with you was my pleasure."

His gaze lingered on me for several long moments before he said, "I suppose I should ask Miss Rigby for another set?"

"Yes," I said, pressing down the strange disappointment his question created. "Her card may be full now, but it is worth making your interest known. If nothing else, it will give you the opportunity to converse with her again."

He nodded, his brows drawn in pensiveness. How I wished to know what he was thinking and whether he experienced the same fluttering in his stomach as I did. Surely it was nothing more than the exhilaration that lingered after dancing a lively tune?

He led me back to where Sabrina and I had been sitting, but the Duchess was no longer there. Once Mr. Montfert had left me to go speak with Miss Rigby, I searched the crowd for Her Grace, surprised by my desire to find her. Our conversation had been...unexpected, and while I held some hesitancy to be around the woman, I sensed her desire to change was genuine.

I spotted her in line for the next set, Rowe as her partner. Annette, too, stood ready for the cotillion with yet another gentleman who had called on her earlier this week. Mr. Montfert and Miss Rigby joined them, and I sat on the sidelines watching with a somewhat forced smile. She had accepted a second dance, and I should have felt joy in that success. But it never came.

I had always striven not to allow jealousy to sour my mood, but after finally experiencing the thrill of dancing with a handsome gentleman, it was difficult to keep the feeling at bay. And I worried that jealousy had more to do with one man in particular dancing with another woman than my inability to join the line.

# Chapter Fifteen

## PHILLIP

THIS WAS AN UTTER disaster. I raked a hand through my hair, staring at the rows of hothouse flowers with pure trepidation. In all the books I had read, not once did I think it prudent to memorize the meaning of flowers to know what sort of message they might convey. The last thing I needed to do was insult a potential bride before I even had the chance to call on her.

I reached for a deep crimson rose, but Apsley whacked my hand away. "I do not recommend that one."

"Why not?"

"Because it is crimson, for starters."

I pursed my lips. "And that means what, precisely?"

"Mourning."

Oh. No, that would not do.

"And," Apsley continued, "a Provence rose is generally taken to mean your heart is in flames." He paused for a moment, a smirk filling his lips. "Is your heart in flames? Have you fallen madly in love with someone and being apart for any amount of time is agonizing? I suppose a crimson Provence would work nicely if that is the case."

Heat crept up the back of my neck. I was *not* madly in love with anyone. At least...not yet. I could admit I found Miss Rigby attractive. Whether or not I could develop deeper feelings for her remained to be seen. I would need more time with her to determine that, which started with calling on her.

I shivered at the mere idea, and it was not the good sort of shiver. No doubt I would make a complete fool of myself. Our conversations at last night's ball had been mostly strained and awkward. The dancing had not been much better.

"What about this one?" I asked, pointing to a rose of a true red hue.

"Unless you are declaring your intent to propose, I would dissuade you. Passionate love may be a bit strong."

Indeed.

"And this one?" I asked, pointing to another.

"A lady would likely take that to mean beauty." Apsley rubbed his chin. "Not a bad choice. Every woman likes to be complimented on her appearance."

"That will do. What else should I add to the bouquet?"

Apsley spent the next quarter hour assisting and teaching me. I had danced with six women at the ball, and as tradition dictated, I would send them each a bouquet. Miss Rigby's, though, made me the most nervous. I needed to pick her flowers carefully so as to not send the wrong message.

"This is overwhelming," I muttered. "How does one not say the wrong thing? Why can a flower not simply mean I enjoyed dancing with you?"

Apsley's cheeks turned a slight pink as he rubbed the back of his neck. "To be honest, most women will not understand the message. And most gentlemen do not consider the meaning of flowers. I may have gotten carried away in my advice."

My shoulders slumped. "I cannot decide whether to be relieved or irritated."

"Perhaps you should just choose the ones you think Miss Rigby will enjoy?"

That was not any easier. I hadn't any idea what Miss Rigby would enjoy when it came to flowers, or anything else, for that matter. She did not open up to me enough to obtain such knowledge.

"If most gentlemen do not concern themselves with it, then how do you know so much about flowers and their meanings?" I asked as we continued down the row. The stuffy hothouse air made my breathing more labored than it ought to have been, and sweat tickled my forehead. I was ready to get out of here.

My friend teased the petals of the violets he held. One dance was all he had participated in last night. "I picked up the knowledge in France while touring the continent."

"You toured the continent despite the war?"

Apsley shook his head. "Not till after Bonaparte surrendered. I spent a few months there."

"Learning about flowers?" I lifted a brow in question. Why did it feel as though there was much my friend did not say?

Apsley cleared his throat, playing with the petals of a daisy with more force. The result left several petals fluttering to the floor. "It is something I simply picked up."

Clearly, he had no intention of elaborating, so I turned my attention back to my task. With less consideration, five of the bouquets came together quickly until one remained. I turned to Apsley. "What sort of flowers does your cousin like?"

His brows furrowed. "What?"

"Your cousin, Miss Scott. Does she have a preference for flowers?"

Apsley's face scrunched. "How should I know what sort of flowers she prefers?"

"She is living in your townhouse," I answered with exasperation. "Surely you know something of her likes and dislikes?" I did not expect him to know everything about her, but how could he not know at least a little? After all, I knew something of Sabrina's habits and interests.

"You've given me far too much observational credit. I could not even tell you what my sister likes, and I live with her all year." Apsley sighed. "Just pick something, will you? We were meant to go to Angelo's an hour ago. I am growing bored. And it smells too floral in here."

"I cannot go to Angelo's today. I have to meet with my uncle and then call on Miss Rigby this afternoon." The statement tightened my chest with nerves. I was not ready for this. Perhaps I needed a round of practice. Would Miss Scott assist me if I asked her?

"You dragged me here without the promise of a reward?" Apsley scoffed, his expression one of severe disappointment. "What am I to do the rest of the day, then?"

I shrugged. "You could make calls with me, I suppose."

"Not a chance. I shan't do anything to make any woman believe I have a particular interest in her. Nor would I want my mother to make assumptions. Calling on ladies is risky business."

"Then I'm afraid you'll have to entertain yourself by other means. My uncle wishes to meet with me once I return home, and my afternoon is engaged. If I am to make any headway toward finding a wife, calls must be made."

"Yes, yes, I quite understand." Apsley gave me a dismissive wave. "The sooner you finish with this marriage business, the better."

Did he mean we would remain friends? I hadn't considered it before, but the idea brought out my smile. Apsley and I were very different, but I enjoyed his company, and it was nice to know our acquaintanceship would not end once I had wed. Uncle would certainly be pleased.

I paid for the flowers and left instructions for their delivery. Apsley and I parted ways, though where he was off to, I didn't know. Once I arrived home, our butler informed me my uncle was waiting in his study, and I trudged up the stairs with heavy feet. Every time we met, it felt like impending doom.

And with good reason. He had yet to tell me if I had balanced the ledgers properly, and every day that passed without his approval set me on edge.

"Enter!" he shouted after I had knocked.

I did as instructed, finding him stuffing a red, leather-bound book into his desk drawer—the ledger I was currently not allowed to look at. Once I had closed the door, he gestured for me to take my usual seat in the chair opposite his desk.

"Well?" he asked. "How did the ball go? You said you intended to find out more about several ladies. Were you successful?"

"I believe so...to an extent."

Uncle's eyes narrowed. "Pray tell, what does that mean?"

I had prepared for this moment. After the ball, I made a list of the women I danced with to present to Uncle, knowing he would ask for the information. A list I hadn't excluded *anyone* from.

My heart pounded as I retrieved the paper from my pocket and handed it to him. What I had done was a risk, I knew, but I had not been capable of talking myself out of it. I had to know if there was even a slight chance... "The women I'm considering."

Uncle unfolded it with haste, his eyes devouring it like ravenous flames. At first, he nodded, seeming pleased with the names presented...until he reached the bottom. His face twisted into a fierce scowl, and he pointed a chubby finger at the paper. "Miss Grace Scott? What is she doing on the list?"

My stomach lurched. "I met her recently, and she seems very amiable. She is Apsley's cousin. I thought, perhaps, with her connections to the viscount—"

"The devil with her connections!" Uncle grabbed for his quill and inkwell. He dipped the tip and aggressively slashed the paper, splattering a thick line of dark ink across it. "She is not eligible as a candidate. I want nothing to do with her family."

"But you said my friendship with Apsley—"

"That is entirely different." Uncle pointed at me, his brows drawn. "The other Scott women ruined Sabrina's chance of marrying an earl. You will have nothing to do with either of them. Apsley is one thing.

His father is wealthy beyond compare, and an allegiance with him would be lucrative. This Grace Scott"—he spat her name with such disdain that my fists clenched— "is worthless. Not enough connection. Not enough dowry. Even if she possessed those things, I would never approve. Tactless family. I will not align myself with someone who brought such humiliation upon me."

I fought the urge to argue. If Miss Scott and her sister were responsible for any embarrassment, it had not come by their own hands. Uncle's forceful ways and insensible expectations were always the culprits to his damaged pride.

Regardless, it would do me no good to speak the truth.

"Very well," I said, feeling as if a hole had opened up inside me. "I have found Miss Rigby the most agreeable of those who remain on the list. She comes from wealth. She is very quiet, but graceful and eloquent. I intend to call on her soon and hopefully learn whether she meets more of your...suggestions."

He nodded, his expression void of the anger that had been there moments before, and I shifted in my seat. I was not used to having his approval, and rather than put me at ease, it felt wrong.

"The Rigby's are a good family. No ties to the aristocracy, but doing business with Mr. Rigby could greatly benefit us. He is in textiles, you know. Great investments in textiles."

"So you would approve of a match with her, then?"

Uncle leaned back in his chair and crossed his arms over his chest. "I will do some digging of my own. For now, you may call on her but do not act too hastily before we speak on the matter again. You are dismissed."

"Thank you, Uncle." Though what precisely I was thanking him for, I wasn't sure. I had gained permission to pursue Miss Rigby, albeit slowly for now, but such permission elicited no excitement from me. I could only pray my feelings changed as I came to know her better.

"Boy."

I stopped at the door, holding it partially ajar. "Yes, Uncle?"

"You balanced the ledgers perfectly." His tone was even, his expression blank. I had never expected him to take pride in my work and success, but it hurt all the same. How could I be so torn, disliking his approval one minute and yearning for it the next? I felt like a wayward boat, tossed about by the sea with no sense of direction.

I waited a moment for him to say more, but when he offered nothing, I gave a quick nod and left the study.

# *Chapter Sixteen*

## GRACE

THE DRAWING ROOM AT Apsley Court was quickly becoming a garden with the number of floral arrangements filling the space. I sat next to Annette on the sky-blue settee nearest the window as Lady Paxton examined each bouquet and read the notes attached to them aloud. Annette seemed to grow more weary with each one, and more bouquets continued to arrive.

"You should be flattered," said Lady Paxton.

Annette crossed her arms. "It is impossible to be flattered when at least half of my callers were sent by my brother. Do you know how utterly embarrassing that is? He made it seem as though I could not get any on my own. I do not even *want* them. I shall get him back for this."

"You will not be getting me back for anything." Rus entered the room, apparently having overheard his sister's threat. His nose scrunched. "My, but it is smelly in here."

"You can blame yourself," Annette spat. "Had you not sent every bachelor within a mile of London to dance with me last night, this room would not look like the offspring of Kew Gardens."

"Come now, Netty. I did not send every bachelor. Just the ones I thought might annoy you most." Rus took a seat in one of the armchairs and stretched his long legs leisurely out in front of him. "You should be thanking me."

Annette scoffed. "Thanking you? That is not what I have in mind at all."

"Fortunately for me, murder is considered a criminal offense by both God and country."

"Newgate might be worth it," Annette mumbled.

Rus leaned forward, catching her gaze. "We both know you would never survive prison or any sort of cage like it. And besides, deep down, you love me."

Annette smiled wryly. "It is so very deep."

"Perhaps I can reel it to the surface, at least temporarily. I have a way to make up for all of this." He gestured to the bundles of flowers decorating the room.

His sister narrowed her eyes. "How?"

"By telling you the message each of these buffoons unwittingly sent in their floral arrangements."

I chuckled. I had forgotten Rus's odd knowledge about plants and their meanings. He had gathered the information while touring the continent and, for whatever reason, clung to the wisdom. I knew very few gentlemen who could have entire conversations about the meaning behind certain flowers. Nor ladies, for that matter, including myself. According to Rus, it was all the rage in France, and much could be conveyed based on the color and type of flower within an arrangement.

Which meant an evaluation of Annette's bouquets would prove highly entertaining.

Annette sat up straighter, clearly intrigued. "Go on."

"Let us start with the one by Mother. Rhododendrons for danger—which is not entirely inaccurate since they are for you—Lavender for distrust, and Pansies for thoughtfulness. How lovely and so adequately unclever. Who is that one from?"

"Lord Kingsley," Lady Paxton answered.

"Ah, well, we cannot be too surprised, can we? A man who wears a canary yellow hat would send something so ridiculous."

A giggle burst from Annette, and she waved him on. "The next one, if you please."

We continued that way for the next hour, Rus telling us the unintentional message of each bouquet and us laughing, often to the point of tears. Even Lady Paxton struggled to retain her composure.

Whatever animosity existed between brother and sister faded for the time being, and I was given yet another glimpse at the affection between them. Whether it was regularly visible or not, the two of them did love one another.

The butler brought in another bouquet, and Lady Paxton immediately picked through the pink roses and blue and white flowers to find the note. Her eyes roamed the card, and then she met my gaze, a smile pulling at her lips. "This one is for you, Grace."

"Me?" I sputtered. "Why would I get flowers? I did not dance—"

My mouth snapped closed. I never expected flowers because I had never expected to dance this Season. But I had, with one man. The bouquet could only have come from Phillip.

Lady Paxton read the name on the card, confirming my suspicions, then finished with the short note. "Thank you for the most agreeable dance of the evening."

Annette gripped my arm. "You danced? When? I thought you had no intention of stepping onto the floor?"

Warmth bloomed through my cheeks, and I shook my head. "I didn't. We never...that is...Mr. Montfert danced with me in the alcove past the refreshment tables. We were still within view, mind you, but he knows about my leg and...well, I suppose he wanted me to have at least one dance and not have to worry about the embarrassment my leg might cause." My smile appeared with the memory. "The man practically danced around me. It was rather sweet of him."

I glanced at my cousins. Annette was staring at me with suggestive, raised brows, and Rus's expression was nothing but smug.

"It did not mean anything," I blurted, knowing all too well where their thoughts had gone. "He is my...friend." Technically, he was my client, but I could not state as much with my aunt in the room. Besides, Rus and Annette both knew the true nature of my affiliation with Mr. Montfert.

Annette turned to her brother. "What do Grace's flowers mean?"

"I will tell you if you want, Grace," Rus said. "But you should first know I was with Montfert when he picked them out, and he specifically asked me for flowers that represented certain words."

My stomach twisted with discomfort. What word would Mr. Montfert have chosen for a message? Did I want to know?

Did I want *everyone* in the room to know?

Curiosity won out. I swallowed. "You may tell me, Rus."

He nodded, but there was no teasing glint in his eyes when he responded. "The pink roses mean grace. The periwinkle is symbolic of new friendship and the magnolia perseverance."

My heart sputtered. Mr. Montfert had chosen a flower that matched my name, but I couldn't help but wonder if he meant more by it. I had never considered myself graceful, despite what I had been dubbed at birth. How could I with a bum leg that kept me from doing things I would otherwise enjoy?

As for the magnolia, I could deduce his meaning well enough. And new friendship? Well, it pleased me that he thought of us as friends.

Lady Paxton brought the flowers to me, and as I held them, I rubbed one of the soft petals between my fingers. Even though Mr. Montfert had taken the time to dance with me, no matter how odd of a dance it was, I still had not expected him to send flowers. His kindness and consideration struck something within me, and a wave of emotion brought hot tears to my eyes.

"Oh, Grace." Annette placed her hand on my arm, her brows furrowed in concern. "What is the matter?"

I shook my head, chuckling. "Nothing. Truly, I am well. I simply did not anticipate this. It was very thoughtful."

"Thoughtful, indeed," said Lady Paxton. "This Mr. Montfert seems like a very kind gentleman."

There was a question in her tone, one I could not answer. I brushed away my tears and swallowed against the dryness in my throat. "He is."

Drat it all, even Rus was watching me intently, his eyes considering. I needed to get a hold of myself before the wrong impression settled so firmly in their minds I would not be able to remove it. Before I could shift our conversation to a safer topic, the butler entered again, this time announcing a visitor.

"Lieutenant Paget has come to call," he said.

"Show him in," Lady Paxton answered promptly.

Well, I could not have come up with a better distraction than Annette's sworn enemy paying her a visit.

The moment he entered the room, the lieutenant's gaze fell on her, and his mouth ticked upward into a wide grin. His navy blue coat matched his twinkling eyes and set off his dark hair in a way that made him objectionably handsome. I doubted even Annette would argue, at least not were she being honest with herself.

The lieutenant bowed, his gaze never leaving my cousin. "Good morning."

Pleasantries were exchanged, and Lady Paxton invited the man to sit down and take tea with us, but he refused the offer. "I am fine, thank you. I am here on business."

Annette scoffed in disbelief, and the lieutenant's brows raised in challenge. Annette composed herself. "Business, you say. I thought perhaps you had come to deliver a bouquet yourself since you failed to send one this morning. But I see you are lacking in manners or perhaps have been gone from Society for so long you have forgotten post-ball etiquette."

"Annette," Lady Paxton warned.

The lieutenant clasped his hands behind him. "I have not forgotten anything."

Annette's jaw clenched. "So you failed to send them intentionally. I should take offense."

"It seems to me you already have." He was grinning now, so wide he dazzled the room with his perfectly straight teeth. "Believe me, Miss Apsley, had I known it would cause you so much displeasure, I would have sent them. You see, I was under the impression any bouquet sent from me would be met with disdain. Trampled or crushed. I was thinking of the flowers. You might say I saved a few lives by forgoing proper post-ball etiquette."

My cousin sucked in a breath, fury burning in her blue eyes.

Rus was on the verge of uncontrollable laughter, and I dared not look at him too long or else burst from amusement myself. The lieutenant seemed to know precisely how to vex Annette, his jabs carefully curated with both sting and wit, then delivered in such a way as to sound courteous.

"I must beg your forgiveness for my assumptions," he continued. "I will rectify the mistake with haste and be certain not to make it next time."

"Perhaps there ought not *be* a next time," my cousin practically growled.

"Annette," Lady Paxton chided. "You will watch your tongue."

My cousin bit down on her lip, clearly struggling to obey. The lieutenant winked at her with a devilish smile before directing his attention to her mother. "I took no offense, my lady. But alas, as much as I do enjoy such wonderful company, I have come to speak with Lord Paxton, should he be amiable to it."

Lady Paxton's smile fell, and a heaviness filled her voice. "I am certain he would not oppose your visit, but I must request that you return another time. My husband is not feeling his best today."

My uncle had been unwell since the ball, and no matter how many times we inquired after the matter, Lady Paxton assured us he would recover. Still, I sensed she was not perfectly honest with us, and if Annette and Rus's frown were any indication, they were not convinced either.

"I am sorry to hear it," the lieutenant responded, genuine concern drawing his brows together. "I wish him a speedy recovery."

"We appreciate that," said Lady Paxton.

Lieutenant Paget hesitated a moment before his grin returned. "Well, since I am already here, perhaps Miss Apsley would care to take a ride with me? My gig is parked not far from Hyde."

Annette looked as though she might explode, and she turned a pleading look to her mother. Lady Paxton fought a smile, and one of her auburn brows lifted. Annette had an agreement to keep, and my aunt would not allow her daughter to back out of it without conceding that agreement.

Annette closed her eyes as if her next words were painful. Perhaps they were. "I would be honored to ride with you, Lieutenant."

"Excellent. Shall I wait by the door while you retrieve your bonnet and gloves?"

"And a chaperone," Lady Paxton added. "Perhaps Eliza would be best."

Annette stood with a forced smile. "Very well, I will fetch my things and my lady's maid."

Rus, who had been quiet through the entire exchange, waited until the two of them had gone from the room before speaking. "The lieutenant vexes Netty greatly." He slumped back against the cushions, crossing one knee over the other. "I approve. She should marry that one."

And the matchmaker in me could not have agreed with him more.

# Chapter Seventeen

## PHILLIP

CALLING ON MISS RIGBY did not go well. The memory of sitting in her drawing room, the minutes passing in silence, made me cringe. The entire affair had been awkward and uncomfortable. It was not that I did not like Miss Rigby. There was nothing inherently wrong with her. She was kind and lovely, but there seemed little to no connection between us, and thus the conversation had been stilted.

When there *was* conversation. Her short answers to the questions I prompted her with did not allow for any sort of depth.

I reminded myself that men had married for far less. I could certainly do worse than a wealthy heiress, and having even a small portion of Uncle's approval to continue the pursuit of Miss Rigby should have been enough to set me at ease.

But it did not.

This decision would determine my future, and I feared I would mold it into something I regretted. I needed Uncle's approval, but I wanted a wife I enjoyed being around. The two were at war with one another, which left me utterly conflicted.

At least, temporarily. When it came down to things, Uncle's say in the matter held the most weight. My reliance on an inheritance left no room for anything else.

My valet helped me dress for the day as I pondered my options. I could tell Uncle that Miss Rigby was not a promising prospect. It would not be a lie given the cold welcome I had received from her mother. Something told me Mrs. Rigby had more in mind for her daughter than the nephew and heir of a man who made his rise into the upper echelons via trade. She had her claws out for a title, something I could not offer.

Uncle would be far from pleased, though, if I could not provide a promising alternative. The list held enough options, but I had not established much of an acquaintance with any of the other women.

I needed another meeting with my matchmaker.

Before heading to breakfast, I quickly wrote a note to Miss Scott, addressing it to Apsley. He would ensure his cousin received it. I appreciated his willingness to overlook the impropriety of the exchange, even if he no longer offered his services as chaperone.

I neared the study, intending to take the stairs to the breakfast parlor, when the sound of voices from within brought me to a halt. I recognized Uncle's raspy, firm tone. It carried the same demand that laced our conversations, but the masculine voice that responded was unfamiliar to me.

"I've acquired the new paper, sir, and the new engravings arrived yesterday. It's a near-perfect match."

"Good, good," Uncle responded. "And it has all been set up? You've spoken to Mr. Cosway?"

"Yes, sir. He intends to have the first pieces completed tonight."

"I'll need this done by the end of the week. The old codger looked mighty weak when I saw him yesterday. He won't last another fortnight, mark my words; we've not much time. Besides, the Restriction Act could be dropped at any moment. The scheme will not work half as well once it does."

"I'll instruct them to make haste, sir."

"Indeed. You will if you know what's best for you."

The second man said nothing to this, and Uncle continued. "I have a lead for our next venture, but we'll discuss it once this is complete."

There was a long moment of silence. "Sir..."

"Yes?"

I could practically envision the rise of Uncle's brows merely by the impatience in his voice.

"I...well, I think this will be my last job for you, sir."

Uncle laughed, the sound almost sadistic. "You think you will walk out on me now, do you? Shall I remind you of the conditions of our arrangement? I pulled you out of the slums, and I can put you back there just as easily. In fact, you and your family will be worse off than before."

My heart pounded. Uncle was a master manipulator, and whoever this man was, he'd been caught in Uncle's web. Even without knowing the nature of their business, the poor fellow had my sympathies, especially with Uncle making threats against his family.

A tiny flame of fury stoked within me. Uncle used the same tactic on me, encouraging my obedience by threatening not only my future but Mother's. He used her well-being to ensure my complacency.

A screech penetrated the air, a chair abruptly scratching against the floor. I backed away as the thump of footsteps grew louder, pressing my body against the wall, but to my relief, the study door was merely slammed closed. I could hear the muffled voices from within, but not with any sort of clarity.

I inched back to the door and pressed my ear to it. Curse my hearing difficulties! I still couldn't understand a word of it.

"He hates eavesdroppers," said a voice from directly behind me.

I jumped, my heart flying into my throat, and turned to find Sabrina grinning at me.

"What are you doing?" I whispered.

"Me?" She scoffed. "You are the one listening in on private conversations. You ought to know better. He will not be pleased if he catches you."

I shushed her. She was right; I knew better. Uncle had hit me with his pocket watch for similar behavior before, though it had been some time since I attempted to listen in on his private business meetings.

Sabrina grabbed me by the arm. She led me down the corridor to a room that served as a guest bedchamber and shoved me inside. I crossed the space and threw open the curtains to let in some light as she shut the door, but even with sunbeams pouring in, my cousin's dark features blended into the shadows.

"What did you overhear?" she asked.

I hesitated. Sabrina did not typically take an interest in her father's business, and I recognized that determined glint in her eyes. I'd seen it before in the man we were discussing. Such similarities between father and daughter prompted my hesitancy to trust my cousin.

I folded my arms. "Why?"

Sabrina mirrored my stance with an exasperated look. "Because I want to know. It is not as if I intend to tell my father you were listening or what you heard."

"You still did not answer my question. Why do you want to know?"

Sabrina bit her lip, considering me. "Can I trust you, Phillip?"

"I cannot think I have ever given you a reason not to."

She came closer—so close that she needed to lift her chin to hold my gaze. "You are my father's heir. That is reason enough for me to question things. I have yet to decide if you will turn out like him."

My brows furrowed. Her words stung, but they did provide me with understanding. I had never considered what Sabrina thought of me. I had never had a reason to, distant as she had been. "You do not want me to become him."

Her expression softened, if only slightly. "I wouldn't wish anyone to become him, and while I would like to think the two of you are very different, my father expects you to follow in his footsteps. To make decisions as he would. There may come a time when those actions prove...unethical. What will you do then? I know he holds the inheritance over you. I know you need it. So tell me, Phillip, are you prepared to do whatever you must for it?"

I opened my mouth, but words escaped me. I did need the inheritance, but Sabrina implied there might be a cost. One I hadn't considered. "Your father has never asked anything unethical of me. He is ruthless, I will admit, but—"

"Just because he has not asked *yet*, does not mean he won't. You may trust me on this. I have been watching my father for some time now, listening without his permission. Wealth and social recognition are all he has ever cared about, and he will say and do whatever is required to have them."

"Such as insist his daughter marry a man over twice her age?"

Sabrina grimaced. "I wish that was the extent of it. My marriage is nothing compared to everything else."

Everything else? I studied her. Sabrina had never opposed her father like this. At least, she hadn't before the house party. Something had changed since then, and not just in terms of her willingness to do whatever her father asked.

I rubbed a hand over my chin. "You said you've been watching him. And listening."

"Yes."

"What have you learned, Sabrina? I know the two of us are not confidants, but I can promise you, I have no desire to be like your father. I need the money—that I will not deny—but I've no intention of taking on his entire persona."

"So, if he asked you to do something that went against the law, that defied your sense of morality, would you refuse him?" Her brows raised in challenge. I wanted to answer with a firm *yes*, but I hesitated. What would I do if faced with such a predicament? I wanted to believe I would never break the law or compromise my integrity, but what if by refusing, I lost everything?

After all, if I lost, so did my mother.

My jaw clenched, and frustration swelled within me. Sabrina's question was fair. I would not put it past Uncle to do something of an illegal nature, and I wanted no part in it. But desperation often made people do things they otherwise would not.

"Your hesitation does not bode well," she said.

I shook my head. "It's not easy for me to answer. You know your father has me under his thumb. I've no wish to see my mother destitute, but I also know she would not approve of us gaining any of this"—I gestured around me—"by me becoming someone I am not. By ignoring my principles."

Sabrina clasped her hands in front of her. "What do you know of my father's will? Are you currently named as heir?"

"Yes, though he threatens to have things changed on a regular basis."

"That is not surprising. Leverage is his key to success. And blackmail." A line formed between her brows. "Father has not corrupted you yet, but if we want to keep it that way, then I need more evidence."

"More? That implies you have some now."

She averted her gaze.

"Sabrina, what do you have evidence of?" I asked, my tone more demanding. "At present, I will inherit all of your father's holdings. If he's involved in something criminal, I deserve to know."

"I agree. You do deserve to know, but I cannot tell you. Not yet, anyway." She sighed, and there was an element of genuine exhaustion to it. "I will explain soon, but I need to be certain of a few things first. It might help if you told me what you overheard."

I shook my head. "Nothing incriminating. Your father threatened to ruin a man, but that is hardly an offense the courts would do anything about if the fellow isn't titled."

Sabrina's shoulders slumped. "I know who the man is. He is neither titled nor wealthy, and this is not the first time Father has threatened him. Did he say anything else?"

"Something about acquiring paper and engravings. Said he needed things ready soon because someone was...well, someone was near death, by the sound of it. He also mentioned the possibility of a new lead. Your father said they would discuss it next time they met."

This piqued her interest. "Did they say when?"

"No. I'm afraid not."

"Drat. I must find out when that meeting is." She met my gaze. "Let me know if you hear anything more. I know it is difficult to understand—likely difficult to even trust me. I have not been very warm toward you in the past. Still, I wish to put an end to my father's machinations, Phillip. He's hurt more people than you know, and I do not want the same for you. To be hurt or to be forced to hurt someone else."

I was uncertain how to respond. My inheritance had always been complicated, but this information, the idea that anything about Uncle's holdings could be dirty, left me feeling unwell. I did not want to become part of some scheme to harm others. "I will inform you should I hear anything, so long as you promise to explain all of this."

"I promise," she said with conviction. "Soon."

Sabrina bid me goodbye, leaving me alone in the bedchamber. Leaving me more confused and worried about my future than ever.

# Chapter Eighteen

## PHILLIP

Days of nonstop rain had not improved my mood. I had not been able to meet with my matchmaker, and the longer I went without speaking to her, the more antsy I became. Worse, I was left with little to do but ponder on what I had learned of Uncle.

Sabrina had promised details but hadn't spoken of the matter again. How long would it take for her to find the evidence she needed?

I ran a hand through my hair and glared out the window of the drawing room at the street below. Rain pounded against the pavement, and the onslaught filled the streets with broad rivulets that sloshed beneath carriage wheels and hooves. Hyde was likely a mess of mud and water. No one in their right mind would venture there in these conditions.

I had sent another note for Miss Scott early this morning, canceling our meeting yet again. But now, I wondered if a better course might be to alter the meeting location. She had insisted upon discretion, which meant being seen together too frequently in public was out of the question. Where, then, could we spend time together in privacy?

"If you scowl like that for much longer, you will have a permanent frown," said Mother. She sat across the room, stitching flowers onto a piece of white linen.

"I miss the sun. I cannot ask a lady to go out in this sort of weather."

Mother met my gaze, her expression blank. Still, her eyes were studious. She had always possessed a quiet pensiveness and the ability to see through me. I both admired and hated it.

"You've been making quite a few calls as of late."

She was not wrong on that front, though I had failed to mention those calls were all to the same woman. I had always believed that, when I decided to court someone, I would be excited to inform Mother. I held no such enthusiasm about mentioning Miss Rigby. In the three times I had visited her at home, my feelings and comfort around her had not progressed. It was too soon to give up, but my hope waned.

I heaved a sigh and crossed the room to take a seat next to Mother. "I have been making calls to one lady in particular."

"Oh?" She smiled slightly, still studying me.

"Yes, but it seems no matter how often I visit her, there is no…" I bit my lip, searching for the right words. Miss Rigby was perfectly acceptable in every way. I could find no fault with her beyond my lack of desire to spend time in her company. Why could my heart not cooperate on the matter? This would prove much easier if I simply fell madly in love with the woman.

"No spark?" Mother finished before I could determine what to say.

My shoulders fell. "She is everything a young lady of sophistication should be."

"But you feel nothing for her." Mother's smile grew. "There are many women in London who are ideal, Phillip. That does not mean they would all make a good match for *you*."

"I suppose not."

Her smile faded. "Your uncle puts too much pressure on you, but you remember what I told you, do you not?"

I reached for her hand. "To make sure my heart is taken into consideration."

She nodded. "I want you to be happy, darling. Your father and I loved one another very much. He would have wanted the same for you, as do I. If this lady you've been to see does not excite you, fill you with hope for the future, then I cannot imagine she is the right choice. Do not make the decision solely based on the things your uncle wants."

"You know his opinion matters a great deal for everyone's future. Mine, my wife and children, and yours. There is much to consider."

She patted my hand. "There always is when it comes to matters of the heart."

Matters of the heart? Perhaps that was entirely the problem. My heart did not feel engaged in Miss Rigby whatsoever. Even with Uncle's approval, I hadn't felt motivated to move forward.

"Then I hope you will excuse me for scowling out the window until I figure it out," I said teasingly. "It seems my face cannot help but reflect the condition of my thoughts."

She chuckled lightly, and we enjoyed one another's company in silence for a time—she pursuing her needlework and I lost to my thoughts.

Musing over my predicament was getting me nowhere on my own. I needed the sun. I needed Miss Scott.

An hour later, Uncle entered the drawing room dressed in a dark red waistcoat and heavy brown overcoat. His beaver hat sat askew on his head, and the chain of his gold pocket watch dangled from his fingers. Mother and I stood in acknowledgment, as was expected of us.

"What are your plans for today?" he asked in his customary sharp tone. The question was directed at me. He rarely acknowledged my mother, let alone spoke to her.

"I haven't any plans for today," I said.

Uncle sneered. "Best be wooing that lady, boy. I do not want to see you idle until the deal is done."

The deal. What a brilliant way to look at marriage. I tempered my irritation so the sarcasm would not come out in my tone. "I called on her yesterday. Once the weather clears, I plan to ask her to go riding if that suits?"

Uncle grunted, his gaze darting to the window and back. "I suppose that will do, but I expect you to make good use of your time. Not sit around. I have business to attend to and will not return until supper. I've left a ledger on my desk for you to balance. See to it today."

"Yes, Uncle."

With another grunt, he was off. Mother reclaimed her seat, and I was sorely tempted to join her. I should take care of the ledger and be done with it, but I stood, rooted in place. I couldn't focus on numbers just now. What good would it do me to ask Miss Rigby to ride when the sun returned? I'd hoped being out of doors and not having the constant glare of her mother might ease the awkwardness between us, but now, I wasn't so sure.

I desperately needed advice. I needed my matchmaker. If we could not meet in Hyde, then perhaps someplace with a sturdy roof to keep out the rain would do. Given Uncle would be gone the remainder of the day and Mother and Sabrina rarely ventured beyond their bedchambers or the drawing room, I had an idea of just such a place that could afford us both protection from the weather and the privacy we required.

Indeed, it was time to send Miss Scott another note.

# GRACE

I KNOCKED IMPATIENTLY ON Annette's door. After receiving one note from Phillip stating we would not meet due to the weather, delivered to me over breakfast by Rus, I had intended to spend the day reading. No sooner than I had picked out a book in the library and curled up next to the hearth, Rus had found me again to deliver a second note. My cousin hadn't asked what either of them contained, but he did make his deliveries with a raised brow and incorrigible smirk.

I could not blame him for teasing me, I supposed. Generally, women and men did not exchange letters like this unless it was with a relative or lover. My client was neither, which Rus knew, but he'd never been one to turn down an opportunity to make a nuisance of himself.

Once he had gone from the library, I'd swiftly opened the note to find Mr. Montfert had changed his mind. He wanted to meet today, despite the rain, and the location request set my heart pounding. An unmarried woman did not go visiting a bachelor at his residence. It simply wasn't done.

Then again, neither was exchanging notes. I had dismissed that impropriety due to the nature of our relationship, but meeting at his home? That seemed to cross a new line.

Yet, the thought filled me with eagerness and excitement. Mr. Montfert had sounded desperate in his letter—almost pleading. How could I deny my client when he needed me most? This arrangement had to go well if I ever wished to have the financial freedom I sought.

I knocked again on Annette's door, bouncing on my toes. Finally, the door swung open to reveal her still in a dressing gown and rubbing her eyes. "For heaven's sake, Grace. What is so urgent?"

"I am to meet with Mr. Montfert today. I need you to ready yourself."

Annette yawned. "I cannot go with you today. Besides, the weather is far too miserable."

"Why can you not go with me?" I asked, ignoring the latter half. If she was not to accompany me, then perhaps it would be best to keep the location of this meeting to myself. My aunt, uncle, and guardian would not approve, and despite Annette's rebellious nature, I suspected she might not either.

"Hmm? Oh, Lieutenant Paget has invited me to the museum at noon. Mother is going to escort me." She grimaced. "Forgive me for not extending the invitation to you, but I knew there was a chance you would have a meeting with your client. Can Rus go with you today? I know he is terribly obnoxious, but—"

"It is quite alright," I said, holding up a hand to stop her. "I'll take my lady's maid with me. Forgive me for waking you."

She shook her head. "It is time I ready myself, but are you certain you wish to go out in this?" She gestured behind her to what I assumed was the window where water droplets beat against the glass.

"I am sure. We've arranged to meet somewhere dry. But never mind that. You do not sound very vexed about an outing with Lieutenant Paget." I raised a brow in question, and Annette shifted on her feet.

"There are worse suitors," she said, though nothing in her expression made the statement believable. She must have sensed my incredulity, for she continued. "The lieutenant and I have called a truce."

"A truce?" I repeated. That seemed rather unlikely. "When did this happen?"

"When we went riding. He does have *some* redeemable qualities." She sounded as if she were trying to convince herself more than me.

"That is good, is it not?"

Annette forced a smile. "Of course. I look forward to discovering more of his...redeemable qualities. Today. While at the museum."

I wished her patience rather than luck, sensing she would need it, and left her to get ready for the day. Lying had never been a talent of mine, but I had no intention of taking my maid with me. That would mean informing someone else of my meetings with Mr. Montfert. It was bad enough that Rus and Annette were aware, though I knew I could trust them. Still, I would not increase the risk of my guardian discovering my scheme.

Nor would I risk him learning of what I was about to do.

I dressed in a warm pelisse and topped my head with a bonnet. Rain pounded against the roof of the townhouse, so I grabbed an umbrella to keep me dry on my journey to the address Mr. Montfert put in his note. The challenge did not lay in facing the weather, however. I needed to get out of the house without anyone becoming aware of my departure.

Too many servants bustled about the ground floor to make a stealthy escape possible. Instead, I entered one of the guest bedchambers and closed the door behind me. The room was not used often, therefore reducing the chance someone might catch me. It was also located on the first floor rather than the second, like my own chamber. If I was going to scale the wall, one less story was preferable.

Besides, I happened to know this particular room had a trellis of Wisteria just outside the window. I had admired the vines from the back gardens more than once.

I slid open the window and peered down at the muddy puddles forming around the shrubbery below. My stomach knotted. It was higher than I had recalled, but I would manage. One leg went over the window sill, then the other, my boots digging into the thick vines until I found a foothold in the wooden trellis. Climbing with the umbrella would be a task, so I dropped it into the bush directly below, and it disappeared into the foliage.

Now to climb.

My first step was shaky. Rain continued to pour from the darkened clouds above, soaking my bonnet and coat before I had made it halfway to the bottom. Finding the trellis between the vines proved a challenge, and what was more, the vines themselves were slick with water.

With a few feet left, my boots slipped, and I struggled to regain my footing. My fingers gripped the trellis, and I fought to hold my weight. I considered screaming for help as my body dangled against the façade of the house. I could give up, but to do so would be as good as a confession. What would Rowe do if he found out what I was up to? Put an end to my Season?

Before I could decide what to do, my fingers lost their hold, and I fell.

I hadn't been far from the bottom. Four—perhaps five—feet at most. But I landed hard on my weak leg and collapsed to the ground with a cry of pain. Gripping the limb, I stared up at the house, waiting. Watching. Someone might have heard, but with the pounding of the rain on the roof and walls, I doubted it.

I pushed myself from the ground, slowly, my jaw clenched with the pain that ricocheted up my leg. Once I had retrieved my umbrella from the bush, I limped around the side of the house, careful to avoid the windows.

Walking the streets was more difficult. I attempted to ease my pain with a slow pace. I was fortunate that Mr. Montfert's townhouse was not more than three streets away. I didn't know the time, but my limp would likely make me late. What would I do if he wasn't waiting for me?

I pushed the worry aside. Mr. Montfert had said he would meet me at the servants' entry on the north side of the house. He would be there. After all the trouble I'd gone through, he had better be.

The wind picked up, sending an icy chill through my body and causing rain to pelt me from behind. Water soaked the hem of my dress, and whatever warmth I might have gained from my pelisse was diminished by the dampness of the soaked fabric.

I arrived at Phillip's home and allowed myself not more than a moment to admire the white Grecian columns framing the door and the red brick wall that was painted with water. After looking up and down the street to ensure I wouldn't be noticed, I slipped through the gate and around the side of the house until I came to a door.

And then I stared at it.

What was I to do, knock? Mr. Montfert had failed to include instructions for after my arrival. What if I tapped on the door and a servant answered? My presence here would be difficult to explain, especially given my drenched state. Despite the umbrella, I looked worse than a long-haired dog after a swim.

Perhaps that was a bit dramatic, but I certainly felt ridiculous. And cold.

I shuddered, taking a step closer to the door, and lifted my hand. It swung inward before my fist ever made contact, revealing a head of familiar brown hair and blue-grey eyes.

# Chapter Nineteen

## PHILLIP

As expected, when I opened the door, I saw Miss Scott. I had watched her lithe form pass by the window, after all. What I did not expect was to find her drenched from top to bottom, the pale yellow umbrella she held doing little to protect her from the onslaught of rain dumping from the heavens. There wasn't an inch of her not soaked. Even her brown hair clung to her face.

I grabbed her wrist and tugged her inside out of the weather. She sucked in a sharp breath, and her face contorted with pain. My gaze immediately fell to her feet, as if I would be able to see her leg despite her skirts. I could only assume that was the source of her pain.

"What were you thinking?" I blurted. "Coming out in the weather like this."

She scowled at me, and I nearly laughed. I had never seen such an expression mare this woman's face. Miss Scott rarely wore anything but a smile.

"What was *I* thinking? Y-you were the one who invited me here."

"Yes, but I did not think you would walk in the rain. Why did you not take a carriage? I'm certain Apsley would not have minded."

"Rus would have a-asked questions. He may be lax in a great many things, but even he would not approve of my coming to see you u-un-chaperoned, and at your home, no less. At a minimum, he would have informed my guardian, and Rowe is f-far more of a prude when it comes to my reputation." She paused, her teeth still chattering. "I do not f-fault him for it since I am his responsibility, but I do not wish to worry him."

My mind was still stuck on one word: unchaperoned. Only now did it occur to me that we were utterly alone in the pantry. Miss Apsley usually tagged along with her, but I realized now it was not appropriate for either of them to come here. Why had I not considered that?

I ran a hand through my hair. "I should not have asked you to...forgive me."

Miss Scott rolled her eyes. "It hardly matters. I came all this way. We might as well d-discuss things."

"Very well, but not here. I informed the servants that I intended to spend much of the day in the library and did not wish to be disturbed. It will be safer there."

Miss Scott placed her hands on her hips. "And h-how do you propose I get to the library without being seen?"

That much I had prepared for.

I retrieved a deep red hooded cloak from where it hung from a hook on the wall and offered it to her. "Take this. It is Sabrina's. If anyone does see you, they will think you are her."

She gave me a skeptical look. "No one in their right mind would ever mistake me for your cousin. Sabrina is quite possibly the most beautiful woman in London, and b-besides that, she does not possess a limp."

My cousin was lovely, yes, but I would not go as far as to name her the most beautiful. In fact—

"Very well." Miss Scott shuddered and slipped the cloak around her despite her argument. She must be freezing.

"Come," I said softly, lifting the hood over her head. "Let's get you to a fire."

Her warm brown eyes stared up at me, hesitant and probing, but when I offered her my arm, she took it. Quietly, I led her from the pantry, narrowly avoiding the servants who bustled about the kitchens. We passed the study and followed the corridor to the library, our pace slow. Miss Scott's hand tightened around me each time she placed pressure on her left leg. She was wet and in pain, and guilt ate at me for both.

I should never have asked her to come, and all to satisfy my concerns about Miss Rigby. I could have waited for advice—waited for the rain to stop and the ground to dry. If the woman caught a cold, it would be my fault.

We entered the library, and I closed the door before leading her toward the fire. Miss Scott removed her gloves and then the cloak. She laid them both across a chair before inching nearer the flames, her arms wrapped about her middle and her teeth chattering.

"Perhaps...perhaps I ought to find you something dry to wear," I said, suspecting she would never agree to it.

Miss Scott faced me. "I-I'll be fine."

I debated calling for tea. A warm drink would help, but it would also risk someone learning of her presence. Still, I hated watching her shiver like this. Perhaps a blanket? But with extra fabric wrapped around her, it would take longer for her clothing to dry.

Lud. What else could I do?

A sudden desire to pull her into my arms accosted me, making my pulse frantic. I shook the idea away and kneeled next to the fire to stoke the flames. They didn't need it, but better to stoke those than the ones burning within me.

Miss Scott patted the top of her head and winced. "My hair must look frightening."

I sat back on my heels and stared up at her. Her hair was a bit of a disaster, but frightening was not the word I would have used. There was something alluring about the way the firelight reflected off of her damp strands and gave her skin an almost glow.

I turned my attention back to the fire. Silence settled around us, and I continued to poke at the flames without purpose, my thoughts a swirl of confusion and my chest tight with...

Well, I hadn't any idea why it felt as though someone had filled me with bubbles that continued to expand. It was an odd sensation I had never experienced before meeting my matchmaker.

"Are you certain no one will find us in here?" she asked, her voice quiet.

"My uncle is out on business and will not return until evening. My mother is home, but she spends all of her time in her chamber or the drawing room on days like this, as does Sabrina." I pointed to a darkened corner of the room with a wide sofa. "You may hide behind there should we be disturbed."

She chuckled lightly. "If you think I can scurry that far before someone sees me, then you overestimate my fleeing skills. Especially at present."

Her leg. She meant because of her leg.

"Is it bothering you terribly?" I gestured to her lower half.

"Unfortunately. I had thought to escape the house by climbing out the window so as to not be seen. I climbed down the trellis from the first floor but slipped on the wet Wisteria vines." She smiled wryly. "In better weather, it would have been a solid plan."

"I cannot believe you climbed out of a window for me. I must applaud your dedication, but may I ask that you not put yourself in danger again?"

"I will make no such promise, Mr. Montfert. I intend to help my client. If that requires climbing out of windows and scaling walls..." She shrugged, but her real smile appeared.

"I admire your bravery. I confess I would have hesitated to do either of those things."

"Yet you would dance with me in a crowded ballroom in a way most would find embarrassing? I think that is far more brave, sir."

Brave? No, I could not claim it. Not once when I danced with her had I thought of what others in the room might think. Certainly, I had known how foolish and silly the entire thing must have appeared, but I hadn't cared. Dancing with Grace was the most enjoyable thing I had done since coming to London.

Miss Scott. Not Grace.

I stood and grabbed the nearest chair to drag toward the fire. Miss Scott sat down, offering me a polite 'thank you' before I grabbed a second one to join her.

"I must thank you for something else," she said. The stutter in her voice had disappeared, at least.

"What might that be?"

"The flowers. They were lovely and so unexpected."

I tilted my head. "We danced, Miss Scott. Is it not an expectation that ladies should receive a bouquet following a ball?"

"Of course, but I...that is, I did not know if our dance counted. It was rather unorthodox, was it not?"

"I can agree with that, but it was a dance, nonetheless. And perfectly deserving of flowers."

"Well," she said, the color in her cheeks heightened, "I thank you for them. They are likely the only ones I will receive this Season."

My brows furrowed. "That is not true. Surely a suitor might send a lady flowers other than after he dances with her?"

"Yes, but you assume I will have any of those." Her smile turned sad. "Given my difficulties with dancing and even walking at times, it is hard to imagine many men desiring to court me, a fact I have resigned myself to." She shifted in the chair, turning to face me more fully, the sadness in her expression disappearing. "Which is why I am more than happy to help you find a match. If I cannot have my own, then what better to do than match others?"

Her enthusiasm should have reassured me. Instead, I frowned. How could this kind, vibrant woman give up on courtship so easily? Her leg had not stopped her from climbing *out of a window*, but she drew the line at expecting suitors? The idea perplexed me, but not as much as her belief no one would ever court her because of her malady. She was still beautiful. Still intelligent and—

"Have I said something to offend you?" she asked, her brows drawn tight.

"No." I shook my head. "Not at all. I simply am not fond of the idea of you giving up on finding a match of your own. You deserve it as much as anyone."

"Mmm, well, society does not take kindly to broken things." She shrugged. "Especially ones that cannot be fixed. I have made peace with it and have a plan for my future. You needn't pity me." She sat up taller. "Now, enough about me. Your letter sounded urgent. Am I to understand you called on Miss Rigby?"

Miss Rigby. Yes, that was the reason I had requested Miss Scott to come in the first place. I had a plethora of questions to ask, a desperate need for advice. But I could not think of a single one, my mind too stuck on her self-proclaimed brokenness. Uncle had often placed the same label on me. As a child, I had even believed it.

But as I grew older, I realized that my worth was not directly tied to my physical struggles. The impairment challenged me, pushed me. It did not define me. What would Miss Scott think were I to confess my disability? Would she believe me incapable of finding a love match, just as she had deemed herself incable?

I doubted it. She had, subconsciously, put that restriction upon herself as a form of protection from disappointment and ridicule, of that, I was sure.

I slid to the edge of my seat and reached for her hands. She gasped when I took them both in mine. Neither of us wore gloves. Her fingers were still cool but not as icy as they had been. I looked into her eyes, and my heart sped as I spoke with conviction. "You are *not* broken."

"I have a limp—"

"Which does not make you broken. Different, perhaps, but are we all not a little different? How boring the world would be if we were all the same."

"Having different opinions, likes and dislikes, is not the same as having a body that does not function properly," she retorted.

I gave her hands a gentle squeeze. "True, but would you tell a blind man he knows nothing of beauty simply because he cannot see?"

"Of course not. Beauty is more than what our eyes can perceive. It can be heard. Felt."

"Indeed. And would you tell a man who is deaf that he cannot appreciate laughter or music, birdsong or words, simply because he cannot hear them?"

She gave me an incredulous look. "I see where you are going with this."

I grinned. "Then can we not assume a woman with difficulty walking or dancing might still enjoy and appreciate those things? In a different way than what is normal, perhaps, but appreciate them all the same. You are not broken because of your struggles, Miss Scott. Were that the case, we might all be considered such, for there are none of us born without imperfections. Some are just more difficult to perceive than others."

Slowly, she shook her head, her eyes locked on our clasped hands. "Sometimes I feel as though I am the only one in the world with such imperfections."

I released one of her hands and tucked my knuckles under her chin, lifting until she met my gaze. "I assure you that is not true."

A small smile pulled at one side of her mouth. "And what of you, Phillip? What are your imperfections? I fail to see them."

My heart pounded hard against my chest. Phillip. She had called me Phillip.

I brushed my thumb over her jaw, and her eyes fluttered closed. I wanted to tell her about my partial deafness. Wanted to explain she was not at all alone. But Uncle had made me swear to keep the problem to myself. Not even Sabrina was aware of it. Before now, I hadn't desired for anyone but Uncle and Mother to know. After all, Grace was not wrong; Society had little patience for broken things, and while I refused to see myself that way, it did not mean others would not.

But Grace was not like the rest of society. She would understand. I *wanted* her to understand.

I opened my mouth, intent on telling her everything, but the door to the library swung open. Sabrina stepped inside, and her jaw dropped when her gaze landed on us.

# Chapter Twenty

## PHILLIP

My hand fell from Grace's face, and I practically jumped from my chair. "Sabrina. I...this is not—"

She held up her hands and backed out of the door without a word. I had never seen my cousin scurry away before, and instinct told me to chase after her. I met Grace's panicked gaze, and she seemed to understand, permitting me to leave her in pursuit of my cousin.

So I ran. Sabrina was halfway down the corridor before I caught up to her.

"Sabrina, wait!" My tone was a whisper but firm enough to stop her. "It is not what you think."

"I do not think anything, Phillip." She refused to look at me, which directly opposed her words. "I saw nothing. I haven't any idea to what you are referring."

She turned to leave, but I reached for her wrist. "She is helping me find a match. That is all."

"Stop talking."

"You know I have little experience among Society. A friend recommended a matchmaker, and Grace—

"*Phillip*. Stop. Talking."

My mouth snapped closed.

"If I were to learn of you having secret meetings with a lady—which I most definitely have not—please know that I would keep the information to myself. However, I would encourage you to choose a better location for said meetings as my father would not take kindly to Miss Scott's presence here under any circumstance."

This I knew, though I did not fully understand it. I wanted clarity on the matter. I released her wrist. "Why not?"

"It is complicated."

"And that is still not an answer."

"I imagine he is still angry about what happened with my sister," Grace's voice sounded from behind me.

Upon glancing over my shoulder, I found her limping toward us, her expression pinched with obvious pain. I went to her and offered my arm for support, guiding her the rest of the way.

Sabrina scoffed and pinned her gaze to the wall. "The two of you are making it very difficult for me to see *nothing*."

"Never mind that," I said. "What do you mean? What happened with her sister?"

Sabrina sighed, shaking her head. "I've no desire to relay all the details. Suffice it to say that I was meant to gain the attention of an earl at that house party last spring, and Miss Scott's sister stole his heart instead."

"So Uncle blames her family for your failure?" I asked.

"Of course, he does. He would throw a tantrum to find you have an acquaintance with Grace at all, I'm certain. She may not have had anything to do with it, but—

"Actually, I might have had a bit to do with it." Grace winced. "I made certain the earl knew of my sister's affections by slipping him pages from her diary."

Sabrina's lips pressed together in an obvious attempt not to laugh. "Well, it seems you have at least found a matchmaker with experience, Phillip."

"And a tenacious one at that." I smiled at Grace, and she returned it, unleashing those bubbles in my chest again.

They popped when the sound of voices echoed down the corridor from the front entry. Uncle's stern tone addressing our butler was accompanied by the reserved one of another man. The same one I had heard in the study days ago.

Sabrina sucked in a breath. "Father is back, and he's brought Mr. Barton. They must be having their meeting." She looked at me significantly, though what she expected me to do, I hadn't a clue. How was I to get Grace out of here with Uncle coming this way?

"The library," I whispered. "We must hide you."

"There's no time. They're coming." Sabrina pushed past me and threw open the door of a linen closet. She shoved me inside, with Grace stumbling along after. To my surprise, Sabrina joined us, closing the door and bathing us in darkness.

Hands gripped my shoulders and nudged me against the wall, pressing me closer to Grace. "Move, Phillip."

"Move where?" I whispered with agitation. "You have pushed us into a closet, Sabrina. And a small one at that. I am not a scrawny boy of twelve."

"You are most certainly a man, Phillip, and I believe Miss Scott would agree with me." In the darkness, I could not see what my cousin was doing, but the quiet shuffling of her skirts suggested she had crouched close to the floor. "There. I've found it."

"Found what?" I asked.

"The door." Sabrina grabbed the sleeve of my coat and tugged me toward the wall. Except, part of the wall was gone. Why was there a door in the closet?

I still could not see, but I followed Sabrina's lead. Grace held tight to my arm, her steps labored as she struggled to keep weight off of her left leg. The space we entered was exceptionally narrow—smaller, even, than the linen closet. Both of my shoulders grazed either wall, forcing Grace to release me. I had to angle my body for all three of us to fit into the space, which left my matchmaker pinned against my side.

"Where does this lead?" I asked, grunting as I shifted to get comfortable, a task I would never achieve.

"Nowhere." Even without seeing my face, Sabrina must have sensed me scowling at her, for she continued. "It's an old servant's corridor. At some point, the house was remodeled, making this hallway useless." She paused. "Well, not entirely useless. At least not to me."

"What is that supposed to mean?"

"Rather than tear out the walls, it was abandoned. Still, it has its perks. I doubt many of our staff even know it exists."

"Because they do not rummage around in the linen closet?" I asked sarcastically. "How did you discover it?"

Sabrina kneeled, which I only knew because my knee dug into her back. "Keep quiet so my father does not hear us."

Before I could question her, she slid a latch across the wall, revealing a foot-wide peephole above her head that allowed in enough light to turn the utter darkness into lightened shadows. I could see Sabrina's silhouette, crouched in front of me, as well as Grace's at my side. The longer I stared, the more my eyes adjusted. The more detail they could decipher.

The peephole peered into the study, situated so that it gave a view of the door. I recognized the maroon wallpaper and gold-accented furniture immediately, having spent a particularly large chunk of time there since coming to London.

Uncle and another man entered the room, and my body went tense. What if we were discovered? I could not fathom my uncle's fury toward me and his daughter, but it would be worse for Grace. I refused to subject her to his ire.

"We need to leave," I whispered. "The corridor is clear now."

"Not yet." Sabrina stood and lifted on her toes to peer out of the hole. "I need to hear this conversation."

I understood her reasoning, but there was no point in risking Grace. Sabrina could get the information she wanted while I snuck Grace out of the house with Uncle occupied. It was our best chance of not being caught.

"Stay, Phillip," Sabrina whispered, apparently sensing my thoughts. "They could leave at any moment. I will distract my father once their meeting is over, but it would benefit you to hear all of this, too."

My jaw clenched. I would never hear anything but muffled conversation. I could barely understand Sabrina's soft voice, let alone the discussion happening on the other side of the wall. Unless Uncle became enraged and started shouting, I would learn nothing.

But I would not tell my cousin this. Not yet, anyway. At some point, we would discuss what we heard today, and I would have to admit the truth.

"What if he sees the hole?" I asked. "This is dangerous."

My cousin scoffed lightly. "I've been spying on him from here for years. He has not spotted it yet. The hole blends into the wall, hidden between two paintings. Father will not notice."

She sounded so certain, and I wanted to trust her. I glanced at Grace, but her face was too shadowed to read anything of her thoughts. What must she be thinking? She had no notion of why Sabrina would wish to spy on her father, or why I would want to remain here.

The gentle squeeze of my arm pulled me from my musings.

"I can wait," Grace whispered. "This sounds important."

"Are you certain?"

Sabrina shushed us. I could hear my uncle speaking, but the words were garbled. In silence, we stood for what seemed like an hour. My feet began to ache, as did my back and shoulders from the awkward angle at which I stood. How servants had used this corridor for anything, I might never know. No wonder it had been abandoned.

"Phillip?"

I almost missed Grace's quiet voice, so I tilted my good ear toward her to hear her better. "What is it?"

"My leg. It...I do not know how much longer it will hold me."

Lud. If the tight space and standing so long were uncomfortable for me, I could only imagine how she must feel, especially after falling off a trellis.

With slow movements, I shifted so my body angled toward her rather than Sabrina. Grace needed less pressure on her leg, and I could think of only one way to achieve that in this cramped space.

I wrapped an arm about her waist, my fingers splaying over the small of her back. She gasped when I pulled her close. The smell of roses wafted to my nose, mingling with the scent of dust. Her dress was still damp in places, though nowhere near as drenched as it had been when she arrived. Still, I felt guilty for taking her away from the warm fire.

"Do you trust me?" I asked in a whisper.

She nodded, and I lifted her against me, supporting her. Holding her.

Grace's hands flattened against my chest, and I was certain she could feel the fast drumming of my heart. I had never been this close to a lady. Dancing in ballrooms or strolling through parks demanded a certain amount of proximity, but this...I had no experience with this.

My body seemed to come alive with awareness. Every intake of her breath pressed her against me. Every exhale sent her warm breath skittering across the skin exposed above my cravat. Her touch, even with the fabric of my waistcoat as separation, created needle-like sparks of warmth that raced through my veins and into my limbs.

The heady sensation spread to fill every inch of me, foreign and spellbinding. All thoughts of my uncle and his discussion with Mr. Barton faded, my focus solely on the woman in my arms. Now that she was closer, the light from the peephole illuminated her face enough that I could see her eyes, their color a rich caramel with dark flakes of gold. Her hair had dried, leaving it wavy and frizzy.

And her lips? They looked...inviting.

I momentarily closed my eyes, bombarded with the images of claiming them for myself. I had never kissed a woman, and the desire to experience a gesture so intimate with Grace nearly overwhelmed me.

Did she feel it too? This fire between us? With little experience in courtship, I could not be certain this desire was not simply the result of our proximity, but something told me it wasn't. Not once had I felt this way in Miss Rigby's company. I had never considered her lips or the smoothness of the skin along her collarbone. I had never felt the urge to hold her close, to caress her jaw.

To kiss her soundly.

My arm tightened around Grace with the thought. Did I imagine the way she leaned into me? No, I could not have, for now my nose brushed hers, every breath filled with her scent.

My voice came out raspy. "Your leg…is it better?"

"Yes." Her response was breathy, and when her gaze drifted from my eyes to my mouth, I felt undone. The need to eliminate the remaining distance grew too great, and softly, I touched my lips to hers, so light a feather could not have matched the movement.

What was I doing? I hardly knew, but the fight to keep myself from her was growing difficult. I wanted more—far more than I should. More than I could have.

"They are finished," Sabrina whispered.

My stomach jolted, and I pulled away from Grace as much as the cramped space would allow but kept a firm hold about her waist. She tensed beneath my touch, the spell between us broken.

"Are they leaving?" I asked.

"Yes. Allow me to go first, and I'll request a moment of Father's time. I will feign some sort of interest in a titled man. That ought to keep him entertained long enough for you to escape." She slid the latch over the peephole, cutting off the little light we'd had. "Grace, if you will wait for me around the corner of the house, Phillip can order the carriage for us. I will ride home with you, and if your family asks, you may tell them I talked you into a ride."

With a plan in place, the three of us inched our way back into the linen closet. Sabrina left first, and Grace and I waited until we heard the close of the study door before venturing into the corridor. Neither of us spoke until we reached the pantry, and even then I only managed an awkward farewell. My mind was too muddled for anything more, my thoughts distracted by the constant replay of all that had occurred.

I imagined Grace felt much the same.

Once she had gone, I informed the footman of Sabrina's need for the carriage, then waited in the entry hall for her. She appeared minutes later, her expression almost weary.

"You owe me," she whispered, slapping my chest with a loose glove before tugging it on. "I will now have to speak to Father again to disabuse him of the notion that I have an interest in Lord Kingsley."

"You have my sincerest apologies and gratitude."

The footman returned and announced the carriage was ready. Sabrina studied me, something in her gaze far too knowing. It had been dark in the abandoned corridor, and she had been too focused on her father's meeting to notice anything.

Hadn't she?

Any hope I had of her being unaware of what had happened vanished with her next words. "I like her, Phillip. I would like to call her my friend, but I fear that you are playing with fire and are well on your way to hurting the both of you." She stepped closer to me after a glance around us to ensure we remained alone. "You cannot kiss Miss Scott unless you are willing to stand up to my father."

"I thought you saw nothing?" I teased, though the words fell flat. I sobered. "I did not kiss her. She is my matchmaker. I had a moment of weakness, but I know she cannot be more."

Sabrina nodded, but her expression was more sympathy and disappointment than belief. "Your mind may know it, but I'm not so sure your heart is aware."

And as my cousin walked away, I feared she might be correct.

# Chapter Twenty-One

## GRACE

I HAD NEVER BEEN one to sleep late, but it was nearly noon before I finally forced my body from my bed to dress for the day. Remaining in my bedchamber would do me no good. I could not sleep, my mind a tangle of chaotic thoughts. And besides, every time I closed my eyes, the ghost of Phillip's touch caressed my skin—my back, my hands, my lips. Yesterday felt more and more like a dream.

A dream I was all too eager to relive.

What a fool I had become. Matchmakers did not kiss their clients.

Not that Phillip *had* kissed me. Not really. His lips had touched mine, true, but could I not attest that to our forced proximity? He had held me close in an effort to offer my leg relief. His actions were that of a friend, were they not?

I could not say what he thought on the matter, but my heart and body certainly felt more than a friend should. In that moment, I had wanted him—his kiss, his touch, his warmth. I wanted to be the woman he embraced, the one he whispered quiet words of affection and regard to each night before bed.

Where had such desires and feelings come from?

I knew the answer, at least to an extent. When with Phillip, I felt at ease and never judged. The way he had abandoned all thought of embarrassment to dance with me at the Morrison's ball had been the start. Then came the flowers I had never expected.

But neither of those things compared to our conversation in his library, where he insisted that I was not broken. Where he looked at me with such tenderness that I could scarcely breathe. Indeed, were any heroines in one of my novels to receive such a look from a handsome gentleman, they would likely swoon.

I had not swooned, and I would not swoon, because Phillip was my client.

Mr. Montfert. Bother. I needed to keep the formality between us; otherwise, my heart might get more ridiculous notions. The reality was that Phillip Montfert needed a wife who would meet his uncle's requirements, and even though I claimed a connection to a viscount, the man would never approve of me.

After what I had overhead, his approval was not something I even wanted. The conversations on the other side of the wall had left me confused but suspicious. Whatever Mr. Perry was involved in, it sounded...criminal.

The idea did not surprise me, and I wondered if the reason Sabrina and Phillip were spying on him was because they intended to take proper action—whatever that entailed. Would Phillip even need a matchmaker if his uncle was sentenced by the courts?

Once my lady's maid had helped me dress and finished my hair, I made my way downstairs. I had missed breakfast, but I had never once been unsuccessful at convincing Cook to sneak me something from the kitchens.

She did not disappoint, and I came away with a stomach full of lemon tarts and fresh bread dressed with honey, enough to satisfy me until afternoon tea. Intending to seek company—and a distraction from my thoughts—I ventured toward the yellow parlor located on the ground floor but did not make it past the central stairs.

Lieutenant Paget descended them with quick steps, as always, an image of handsome perfection. His steps slowed when he glanced up and took note of me, and a genial smile flitted over his face. "Good afternoon, Miss Scott. How are you today?"

"Well, I thank you. Have you come to call on Annette?"

He shook his head. "I believe she is out making calls herself with your aunt today."

My lips pinched together. I should have been with them, but the need for rest had chased any thought of it from my mind. If only staying abed had done me any good, then my conscience might have been clear. As it was, staying in my room had only provided me with more time to think about Phillip.

Mr. Montfert.

Drat it all.

The lieutenant clasped his hands behind his back. "I came to see your uncle. He is looking much better today."

My uncle's health had improved over the last few days, and he had finally joined us again for dinner, but I gave the lieutenant a curious look. "How do you know he looks better? Have you been visiting him?"

He smiled. "I have. I've taken the time to see him after my outings with your cousin. Lord Paxton and my father have always been particular friends, and I find his political stances intriguing. It has been very informative to gain his perspective on things."

Ah. So, it would seem Lieutenant Paget did have an interest in politics, and he might even favor abolition. Annette would be pleased to learn of this development, assuming she did not already know. I'd had the opportunity to watch them together the last two weeks, and while Annette still kept walls around her, I could tell she had softened toward the man. It would take time, and a great deal of patience on the lieutenant's part, but the two of them had potential.

"It is always good to gain a better understanding of others' perspectives," I said. "We learn much that way, especially how to have empathy for those around us."

"Indeed, and I believe empathy is a virtue worth nurturing. It is something I strive for." He tilted his head, sending a strand of his dark hair onto his forehead. "Might I ask a favor of you, Miss Scott?"

"You may."

"I will be busy attending to business the remainder of the week, and I wondered if you might let Miss Apsley know not to expect me for some time." His lips quirked up on one side. "I should not wish for her to forget me while hosting her numerous suitors in my absence."

I chuckled for two reasons. One, Annette had fewer callers now that Lieutenant Paget was making headway. It seemed between his determination to win her over and Annette's to keep the others at a distance, many of them had given up. It likely helped that Rus was no longer sending bachelors to call upon. Second, I was positively certain my cousin could not forget the lieutenant, even if she wanted to.

"I will inform her, unless you would prefer to write her a note?" I raised my brows. "My stealth for delivering notes of a private nature is well-practiced."

My sister would agree. Never mind that the notes I had delivered on her behalf were without permission. And stolen from her diary. I might have felt guilty for sneaking behind her back had my efforts not helped her find happiness with a man she loved.

The lieutenant looked pensive. "You know, I think I shall take you up on that offer. Would it inconvenience you if I were to write her a letter before leaving?"

"Not at all." I gestured toward the parlor. "Please."

The lieutenant stayed another half hour, writing his note to Annette while I embroidered a cushion, a maid serving as our quiet chaperone. Once he had gone, I gave up the pursuit and settled near the hearth with a book instead. Usually, a novel could sweep me away from all my troubles, but no matter how engrossed I was with the story, my mind inevitably wandered to Phillip.

When would I see him again?

Perhaps if we met and spoke of Miss Rigby, the renewed focus would put an end to my ridiculous musings. I had gone to his house for that very thing, and we had not even spoken of her. Instead, Phillip had spent his time reassuring me.

A chill swept over my arms. I had never told anyone how often I felt broken, and more specifically, alone in that brokenness. It seemed everyone around me was perfect and whole. None of my family had ever understood my struggles. I had not wanted them to, forever keeping most of my pain and sadness hidden.

But Phillip saw through me in ways no one else did, and something in the way he spoke made me feel heard. Understood, even. How could that be when the man was, so far as I could tell, utterly perfect himself? I could find no flaw in him, and each time he went out of his way to make me comfortable or smile, I only added to his list of qualities.

Lady Paxton and Annette returned, the former greeting me before announcing her intention to check on her husband. My parents had possessed a very loving relationship, and I saw the same in my aunt and uncle. While I had never met my paternal grandparents, they had raised their boys to respect and cherish their wives. With such examples in my life, including the relationship my sister had found with her husband, how could I ever settle for something less?

Annette plopped onto the cushion next to me and slumped into an unladylike slouch. "Did I miss anything diverting while I was out?"

"Yes. Did I miss anything diverting while not being out?"

Annette sat up straight. "Visiting the Angstons was a bore. What did I miss?"

I slipped the lieutenant's folded letter from my pocket and held it up. "Your beau was here. He left you this."

Annette snatched the paper from my hand. "The lieutenant came? What was he doing here? He knew I would not be home for callers today."

I shrugged, watching her eyes pour over the note. "He said he came to visit your father. That is all I know. Well, that and he insinuated he found your father's political stances intriguing."

"I've no doubt." Annette's brows furrowed, and she scoffed. "He says he wanted to reassure me of his unwavering adoration and to ease the burden of my pining during his absence." She crumbled the note into a wad. "What rubbish. I shan't pine for him even a second. No, I shall be glad for the reprieve."

"So...you are not happy about courting him? Forgive me, but I thought you were beginning to find him amiable?"

My cousin's eyes rounded. "I am—I do find him amiable."

The words came out so forced that I raised a brow. "That is convincing."

"I like him very much. When he is not vexing me."

"Which seems to be always."

"No. It is not—there are...moments. Very rare, glorious moments."

I narrowed my eyes. "I do not know what is going on between the two of you, but it sounds rather complicated, and I wish you the best."

Annette reared back. "As a matchmaker, should you not sound more optimistic about my prospects?"

"I would if I believed you wanted such prospects. It saddens me that you feel I cannot be confided in."

Her expression softened. "Oh, Grace. It is not that at all. I simply"—she heaved a sigh—"you are right. It is complicated, and you already have Mr. Montfert to fill your time. I do not want to burden you with this—not when it will amount to nothing."

I was not certain what to believe, but it reassured me to know Annette's secretive behavior did not stem from distrust. "Very well, but know that if you change your mind and need someone to lay those burdens on, I am rather good at listening."

"You are, Grace." She smiled and reached for my hands. "And I will keep that in mind."

# Chapter Twenty-Two

## PHILLIP

THE RAIN HAD FINALLY stopped. For the past two days, I had watched through my bedchamber window as the puddles vanished and the mud returned to solid ground. Despite the sunny sky, I felt caged in endless torment, my mind and heart warring on a chaotic battlefield of emotion. I knew what I needed to do, but the memory of holding Grace, of nearly kissing her, put a bullet in what had once been my priority.

How could I court Miss Rigby when my thoughts constantly wandered to another woman?

Not that I could call my visits to Miss Rigby anything akin to courtship. I knew her no more now than I had the first night we met. A quiet disposition was nothing to find fault in, but the woman's shyness made it deucedly difficult to come to know her at all.

After bemoaning my troubles alone in my room for over an hour, I decided to find a distraction in the library. Which proved useless, for all I could think about was Grace's dripping wet hair and the soft glow of firelight on her cheeks.

"She's my matchmaker, confound it." I paced in front of the empty hearth. This was not a situation I expected to find myself in. Grace was meant to help me find a match Uncle would approve of, not *become* the match I wanted.

My feet halted, and I ran a hand through my hair. "It is worse than I thought. I'm contemplating marriage."

The realization hardly came as a surprise. The way I felt in Grace's presence was unlike anything I had experienced before. More than that, I worried about her incessantly. I wanted her to see how deserving of love she was, despite her weak leg. Despite how broken she believed herself to be.

And I wanted to be the man who showed her.

What had I gotten myself into? This was all Apsley's fault, convincing me a matchmaker was a good idea. I should have kept trying on my own. I should have...

A long groan escaped me. The idea that I would have found success without assistance was laughable. Even with Grace's advice and prompting, I had made no headway with Miss Rigby or any other woman. Surely that was evidence enough of how I would have floundered. At least with her help, I had found a woman who met Uncle's approval.

"But I do not want that one," I muttered, resuming my march.

"If you continue talking to yourself, my father might send you to Bedlam."

I stopped at the sound of Sabrina's voice. She crossed the library, her lips quivering with a knowing smile that served to agitate me further. I had not seen her since the day Grace was here, which meant I was still in the dark about my uncle's meeting. Sabrina likely assumed I had heard everything.

"Perhaps I should be sent off," I said. "I truly may go mad."

"Why is that?"

I drew in a deep breath and let it out slowly. Sabrina could guess at my problem, I was sure, but I still hated admitting it aloud. Why did I feel so incapable of handling anything on my own?

"This is about Miss Scott," said my cousin when I remained quiet.

"I know I cannot consider her." My tone came out defensive, which made Sabrina's smile widen.

"Knowing something does not make it easier to accept."

"Yet I must," I countered. "I have nothing to my name but the possibility of your father leaving me his assets. You and I both know he would not hesitate to change his will should I not comply with his wishes. I cannot consider Miss Scott. He has made his opinion of her clear."

"You asked him?"

"Not directly. I simply offered him a list of the women I was considering after the Morrison's ball. He crossed out her name with such force that I dare not attempt to ask him again."

"Her dowry is rather modest," said Sabrina. "She does not come from great fortune. Her father was a gentleman, of course, and well-liked and known among the *ton* as the second son of a viscount, but that is where her qualifications end. Father would not consider it enough even without his feelings toward her family."

I took a seat in one of the highback chairs, slumping into the cushions. "I know."

"What do you intend to do?" she asked.

"Continue courting Miss Rigby and hope she not only accepts my suit but that, in pursuing her, I will forget Miss Scott." I would not forget. That much I could be sure of.

"There is another option."

I propped my head up with my hand and stared at her. "Pray tell, what is it?"

"Do not do what my father wants." Sabrina sat down in the chair on my right when I scoffed. "You feel trapped. I understand, Phillip; I have been there. But there is a chance to put an end to it. You heard his discussion with Mr. Barton."

And there it was. The topic was bound to come up eventually.

I bit my lip, indecision playing through my mind. I could tell her the truth. I should tell her, but fear kept my tongue from forming the words. I had carried this secret for so long that divulging it now was akin to jumping into the dark depths of the ocean. I hadn't a notion of how she would respond—how anyone would respond—and the idea of being shunned frightened me more than I cared to admit.

I rubbed my chin and averted my gaze. "I did not hear very much."

"Of course, you didn't." Amusement laced her tone. "You were a bit distracted."

"I was quite distracted," I said, allowing her assumption to take root. It was far safer than telling her the truth. "Would you be so kind as to fill me in on what I missed?"

"Gladly, so long as you promise to keep the information to yourself."

I folded my arms over my chest. "Why would I tell anyone?"

"Because, Phillip, despite my desire to trust you, you've offered me no reassurance that you would ever oppose my father. I do understand your reasons, but you cannot expect me to fully confide in you because of it."

She made a fair point. Sabrina and I were only beginning to forge any sort of relationship. It was tenuous at best, and it was me who struggled to tear down the wall between us. How could I while under Uncle's constant supervision? "I will say nothing to him about this. I cannot go against his wishes, but I would never put you in his line of fire."

"No? Not even if he threatens to take everything away from you?"

I shifted in my chair. There was a reason my uncle so easily kept me under his thumb, and Sabrina understood what was at stake for me.

She understood how secrets and blackmail could force a person to do something against their morals and resolve.

She patted my arm. "Relax, Phillip. I intend to tell you everything. I simply wished for you to have a bit of introspection. You recently offered me the same, if you will recall, and I hoped to return the favor. I suspect there may come a time when you are forced to choose between your inheritance and integrity. Better to be ready for it now than caught unprepared later."

I nodded. "Allow me to amend my statement then. I will tell him nothing unless I have no other choice."

"That will do for now," she said. "I suppose given your inattentiveness, I must start from the beginning. Mr. Barton has been working with Father for years. He hired the man to oversee several of his schemes, none of which are legal in nature."

"Schemes?"

"Yes. I discovered the first of them years ago when I overheard Father hire a man to create a series of engravings. He became particularly interested in printing, too, buying all manner of books and the like on the topic."

"What sort of engravings?"

"I cannot say other than he ordered them several times and was particularly fussy about them. His need for perfection has never wavered, so I did not concern myself with any of it until after the house party last spring. Since then, I've done a fair amount of digging. And spying." She smiled wryly. "There is a great deal more to uncover, but the short version is that my father has been tricking people out of money through fraudulent means. Their meeting was about their next target."

My jaw dropped. "He is committing fraud?"

"Oh good. You look genuinely shocked. I confess I hadn't mentioned any of this to you before because I did not know if you were already aware and perhaps in on it too."

"Of course, I'm not!"

She shushed me, nodding toward the open library door. "Yes, I realize now your moral compass is far too stuffy to have been anything but ignorant on the matter."

"I am not *stuffy* and neither is my compass."

Sabrina chuckled. "Not completely, I suppose. You did sneak a woman into the house and nearly kissed her in a dark corridor. You are quite scandalous, Phillip."

My face heated. "You know I did not bring her here for that purpose. It merely...happened. A mistake."

Sabrina shrugged. "I am not so convinced it was a mistake, but let us agree to disagree for the time being. I intend to see my father brought to justice. The number of people he has harmed with his actions is reprehensible, and if someone does not bring his crimes to light, he will continue. My obstacle, at present, is most of my evidence is either circumstantial or lacking in physical proof. I overhead much of it myself, and the word of a disgraced duchess will hold no weight in court. I need something more...something tangible to prove it all. You've seen Father's ledgers. Is there anything suspicious in them?"

"Suspicious? No. Everything I've looked over has been balanced. There was nothing out of the ordinary. I—" My brows furrowed.

"What is it?" Sabrina asked, shifting closer to me, her eyes wide with an odd sort of enthusiasm. "You've thought of something. I can tell."

"There is one ledger your father has never permitted me to see," I hedged, "but that does not mean it contains anything incriminating. He's only just allowed me to look at anything regarding the finances. That ledger may simply contain more sensitive numbers and dealings."

Sabrina scoffed. "Yes, very sensitive, I'd imagine. Do you think you could steal a peek at it? Even inquire after the ledger? Father's response alone could prove telling."

"I won't make you any promises, but if the opportunity should arise, I will ask about it." I held my hands up when her face lit with excitement. "If, Sabrina. I cannot go poking around in your father's business, especially if what you say is true. We should both approach this with caution until we have irrefutable evidence."

Her shoulders sagged. "Very well. I will agree to take care, and I will not hound you about the ledger...much."

"Thank you."

"However, might I mention that, should we prove successful in this endeavor, you will no longer be so restricted in whom you can marry." One of her dark brows lifted. "Do not let your heart give up quite yet."

At present, my heart not giving up was precisely the problem. I didn't dare give it more hope. If Uncle was deeply involved in the kind of fraud Sabrina suggested, then he had been so for years. He had also gotten away with it. Much as I disliked to admit it, the man was intelligent enough to cover his tracks. The odds of us finding enough evidence were slim.

I could not risk my future on a slim chance of success. For now, pursuing Miss Rigby was my only option, and I would begin anew as soon as I had another meeting with my matchmaker.

# *Chapter Twenty-Three*

## GRACE

I HAD NEVER BEEN nervous about receiving a note from Phillip. I had also given up trying to think of him as Mr. Montfert. No matter how I chided my thoughts, they inevitably shattered that particular formality with the memory of a dark, hidden passage. I could hardly be blamed for the struggle after what happened, but so long as I kept my spoken address formal, eventually the conflicting feelings I harbored would disappear.

At least, that is what I told myself.

Having an affection for Phillip Montfert was out of the question. I held him in high regard, yes, but I could not allow it to become more. He was my client. So long as I remembered that, all would work itself out.

I folded his note and tucked it into the pocket of my dress. Hyde was lovely this early in the morning with the only disruption to my peace the song of birds singing and fluttering eagerly between the trees. Sunlight glistened off the damp grass, and after so much rain the past week, more flowers had blossomed in rich colors, giving the air an almost sweet scent I could taste.

The cold stone bench beneath me provided a nice respite for my leg. I had walked here again, this time at a slow pace to minimize the pain, but even after days of rest following my excursion to Phillip's townhouse, the limb ached.

I pulled the small notebook I was using to take notes out of my reticule and glanced over the list of my client's qualities. I'd added many to it since the day I met Phillip. There were words like handsome, intelligent, well-read, and honest. Those I could attribute to many of the men of my acquaintance.

But there were others, ones that made my heart sputter and always seemed to hold my attention. Like warm and strong. Neither of those things should be on the list at all because they were not qualities I should have ever been close enough to the man to notice.

Neither did knowing that Phillip smelled of something earthy with hints of citrus help keep my thoughts where they should be.

I blew out a slow breath through puffed cheeks, my gaze moving farther down the list. Phillip was also patient and kind. He supported and showed his care through tender words and touches. How had a man raised by Victor Perry turned out so completely different from his guardian? Phillip's uncle was one of the most conniving and cruel people I had ever met. Once Phillip inherited, would he turn into a similar monster with no thought for anything but fortune and social standing?

No, Phillip was too good of a man to become anything like Mr. Perry. That his uncle had gained at least some of his wealth by illegal means fit his character.

What did Phillip and Sabrina intend to do with the information?

I bit my lip, gently closing the notebook. Sabrina was a conundrum. Our time together at the ball had been pleasant. She was nothing like the woman I remembered, who had been eager to make an impression upon society and bask in the attention. No, Sabrina had secluded herself from the crush, and her demeanor was no longer one of a high-stepped duchess.

And she had found me and Phillip alone in the library. She could have run with that information and devastated my reputation. Instead, she had escorted me home to ensure my family had no suspicions about my absence.

Perhaps I was not ready to trust Sabrina completely, but she had changed. It seemed for the better.

"My, you look rather pensive today, Miss Scott."

I glanced up at the sound of Phillip's voice, and the smile he wore squeezed my stomach. Why must he be so handsome?

"I suppose I am." I slid to the left side of the bench to make room for him. His brows furrowed, and he hesitated a moment before taking a seat next to me. Normally, we met in the clearing, a place secluded where we would not be disturbed by anyone venturing to the park this early in the morning. But upon receiving his note, I decided it would be best that we not meet there when I had no chaperone.

Since neither Annette nor Rus could accompany me, and I had no intention of bringing along a maid, a bench well within the eyes of the public would have to do.

"Tell me, Miss Scott. What is it that so fully consumes your thoughts?" His leg pressed into mine as he angled himself to face me, and warmth spread through my body.

I shifted closer to the edge of the bench. Much farther, and I might fall off. "There is a great deal on my mind. I admit, I do not know your intentions anymore. After the things we heard from your uncle...well, it changes everything, does it not?"

"For now, it changes nothing. We do not have enough evidence to pursue anything. Regardless, you needn't fear. I will pay you for your help, no matter what."

Payment was the least of my concerns.

"But you intend to keep looking? For evidence, I mean." I hated how hopeful my voice sounded. If Phillip was free to choose a wife with no expectation from his uncle, would that mean I stood a chance? It was a ridiculous notion and one I should not allow myself to cling to. Nonsensical as it was, I could not help it. I had never believed I would marry, but the man beside me had made it clear he did not consider me broken. That I should not give up on finding a match for myself. Did that include him as a possibility, or had I mistaken his interest in me for something more akin to friendship?

"Sabrina is intent on it," said Phillip. "I must tread more cautiously. There is much at stake, and not simply for myself." He drummed his fingers against his leg. "May I ask for your discretion, Miss Scott? Please keep the things you have heard to yourself. At least, for the time being."

"Of course. I would never betray your confidence."

He smiled slightly, his tone soft. "I know. Tell me, how are you faring today? Has your leg recovered?"

"Well enough, but let us focus on you. Last we met, we did not...well, we never had a chance to discuss Miss Rigby. I would like to know your opinion of her and whether pursuing her is still something you want. Or if another woman...that is to say, a woman from my list. Not myself, of course. Even after...not that anything happened, but if someone else might interest you, then we could discuss her instead."

Good heavens.

Phillip stared at me. I averted my gaze, but I could still feel his attention on me. My cheeks were warm, and there was no way he could miss my embarrassment.

"Miss Scott?" His gentle tone tugged at me, but I kept my gaze forward. If I looked at him, I would feel things, and there was no telling what those things might be. Likely things I shouldn't. Even sitting this close to him set my heart to pounding. Why I had ever believed I could forget what occurred in that corridor, I did not know. Clearly, my body could not, even now as it relished in the ghostly memory of his touch, his warmth, and his breath on my skin.

And drat it all if he smelled just as good today as he had then.

I closed my eyes and drew in a slow breath. Perhaps the best course of action was not to ignore what happened, but to acknowledge it and move forward. How did one begin such a conversation?

Fortunately, Phillip took the reins. "Miss Scott, if I have made you uncomfortable, I apologize. It was never my intention—"

"You haven't." I turned to face him and took in his weary expression. He was worried, and this awkwardness between us would never fade until we addressed the cause of it. "You haven't made me uncomfortable. What happened at your townhouse was..."

Was something. I did not know how to describe it; at least, not in a way that would make things better.

"I would say a mistake," said Phillip, "but I've no wish to offend you."

I smiled wryly. "Mistake would imply that anything happened. We both know our proximity was a matter of being in a confined space and your honorable intentions to make me comfortable. That is all. Right?"

I hated how uncertain I sounded. It was embarrassing, especially with how Phillip studied me. Had I made more of this than I should have? What if the things I felt were one-sided?

"Of course," he said finally. "I've given the matter a great deal of thought and concluded our...moment in the corridor was simply born out of comfort. True, I had hoped to give your leg respite from standing, but more than that, I think of you as a friend. I am not generally so at ease with ladies, largely due to my lack of experience, but you are different."

"And because I am your friend and you do not see me as a potential wife, you are not burdened with the expectation to impress. Is that correct?"

He studied me for another long moment. "Yes. That must be it." He smiled, though it seemed somewhat forced. "There is no reason not to act myself with you. I can relax, which removes much of my anxiety, I think. Your company is always refreshing and comfortable, which is why..." He swallowed, then cleared his throat. Still, he did not finish.

I shoved down my disappointment. "Which is why we should put what happened—or rather, what did not happen—aside. We are friends, and I say as both your friend and your matchmaker, it is time we spoke of Miss Rigby."

He nodded. "I have called on her several times since the ball."

"You have?" My jaw clenched as I fought the jealousy coiling within me. "Good. How did it go?"

"Not well, if I am to be honest. Miss Rigby is kind enough, but I find it difficult to persuade her into conversation. And her mother..." Phillip rubbed a hand over his neck. "She is never happy with my presence. I do not think she welcomes my suit."

"And what of her father? Her mother may oppose, but in reality, the decision comes down to him."

"I've made no contact with the man. I suppose I should try." Phillip sighed heavily, as though the weight of the world rested on his shoulders. I wanted to ease his burdens. Unfortunately, the only way for me to do that was to help him find a wife. The monster of jealousy living inside me did not take well to that fact.

"You are hesitant," I said. "What is it about Miss Rigby that gives you pause? Is it merely her parents or something more?"

Phillip chuckled. "More like something less. I cannot even explain, as I barely understand it myself. She is a beautiful woman, but there is no"—he lifted his hands and dropped them into his lap with exasperation—"no desire? No wish to hold her close or share my deepest thoughts and secrets." His gaze fell to my lips. "No wish to kiss her."

Oh dear. I was not the only one struggling to forget, then.

Phillip shook himself from a trance. "What do you advise me to do? How can I get to know Miss Rigby better when she is so shy? Surely, if we learned more about one another, the rest would fall into place?"

"Perhaps," I answered honestly. "You find her amiable. People have married for less. But I do think Miss Rigby, while shy, could be persuaded out of her shell." I tilted my head and grinned. "With enough persistence and charm."

Phillip laughed, shaking his head. "Persistence, I can manage. Charm is another thing, entirely."

If he did not think himself charming, then he might be a touch mad.

"What if we made a list of questions for you to ask Miss Rigby? Questions that might pull her into conversation and afford you more clarity? Then you needn't waste time coming up with things to talk to her about. You can even take the list with you."

He reared back. "You do not think she would find my bringing a list of questions with me odd?"

"She might, but I imagine if you explain your nerves, she will understand. She might even think it is *charming*."

"Would you?"

My brows tightened. "Would I what?"

"Would you find it charming if a man brought a list of questions with him while courting you? If he proclaimed his ineptitude for social calls but could not forgo his desire to see you? To be near you. Is it not important for us to present our strengths as a potential suitor rather than declare our weaknesses? I assumed a lady of quality would want strength in a husband."

There was something vulnerable about his question, though what, I could not pinpoint. His blue eyes watched me carefully. He clearly valued my opinion on this, but I also saw in them genuine fear. Everyone had their secrets—their weaknesses—and although I had told Phillip I saw none of his, surely they were there. Simply well-hidden.

I glanced beyond the path to the blooming flowers, considering his question and my response. "There are many ways to define strength, Phillip. And weakness, for that matter. I would never shame anyone for realizing their faults. Their inadequacies. We all have them, and it is not until we accept them that we can change. How else are we to better ourselves if we first do not admit our imperfections?

"If I were ever so fortunate as to have a suitor, one whose regard I returned, then I would accept him as he is, just as I hope he would accept me." I lifted my leg and nodded to it. "I will never be without this physical flaw. Sometimes I can hide it well, but it is still a part of who I am. It is an imperfection that can never be fixed and one I will live with the rest of my life."

"And you never hesitate to tell people about the malady." His words were a statement, not a question, as if he knew this by observation.

"Why should I? They are bound to learn of it eventually, and besides, I would rather they know from the beginning. Having the knowledge up front tends to separate those who would look down upon me for it from those who would not care a whit about the ailment. The former does not stick around for long, which has little bearing on me. Anyone who would judge me poorly for an ailment beyond my control is not someone worth having in my life anyway."

Phillip stared at me, his blue-grey eyes filled with something akin to admiration. It made my cheeks warm and unleashed flutters in my chest. He could not look at me this way—not if we were to remain friends.

"You are very brave," he whispered.

"It is not bravery. I cannot hide my limp all of the time if you recall. It is easier to tell the truth and not worry over people's opinions." I opened the notebook and retrieved a pencil from my reticule. It was time we got to work before Phillip found something else to compliment me on. Or another reason to look at me the way he had. "So, let us make a list of questions. What would you like to know about Miss Rigby?"

# Chapter Twenty-Four

## PHILLIP

Over the next week, I met with Grace four times, taking up our new place on the stone bench in Hyde. In some ways, I missed the privacy of our clearing, where we could talk without worry of early-goers overhearing. I also understood why such a meeting place could prove dangerous. Knowing Grace could never be anything more to me than a friend had not stopped my thoughts from thinking of how she had felt in my arms or the warmth of her body against mine.

The public space at least kept me from doing anything terribly...irresponsible.

Besides, it would do neither of us any good to act on the feelings I seemed unable to suppress. The last thing I wanted was to hurt her, and given Grace's struggles to believe herself deserving of courtship and marriage, a kiss from a man like me, who could have neither of those things with her, would only lead to heartbreak.

Once I had dressed for the day, I headed for the breakfast room and found Mother seated at the table. I kissed her cheek, and she offered me a soft smile. She was the daily reminder I needed to stay strong during my meetings with Grace. Following Uncle's demands was not solely for my benefit. I wanted my mother to have a life of comfort, and there was but one way to achieve that.

After breakfast, I went to the study, per Uncle's request. We had met more frequently as of late, and discussed his investment ventures and his many trade assets, in addition to the funds produced by his country estate. I'd even made suggestions for improvements that were met with approval. My knowledge and understanding of his holdings increased with each passing day, a sign he was beginning to trust me, whether he admitted it or not. At least that boded well for my future, although I would never feel secure until I inherited. So long as my uncle lived, he would hold my destitution over me, use it to manipulate and coerce. None of it would end until he was in the grave.

A bleak prospect, but one I had lived with for years. It would be some time before I felt any sort of peace in my life. All I could do was keep the man happy, or at the very least, satisfied.

Uncle bid me enter, and I took up my usual seat across from him, his large oak desk separating us, while Mr. Grenville, Uncle's solicitor, occupied a chair near the window. The man often joined us for meetings, but with his quiet disposition, I knew little about him. I supposed it made sense that my uncle would hire a man of business who would do his bidding without question.

"We've much to discuss today," said Uncle, crossing his arms over his chest. I noticed the presence of the red ledger sitting on the corner of the desk, and my heart tripped at the memory of Sabrina's request. This was the first I'd seen it since our discussion, but I would not act rashly. I had promised to inquire after it only should I have the opportunity to do so without raising suspicions.

Uncle leaned back in his seat, studying me with his fingers steepled. "You've done well these last few weeks. Not perfect. There have been moments that struck my patience and made me reconsider things, but I cannot deny you have a good head on you when it comes to business."

"Thank you, Uncle." I did not know what else to say. It stung that he had ever questioned my intelligence, but much of it came down to my hearing difficulties. In my youth, tutors had struggled with teaching me, reporting the slow progress to their employer, and it was not until I understood the source of my difficulties that I began to find ways to overcome them. Still, Uncle had often grown impatient with me, and rather than give his understanding, he had labeled me as broken.

Broken. Worthless. And a plethora of other insults rattled around my mind, forever reminding me of how far beneath him the man believed me to be.

Uncle leaned forward and rested his elbows on the desk. "You will accompany me to my next meeting with investors. There is a good chance this new venture will prove exceptionally lucrative. Do not disappoint me by butchering it. I can have Mr. Grenville here within an hour to make changes to my will."

I glanced at Mr. Grenville, whose expression remained indifferent, then nodded, the threat settling over me far heavier than it usually did. Uncle had been testing me for years, but this felt more substantial.

"I understand," I said.

"Good. The meeting will take place next Tuesday at half past two. I will give you information to look over in the meantime so you are prepared. Study it, Phillip. I expect you to know every detail about this deal."

"I will study it diligently." My gaze wandered to the ledger resting on the corner of the desk, and my pulse spiked. If I was going to ask after it, now was an opportune time. Uncle was in a better mood than usual and had complimented me more than once, a scenario unheard of.

"Is there anything else you need from me? That ledger has not been balanced." I nodded toward the thing, hoping my expression remained stoic despite my pounding heart.

Uncle's eyes narrowed. "Not yet. Perhaps if all goes well with this meeting, we might look at it together. *If.*"

The response held a great deal of uncertainty, but I would not get a more firm answer from him.

"Until then, you are to further your courtship efforts," he continued. "Mr. Rigby will be present at this meeting. It would do well for you to have made some progress before then. I've spoken to him on the matter of his daughter. He is...reluctant but not beyond persuading."

"Miss Rigby is amiable, but her mother has not welcomed me with much enthusiasm. Perhaps we should consider someone else. Someone more open to the idea of marrying without a title."

"Someone else?" Uncle's mouth turned down, his eyes hard.

I leaned forward, placing my palms flat on his desk. "Yes. Surely there is another who would satisfy your expectations. And Miss Scott presented several options—"

"Miss Scott!"

My mouth snapped closed. I had been careful, so very careful, not to mention Grace anytime Uncle was home, but after spending so much time with her, the words slipped out. She occupied my thoughts too thoroughly to have believed I could keep our interactions secret.

Uncle rose from his chair, towering over me, and his fingers dove into his pocket to retrieve his watch. The gold chain dangled between his fingers, and my body froze. Memories rushed back to me, and the chain whipped through the air before I could break myself free. He struck my hand, and I withdrew it from the desk with a hiss of pain.

Even Mr. Grenville sucked in a breath, though he said nothing.

"I told you to stay away from her, boy," Uncle growled. "Did I not make myself clear?"

I cradled my hand to my chest, my skin burning, and ground out a response. "Yes. You have made yourself clear."

Uncle reclaimed his seat, his expression relaxed. "Good. Once Mr. Rigby understands the prospect of this venture, I suspect you will find your endeavors successful. Even the wife will not object to you once they see the fortune to be made and benefit from such an alliance."

I forced myself to smile. "Then I will persist in calling on Miss Rigby."

Even if everything inside me recoiled at the idea.

"WHAT HAPPENED TO YOUR hand?"

Out of instinct, I folded my arms, tucking the hand Uncle had struck beneath my coat. The reaction did nothing to dissuade Sabrina, and she approached me with determined steps. She unfolded my arms and inspected my hand, her dark brows furrowed.

"He's hit you again, hasn't he?"

I pulled away from her. It had been a full day, but still, my skin stung. Red marked the area and likely would for some time. But I had no wish to talk about it. "You wanted to speak with me?"

Sabrina scowled at me but let the matter drop. "Have you learned anything more? I'm stuck."

"Stuck?" I repeated. That did not surprise me. Uncle was too intelligent to leave crumbs. Whatever schemes he was involved in would not be easy to prove criminal. "I have heard nothing more, but I did ask about the ledger."

At this, she straightened. "You did?"

"Yes, but he would not permit me to look at it."

"He would not allow you to have the ledger?" Sabrina paced back and forth, the swish of her green skirts warring with the crackle of flames in the library's hearth. The weather, while dry, had presented too chilly for me to ask Miss Rigby for another ride through Hyde today.

Besides, I had not recovered from the first one three days ago.

The list of questions created by me and Grace had proven exceptionally helpful in establishing a flow of conversation, but it wore on me to constantly initiate it. Miss Rigby simply was not inclined to converse with me without prodding.

"Are you listening?" Sabrina asked.

No, in truth. My mind had wandered, and it was difficult to maintain focus when she paced, her words garbled half the time when she moved to my left.

"Forgive me." I clasped my hands behind my back, giving her my full attention. "What were you saying?"

She glared at me before answering. "I was saying that my father's behavior is suspicious. He's so secretive about this ledger that I'm inclined to think it contains evidence against him."

I shrugged. "Perhaps. But your father has always been rather secretive with his finances. I was not permitted to see anything until recently if you recall."

Sabrina stopped pacing and pointed at me. "More evidence. The fact that he is slow to let his heir see anything says much about his business practices."

I rubbed a hand over my face. Sabrina may well be correct, but if we could not prove my uncle's practices were criminal, it did not matter. I was not particularly optimistic we would uncover anything. Time would tell.

"Your father stated that if all goes well with the upcoming meeting with his investors on Tuesday, we might discuss the ledger and its contents. We will have answers soon enough."

Sabrina's laughter took me by surprise. "Might? Come now, Phillip. When has my father ever followed through on a *might*? You know he employs that word simply to placate. He has no intention of allowing you to see the inside of that ledger. At least not anytime soon." Her pacing resumed. "I cannot wait. I must know what is in it. Stealing it is the only option."

"What?" I intercepted her and stopped her with a firm hold on both shoulders. "No, Sabrina. We cannot take the ledger. If your father found out, he would be furious. I cannot take that risk."

Sabrina rolled her eyes. "I never said *we* had to steal it. I am perfectly capable of doing so on my own. He goes out enough; it shall be a simple task. All I need to know is where he keeps it."

"Information I cannot give you. I have only seen it in his presence. He once tucked it into the desk drawer, but I doubt he keeps it there, and anytime I have visited the study in his absence, the ledger was not within sight. If it contains the sort of information you suspect, he is not likely to leave it available for prying eyes."

Sabrina pursed her lips. "Well, I won't know until I search for it myself."

I gave her a pleading look. That she purposefully ignored.

She pushed past me toward the door, and my stomach seemed to lurch after her. "Sabrina!"

My cousin turned to face me with a grin, her hand resting on the edge of the door. "Relax, Phillip. I have no intention of searching the study right *now*. I am not an imbecile. I'll wait for the opportune moment."

With that, she vanished from view.

# Chapter Twenty-Five

## PHILLIP

Every time I saw Sabrina after our discussion in the library, my chest tightened with a strange mixture of trepidation and anticipation. I had no doubt she would do as she said and search the study. Not knowing when she would take up the endeavor was nearly as tortuous as seeing Grace. Despite what I had told myself, some part of me hoped my cousin succeeded in finding her evidence, even if doing so put my financial security at risk.

Because it also meant I would be free to marry whomever I wished. It certainly would not be Miss Rigby, nor many of the women I had made an acquaintance with over the last two months. Only one of them stood out in my mind. Only one left me longing for her when we were apart.

But such thoughts were dangerous. Not only would exposing my uncle as a fraud have ramifications on the family's reputation, including myself, but there would likely be recompense to pay. Without knowing how much of our income was the result of unscrupulous business practices, I hadn't any idea what the courts would require from us in terms of restitution. A scary prospect, indeed.

I passed Sabrina on my way out of the townhouse. Her eyes sparkled with a knowing gleam, as if she could sense my uneasiness about her plans. Today, I could let my worries rest for a time. Uncle had declared he intended to use the study for most of the day, which meant Sabrina could not do anything brash.

Still, my mind wandered to that blasted ledger, even through my fencing practice with Apsley. My friend watched me remove my coat with a smug grin, having taken a victory without much of a fight on my part.

"You are more distracted than usual," he said as we sat down.

"I hide it well, I see."

"You hide nothing, my friend." Apsley leaned back, resting against the wall. "Tell me what it is. Courtship troubles? Or is there something more pressing on your mind?"

How much should I tell him? Apsley had become a good friend these past few weeks. We spent a great deal of time together, and while he liked to jest and tease, I trusted him.

"Some of it is courtship troubles," I said. "My uncle has approved of me calling on Harriet Rigby. She comes from wealth and has no blemish to her name. Uncle has even invited her father to an upcoming investment meeting with the hope that it will garner his approval of my suit."

Apsley nodded, seemingly impressed. "That all sounds like good news. Forgive me for failing to understand your dejection." He turned away from me, his gaze focused on the empty room. "Unless, of course, the struggle is that you have an interest in someone besides Miss Rigby. Someone, say, you do not believe your uncle would approve of?"

How had he guessed so easily?

He faced me again, and my gaping must have been evidence enough of my question, for Apsley chuckled. "I may not be a romantic, Montfert, but I am not blind. The time you called on Grace, and how you speak of her when we come here, has provided more than enough proof of your developing affections."

I swallowed, heat rushing up my neck and into my ears. "I did not realize I was so obvious."

Apsley shrugged, but his smirk remained in place. "Perhaps not to everyone. It helps that Grace looks at you with the same sort of besotted interest."

"She looks besotted?" I shook my head, quelling the ridiculous hope blooming in my chest. "It hardly matters. Uncle made it clear I was to marry someone with either title or connection. Or both. I care for your cousin, but he has made his disapproval clear. He will not waver in his expectations."

"Expectations are the bane of our existence." Apsley sighed, and I suspected the statement burdened him more than he let on. His chap-fallen expression disappeared quickly, however. "So, you do not intend to marry her anyway? Proclaim love more important than money, as any hero of a romance novel would?"

That brought out my laugh, something I had sorely needed. "No, I've no intention of doing something so grand. I am not the hero."

Apsley pouted. Genuinely pouted. "Whyever not? If anyone were to appreciate a gesture so disgustingly romantic, it would be Gracie."

"Appreciate?" I lifted a brow. "Perhaps the sentiment, but I can scarcely believe any woman would appreciate a life of financial destitution, which is what my future would entail were I to marry her. My uncle's threats are not given without intent. He could disinherit me in a heartbeat, cut me off with nothing to my name. I cannot, in good conscience, ask Grace to live that way. Nor my mother. I can think of nothing more dishonorable."

My words sobered him, and this time when he sighed, it was rather heavy and sympathetic. "I do not envy your position. Perhaps tonight will afford you more clarity. You still plan to attend Lady Davenport's dinner party, do you not?"

"I do. I thank you for securing the invitation. Any chance I have to further my acquaintance with Miss Rigby is helpful."

True to his words when we first met, Russell Apsley had ensured I received a number of invitations this Season, but this one was the most beneficial. I had not seen Miss Rigby at any social event since the ball, and certainly not in Uncle's presence. He would watch both of us tonight, undoubtedly.

"Your optimism is commendable," said Apsley, "but I would like to remind you that, while I will not be in attendance, my cousin will."

Grace would be there. I had not thought of that.

I put on a disingenuous smile. "Wonderful. My matchmaker can assist me in wooing Miss Rigby."

Rus's auburn brows lifted high on his head. "Very well, but do not hurt her, Montfert. If you have not done so already, be certain she knows there can be nothing between you." The warning in his tone was clear. Rus was not her guardian, but he cared for her as he did his sisters.

With a protectiveness generally shadowed by his determination to annoy them at whatever cost.

"Hurting her is the last thing I want," I said. "But she is well aware of my Uncle's requirements."

Apsley nodded. "I wish there was more I could do to help."

"I appreciate that, but I will manage." Or so I told myself repeatedly even after leaving Angelo's to return home. Marrying Miss Rigby was a simple solution. It would satisfy Uncle and, hopefully, secure my future. What it would not secure was my happiness. Perhaps the two of us could come to an understanding and have a life of contentment, but such a prospect paled in comparison to the scenarios my mind concocted were I to marry someone else.

Were I to spend a lifetime with Grace.

I suspected nothing would ever cure me of being drawn to Grace Scott. My days would be spent thinking about her, missing her. Once I proposed, I would have no reason to ever see her again, no need for a matchmaker or the pleasure of her company. Perhaps that was for the best given the way my heart reacted at the mere sight of her.

How would I ever move past the resentment of marrying another?

The thoughts weighed on me even as I entered my townhouse, distracting me enough that I nearly collided with  Mrs. Ellis. Today she must have remembered her husband's passing. She had donned black.

The elderly woman glanced up at me with a wrinkled smile, and I bowed in greeting.

"How are you today, Mrs. Ellis?"

"Well, I thank you," she replied in that shaky voice of hers. "Forgive me for my quick escape. I've just met with Mr. Perry, but I must be off. I'm to take tea with Lady Hartley."

I highly doubted any escape of hers could be classified as quick given her advanced age, but I shifted out of her path and bid her farewell. What business Uncle could have with the woman was beyond me. I had seen nothing in the ledgers I looked over. Was it possible their business rested within the red ledger?

The notion tightened a knot in my stomach, though I could not pinpoint precisely why. The feeling stuck with me the remainder of the afternoon, and finally dissipated as I readied for the Davenport's dinner party.

Both Miss Rigby and her parents would be in attendance tonight. This was an opportunity to gain some favor before the meeting in a few days. The pressure filled me with nerves, and I gave the list of questions Grace and I had created a glance over before making my way downstairs to the foyer. I had asked Miss Rigby the majority of them, and it seemed a waste not to finish.

Uncle and Sabrina joined me, but we had scarcely made it out the door before Sabrina complained of a headache. She put on a dramatic show, pressing her hand to her head. "I feel a trifle faint. Perhaps I ought to stay home tonight. Spend the evening resting."

I narrowed my eyes. She would not be resting, of that, I was certain.

"You staying behind is not the worst idea," said Uncle gruffly. "I do not need your stained reputation causing problems for me tonight."

The rumors surrounding her and the ducal family had not diminished as she had hoped. Worse, Uncle had caught wind of them and made his embarrassment from the matter no secret. Never mind that he was the one who had pushed her to behave in a way to have created such rumors in the first place.

Sabrina smiled but could not hide the fire in her dark eyes. "Enjoy yourselves, then."

Once she had returned indoors, Uncle and I entered the carriage and made the short journey to the Davenport's townhouse. I looked up at the white façade, counting the windows and taking a slow breath to calm myself.

It did little good.

My heart beat a quick rhythm as the butler welcomed us inside and took our hats and coats. We were led into a spacious drawing room with earthy pink wallpaper and deep red furniture. A single, candle-lit chandelier afforded the space light, in addition to what came through the two bay windows on the west wall. Lady Paxton and Rowe Apsley stood in front of the closest, but beyond them, Grace and Miss Rigby conversed.

Well, Grace conversed. Miss Rigby merely smiled, her lips still while Grace waved her hands in animated gestures. I wondered what sort of story she was telling the woman, though it was clearly a delightful tale with the way the light from the setting sun twinkled in her eyes.

I greeted the host and hostess, then made my excuses to join the two women. Miss Rigby smiled softly when her gaze met mine, but Grace's lips pulled wide. My heart reacted as expected to such a warm greeting, and I required a moment to temper its erratic beat.

"Good evening, Miss Rigby, Miss Scott. I hope you are well."

"Yes, thank you," said Miss Rigby, dropping her gaze.

Grace frowned. "We are both well. How are you, Mr. Montfert? Miss Rigby was just telling me the two of you took a ride earlier this week. It is nice to finally have some warm weather, is it not?"

"Indeed." I clasped my hands behind my back. "I hope next week proves equally warm. I would fancy another ride or two in Hyde if Miss Rigby is amiable."

The woman looked up at me. Her lips parted, but she hesitated to respond. Blast. It was one thing to pursue a courtship with the notion of a mutually beneficial marriage in mind, but I had no desire to force my attention upon her. I had hoped after spending time together she would feel comfortable with me. Comfortable enough not to hesitate.

My stomach pinched. I had asked Miss Rigby a great many questions, but not once had I asked for her opinion of marriage. Not once had I asked if she would welcome a suit from me. What if her heart belonged to another? The entire idea made me queasy. Why had I not considered the possibility before now?

"If the weather holds," she said quietly, "I would find that agreeable, Mr. Montfert."

The answer should have relieved me, but it did not. What I needed was a moment of privacy with her to determine some things. Things that felt urgent. Uncle expected me to propose to this woman. I could not do so if her heart was already engaged. I understood what it felt like, and I would wish it upon no one.

"Perhaps Miss Scott would care to take a ride as well." Miss Rigby's words startled me out of my thoughts. The woman never prompted conversation. She glanced between Grace and me as if waiting for either of us to respond. What could I say? I did not want her to get the wrong impression of where my intentions lay, nor did I wish to seem callous.

I cleared my throat. "I would be honored should Miss Scott be open to the idea."

Dinner was announced before Grace could answer. Miss Rigby and I were paired as companions, and I did my best to make conversation with her throughout the meal. All the while, my attention constantly wandered to where Grace sat, each smile pulled from her by her dinner companion a stab of jealousy.

During port, I joined my uncle in conversing with Mr. Rigby. He was a stout man with an expression rarely devoid of a frown. His eyes seemed to hold judgment anytime he looked at me, always assessing, but near the end, his mood lightened somewhat.

"Your uncle says you have a good head for business," the man said and then took a long drink of his port. "I take it you stand to inherit?"

It was a question, but Mr. Rigby seemed to already know the answer. I imagined Uncle had informed him of my status in his will.

"Indeed, so long as I prove worthy of it." I said it with jest, though it was entirely truthful. Both Uncle and Mr. Rigby laughed.

"You will be a wealthy man then," Mr. Rigby continued. "A profitable estate and some rather lucrative holdings. The sort of man worth allying with." He raised an expectant brow. I should not have been surprised by the line of questioning. Uncle had said he would speak to Mr. Rigby about the matter of me courting his daughter. Having Mr. Rigby's favor, as it seemed I was gaining, was precisely what I needed.

"I should hope so," I answered. Best to keep things vague and optimistic.

Mr. Rigby eyed me. "My wife has also mentioned you have called on my daughter several times."

"I have. Miss Rigby is…lovely and good company." My cheeks were going to ache if I kept forcing myself to smile.

The man grunted, leaning back in his chair. "Well, perhaps you and I should have a private discussion soon."

Something squirmed within me. "Soon, sir. Though, I would like to discuss things with Miss Rigby before—"

"Discuss what?" Mr. Rigby demanded. "You either wish to marry my daughter or you do not. I am not in the business of toying with time. I ask you not to waste mine."

My hands came up in a placating gesture, and heat filled my cheeks. The entire room focused on our conversation now, and I had not wanted an audience for this conversation. I lowered my voice. "Forgive me. I meant no offense. I only wished to verify that Miss Rigby's affections were not otherwise engaged."

"Her affections?" Mr. Rigby huffed, and his voice grew louder than before. "I have been looking to marry her off for some months now. Arrange things. Her feelings on the matter are irrelevant. Her marriage is at my discretion."

My jaw clenched. Mr. Rigby was not unlike Uncle then, using his daughter as a pawn. Allying myself with the man did not sit well with me, but I, too, had little say in my future. And after such an open discussion in the presence of so many, I was backed even farther into a corner.

I glanced about the room and noted most had turned back to their own conversations and port. Except Rowe Apsley. He watched me with solemn intensity, and I wondered if his brother had hinted at my affection for Grace. He was her guardian, after all.

What I wouldn't give to have a conversation about marriage with him instead of Mr. Rigby.

Once they had their fill of port, the host declared we would join the ladies in the drawing room. A jovial parade headed in that direction, but Uncle caught me about the wrist and held me back. He waited until the corridor was vacant before speaking.

"You crossed a line," he growled. "Rigby was nearly in your pocket, and you brought up his daughter's possible affections for another man? What nonsense."

"I still intend to speak with her," I said. "I will not force her to marry me."

Uncle took a step forward. I had grown taller than him years ago, but he possessed a set of broad shoulders that still made him feel like a towering tyrant. Perhaps it was the memories of my younger self cowering in fear, or the ghostly sting of his pocket watch chain, but his proximity caused my entire body to tense.

"If this is about that Scott woman—"

"She has nothing to do with this," I interjected, though it was only a half-truth.

"I saw the way you looked at her when we arrived. I am not a fool." He shoved a finger into my chest. "Listen to me, boy. I know you've a broken ear, but hear me when I say this: you *will* marry the Rigby girl. Her father and I have discussed things extensively. An alliance is just what we need to propel our income to another level. A connection with that family will cement all of it, and I will not have you ruining things now."

"And if I should refuse? Whoever you have in mind for heir may not be inclined to marry her either."

Uncle gripped a fistful of my cravat and coat, yanking me closer, his nose wrinkled in a fierce scowl. "If you refuse, I will kick you and your mother out onto the street and marry the girl myself. I am not so old as to be incapable of taking another wife. Perhaps a third time will prove more successful. Someone so young and quiet—I could mold her into just the sort of obedient wife I want."

Over the course of my life, there had been countless times when I experienced fury for my Uncle's behavior—for his sharp, unfeeling words. They all paled in comparison to the hot anger I felt now. Miss Rigby did not hold my heart, but I cared about her and would not allow her to be shackled to this man. She did not deserve the kind of future such a union would entail, and while I did not know if either of us could ever see one another as anything more than friends, it was better than the suffering she would endure married to my uncle.

"Fine," I said through gritted teeth. "I will marry her."

Uncle released me with a huff. "Good. I expect you to propose within the week. And I will remind you to keep your hearing difficulties secret until the vows are exchanged. We don't need to hand Rigby any excuse to reconsider."

"Yes, Uncle."

He knocked his shoulder into mine as he passed. I was expected to follow, but my feet remained rooted in place, my gaze pinned to the floor. Demands had ruled my whole life, but never had I been given an ultimatum that affected more than myself and my mother. It felt disgusting and cruel.

I drew a breath, pulling my gaze from the floor, ready to face what awaited me in the drawing room. Instead, my heart leapt against my chest as my eyes locked on a pair of warm brown eyes.

And based on her expression, Grace had heard everything.

# Chapter Twenty-Six

## GRACE

"Grace." The way Phillip whispered my name sent a flurry of chills across my skin.

His conversation with his uncle should have been private, and I had not intentionally listened in on it. Lady Davenport had asked Annette to play a number on the pianoforte. I had gone with my cousin to the library to fetch some sheet music, but upon our return, we'd discovered a page was missing. I had then gone back to the library to search for it, with success, only to stumble upon a heated argument in the corridor.

Not wishing to interrupt, I had pressed myself into the shadows until Mr. Perry left, leaving Phillip alone with the most dejected expression I had ever seen. I had wanted to reach out to him, to comfort him, but the words I had overheard kept my tongue-tied.

"Grace," Phillip repeated, taking strides toward me. He stopped not more than a foot away, and even in the darkened corridor, I could see the plea in his blue eyes. "How much of that did you overhear?"

"All of it," I whispered, clutching the page of sheet music to my chest.

Phillip ran a hand over his face. "My uncle is adamant about me marrying Miss Rigby. You have assisted me so much already, but is there any chance you could speak to her? Make sure she does not have an affection for someone else? It would set me at ease to move forward if I knew."

I blinked, attempting to process his words. It was noble of him to consider Miss Rigby's feelings. His uncle certainly did not care about such things. I had no qualms about discovering the information for Phillip, but...

"You are deaf?" The question stumbled out of me, and I snapped my mouth closed.

Phillip winced. "Partially deaf. I cannot hear well in my left ear. Conversation is often garbled at best."

Which was why he had not heard me that day in Berkeley Square. It was why he always positioned himself on the left side of those he was conversing with. I recalled a number of occasions where he moved without reason or turned his body at such an angle that he pressed against me. Now, I understood; he'd done so in an effort to hear better.

"Why did you not tell me?" I asked.

He stared at me for what seemed an eternity, silence encompassing us from all sides. In the distance, light chatter echoed from the drawing room. We needed to return, and soon, else arouse suspicion.

"I've been ordered not to tell anyone since I was a child," he said finally. "Society, as you well know, often does not treat those of us who suffer such ailments with the kindness they ought. It is a difficulty I would rather keep secret."

"But why did you not tell *me*? Surely you must know I would never judge you for it? That I would not think poorly of you?"

"Of course not. I just..." He sighed, averting his gaze.

"Are you embarrassed by it?"

"Sometimes," he replied, still refusing to look at me. "I grow frustrated with myself, and I worry how people will respond were I to tell them. I hate that there is nothing I can do to fix it, and I do not want pity. Uncle is convinced that to reveal the malady would be to give society an excuse to shun me. To mock me. Even he has been slow to withhold judgment, proclaiming me unintelligent and broken."

"Broken," I repeated softly. "You told me I was not broken."

He took a step closer, the tips of his boots disappearing beneath the hem of my gown. "I meant it, Grace."

"Does that apply to yourself as well? Do you agree with what your uncle says? That you are broken?"

"No," he said firmly.

I wanted to believe him, but how could I? He kept his ailment hidden from the world. Why would he do so if he thought himself as capable as anyone else? He'd admitted to being embarrassed by it. Did it not follow that embarrassment stemmed from insecurity?

"If you truly believed that, you would not hide it from everyone, but especially not from me." I met his gaze, blinking away the cloudy haze over mine. "How can you say you do not believe yourself broken, or me for that matter, when you cannot even tell others of your struggles?"

"It is more complicated than that, Grace. Much as I hate it, I need society's good opinion. We all do."

I pinched my lips together and nodded. "And they cannot have a good opinion of you when you are not whole? When they know you are broken and afflicted with a condition beyond your control?"

"That is not what I meant."

"Is it not?" My voice raised with my anger. "Hiding our struggles does not make them go away, nor are we less for having them. Broken or not, I am capable of strength and intelligence, independence and happiness."

"But not capable of courtship? Of having a marriage based in love?" He smiled sardonically. "Did you not tell me that you did not expect those things for yourself because of your leg? It is the height of hypocrisy for you to criticize me, Grace. Whether you care to admit it or not, you allow your leg to hold you back. You allow society's opinion and expectations to dictate your future. So forgive me if I prefer not to give them such an opportunity."

*You allow your leg to hold you back.*

His words stung because I felt them deeply. They rang with truth—a truth I had not been ready to hear. I used my leg as an excuse to believe I would never marry. Only recently had I allowed myself to consider, even briefly, that I might have been wrong.

I backed away from him, my lip trembling.

Phillip's expression softened. "Forgive me. I should not have—"

"No, you are right." Despite my valiant efforts to prevent it, tears tumbled down my cheeks. "You've no need to apologize, but I must go."

"Grace."

I rushed past him, and he made no effort to stop me. Using my sleeve, I wiped away the tears, though I doubted I had rid my face of all evidence. That notion was proven correct the moment I stopped into the drawing room, for Rowe took one glance at me and rushed to my side.

"What happened?" he asked.

"Nothing." I forced a smile. "My leg is aching. Might we leave?"

I had used the excuse often enough, Rowe had no reason not to believe me. My leg always ached, in truth, and it was no more unpleasant now than when I sat in the library reading. But I needed to leave. I could not stay here and face Phillip, nor could I watch him spend time with Miss Rigby.

My leg did not hurt nearly as much as my heart.

THERE WAS SOMETHING COMFORTING about curling up in a blanket next to a glowing hearth, but today, even the warmth and security of those things did not ease my melancholy. My argument with Phillip played over and over in my mind, robbing me of sleep. Days had drifted by in a fog of unfeeling existence.

Had he proposed to Miss Rigby by now?

Mr. Perry had given him a week to do so, and if there was one thing I had learned about Phillip Montfert, it was that he obeyed his uncle. I understood his reason. The threat of being disinherited was too much for him to ignore, and Phillip was too honorable of a man to allow his uncle to wed Miss Rigby instead.

That particular threat had nearly made me gag when I overheard them in the corridor. The callous way Mr. Perry spoke indicated a life of misery for anyone unfortunate enough to be called his wife. I thought of Sabrina and how the man had treated her at the close of the house party we attended last spring. Mr. Perry cared nothing for the women in his life.

But those were not the worst of my thoughts.

No, Phillip had implied that berating him made me a hypocrite, and he was right. I had never shied away from telling people about my leg, or how I had come to have such a condition. I had always thought accepting my limitations was fair, that I needn't be able to do everything to live a happy life. I still believed it.

In a physical sense, there were simply things I could not do, or at least not do as well as others. There was nothing wrong with accepting that and understanding those limitations to keep myself from enduring more pain.

Phillip had not spoken of physical constraints, however. I had decided years ago that my inability to dance or take long walks put me at a disadvantage when it came to courtship. I was not wrong to assume it, but I had allowed the idea to grow into a monster that insisted no man would ever wish to court me at all. As if such disadvantages could not be overcome in other ways.

Dancing and long walks were not the only way to fall in love, and yet I had allowed my romantic notions to sweep me away so far I had lost sight of that. Love knew no constraints. It found people no matter their station or struggles. Why had I believed I was different in this regard?

"Hypocrite," I muttered. The word was appropriate, and even though it pained me to hear it from Phillip, I was glad for his words. I only wished the argument had not driven a wedge between us.

I blinked back tears with a humorless laugh. What had I expected of the future? Phillip had made it quite clear he would marry Miss Rigby. He had no choice but to satisfy his uncle's demands. I should not have assumed that, once my service as his matchmaker concluded, we would remain friends.

It was better we split ways now.

A light tap on the library door drew my attention. Rus peered inside, his expression as somber as I felt. He crossed the room, and I noted he held an envelope. My heart sputtered.

"Yes, it is for you," he said, taking a seat next to me.

I snatched it from his hands and started to open it…then realized Rus was still here. Watching me. Why was still here?

He read the confusion on my face and smiled wryly. "Go ahead and open it. I already know what it contains. Montfert told me himself."

Our notes had always been private. Not that there was anything untoward in them, but I preferred Rus did not know all of my business. Phillip telling him about the contents did not bode well.

I opened the envelope and found two things: a banknote with the sum of 25£ and a short note.

"To my matchmaker," I read aloud. "Thank you for your dutiful services and assistance in my success. As we never discussed your compensation in great detail, I have taken the liberty of providing what I hope is adequate payment." My voice cracked.

Adequate payment. It was more than I ever expected. Once again, Phillip had proven his generosity. His honesty. Drat him.

"I wish you the best in your future endeavors and will not hesitate to suggest your services to others who may stand in need of it. All the best, PM."

I drew in a shaky breath. That was it, then. We would both move on with our lives, perhaps never speaking to one another again. The idea left me hollow and depleted.

Perhaps not terribly depleted, as my tears began to spill over. I brushed them away, not wanting Rus to be stuck with a watering pot, but they kept coming. Rus stood, and with a gentle kindness I so rarely saw from him, pulled me to my feet and into his arms. I stayed there for several minutes until I regained control of myself, then pulled away.

"I'm so sorry, Grace," said Rus.

"For what?" I asked. "You delivered my first client. I got what I wanted: my very first payment as a matchmaker. It is something to be celebrated."

He tilted his head, a knowing look in his eyes that threatened to unravel me. "Had I known...I should have let you do this on your own. Had your first client been a portly man without hair, you might not have lost your heart in the process."

"Is it so obvious?"

"Is it obvious that you and Montfert fell in love with one another?" He laughed. "Disgustingly obvious, Gracie. He speaks of you often enough, and watching the two of you together was highly indicative in itself. Never mind that he practically admitted it to me when I questioned him on the matter. I only wish...I wish something could be done to set things right."

"There is nothing to be done but move on," I said, shaking my head and ignoring his statements. Knowing Phillip had admitted his feelings to Rus did me no favors.

"Very well, but I do not care to see you crying. It makes me deucedly uncomfortable. Let us find something to distract you, yes?" He snapped his fingers. "I've got it. You can help me plan my next act of revenge on Netty."

"Is it not her turn for revenge after all the unwanted suitors you sent her?" I had never been good at keeping up with their antics.

"*No.*" He held up a finger. "No, it is my turn. Do you know I went to White's last night only to be mocked because of stains on both of the armpits of my coat? I was not sweating, mind you, and the stains smelled suspiciously of strawberry jam. *Jam*, Gracie. She stained my pits with jam. What sort of sister does that?"

"The kind seeking revenge, I imagine," I answered with a chuckle.

"Indeed. So, I must plot my own, and—"

"Your plotting will have to wait," came Rowe's voice from the doorway. "I have news."

Rus's smile faded, and he hastily rounded to face him. "Has the doctor finished?"

Lord Paxton had forgone the dinner party due to a cough and had remained in his chamber ever since. This morning, the doctor had been called, and I feared it meant his condition had worsened.

"He sounds better today," said Rowe, "but Dr. Montgomery said it is to be expected, this constant up and down. Eventually..."

Rus swallowed loudly. "How long?"

"Months at the least. Father has requested to return home to Kenwick, and Mother agrees it is for the best. He will rest more peacefully there. More comfortably."

I had not thought my heart could be torn apart more than it already was. My uncle had always been rather doting on his children and even his nieces. To lose another father figure in my life so soon after my own's death...well, months seemed far too short a time. Still, I was grateful the state of his health was not worse. My father had passed so suddenly that Amelia and I had not had the opportunity to say goodbye.

"How soon are we to depart?" asked Rus.

"Three days time, but Father has asked that Grace and I remain. He has some business that needs settling. Nothing of great import, but he preferred me to do it so you could return with him. He wants you at his side, I think." Rowe met my gaze. "He also wished not to interrupt your first Season. Annette will return home, but there is no reason for you not to see it through since I must stay anyway."

Rus nodded absently. He seemed almost in a state of shock. I reached out and placed a hand on his shoulder, which shook him out of his trance. He smiled slightly at me, then patted my hand. "Not to worry, Gracie. We will come about. Do not get into too much trouble without me."

He winked before excusing himself to go speak with the staff. Preparations for departure would begin immediately. I considered protesting, to proclaim my desire to leave London as well. With Phillip proposing to Miss Rigby and most of my family leaving, what purpose did I have here?

"Grace, are you well?"

Rowe. I had forgotten he remained in the room with me. "I will be. It is I who should be asking you that, anyway."

He crossed the room to my side and heaved a sigh. "I have not been the most attentive guardian since we came to London. You've been left on your own far too much. Leaving the dinner party early reminded me of my duties, and I apologize for—"

"Rowe, please stop. You have been nothing but the best guardian to me. I have not been alone much at all. I've had Annette and your Mother for company. I've enjoyed myself. What more could I ask?"

"A great deal more," he said with a sad smile. "I had intended to introduce you to..." He rubbed a hand over the back of his neck, his cheeks tinting. "Well, to potential suitors. I failed in that regard. Although, Mother mentioned you had a gentleman caller a few times. If I had to guess, it was the same one we saw in Berkeley Square?"

One of his auburn brows lifted teasingly.

"As I told you then, he is only a friend. It seems he is to marry Miss Rigby."

Whatever amusement his expression had held disappeared completely. "I did overhear him speaking of that very thing with Mr. Perry during port."

There was more to the despondency in his expression than sympathy and sadness for me. I had once wondered if perhaps Rowe held a *tendre* for Miss Rigby, and I found myself pondering the notion again now. Perhaps we were both meant to walk away from this Season a little bit heartbroken.

# Chapter Twenty-Seven

## PHILLIP

"Numbers?" I rubbed a hand over my face, gripping for patience. "You realize most ledgers contain numbers, do you not? That is their purpose."

Sabrina glared at me. "Yes, Phillip, I do realize that, but I was not raised with knowledge of balancing ledgers or how to manage funds. It is all gibberish to me, which is why I copied a page or two for you to look over."

She extended the sheets of foolscap toward me, and I took them with a sigh. I should not have been so frustrated with her, but between her efforts to discover evidence against Uncle and my argument with Grace, not to mention my impending proposal and investment meeting, I was a total wreck. I could not handle one more thing on my shoulders.

I sat down at a table in the corner of the library with a heavy thump and held up the first page so it caught the light pouring in from the window behind me. There were four columns: two with numbers and two that categorized them. Even at a glance, I knew they did not pertain to anything regarding the household and must be related to Uncle's business ventures. It was not unusual to keep separate ledgers for such things, but generally, there was a master ledger that combined them both, giving one an overview of all assets.

I had spent the last few weeks balancing the master ledger in addition to the household ones. My memory wasn't perfect, but none of the things listed here seemed familiar. In fact, as best I could tell, they weren't expenses at all, but rather income.

"What is it?" Sabrina leaned toward me from the opposite side of the desk, which made her face hover close to mine. "You are thinking, and I want to know what it is you are thinking about."

I pulled away from her in annoyance. "I need more than a minute to look at it, Sabrina."

She glanced at the clock. "Will two minutes suffice?"

I rolled my eyes. I was starting to understand what Apsley had said about sisters. They could pester a man to insanity.

My cousin graciously afforded me five minutes before begging for my thoughts again. I shook my head and set both sheets on the desk. "I cannot account for these. There is nothing about them in the master ledge your father had me balance."

"That is suspicious, is it not?"

"Yes," I hedged. "It is, but this is not evidence of a crime, Sabrina. It will do nothing to prove your theory."

"It is not a theory." She planted her hands on her hips, her dark eyes boring into me. "I know he is guilty, and there are rumors about people who have suffered financially because of his dealings. I will not stop until this is all settled."

My head ached, and I rubbed my temples as if to relieve the pain. "He is your father. If—and I do mean if—you find what you are looking for, it will likely see he is transported if not handed a death sentence."

"I am aware. Should I stop because of this? Feel sympathy? My father has never shown me an ounce of regard. Why would I spare him any?"

"He is still your father."

"By blood, perhaps. Unfortunately, I cannot escape that fact. And do not tell me you feel differently."

She was right; I could not deny it. Were Uncle to go to prison, or worse under proven charges, I would experience no sympathy for him or sorrow. He was cruel and unfeeling. A selfish being whose sole purpose was to further his own precedence and wealth.

I nodded slowly. "We can do nothing without more evidence. For the record, I do believe you. Something is certainly amiss, but we cannot know the depth of it without more. Nor can we make a move. Taking this to the courts without enough evidence would spell disaster for both of us. You understand that, do you not?"

Sabrina reached for my hand and gave it a squeeze. The gesture took me by surprise. She had never shown me much affection, but over the last few weeks, she had been far more open. It reflected how much she had changed.

"I know, Phillip. Just as I know my father has hurt you physically at times. I do not wish to see that happen because of me"—she gestured to the paper—"because of what I'm trying to do. Nor do I wish to see him disinherit you after all you have endured."

"I thank you for the consideration," I said softly. "But the truth is your father will always find fault with me. My future will never be secure until he has passed on. Guilt eats at me for even thinking of such a time—for looking forward to it—but I cannot lie that it will bring me a peace I have never been afforded. Your father believes I am broken, and as such, he will never view me as worthy of all he has built, no matter how I strive to prove him wrong."

Sabrina scoffed. "His definition of broken is vexingly skewed. What fault could he possibly find in you? Even I know you to be intelligent and hardworking. You do everything he asks of you."

I swallowed, my argument with Grace pushing itself to the forefront of my mind. Even after days of mulling over everything, her words lingered. Perhaps because I knew she was right, to an extent. Keeping my ailment a secret only suggested I was ashamed of it. Embarrassed by it. Those things reinforced Uncle's belief that I was broken, a stigma that deep down, despite my efforts, I believed it too.

More than once, I had seen Grace bravely tell others of her struggles without fear of repercussion. I still believed fear was warranted considering how many members of the upper class behaved and judged, but giving fear such credit did not mean it was worth heeding.

"Sabrina, there is something I wish to tell you."

My cousin tilted her head, her dark brows furrowing, likely due to the waver in my voice.

"I...I am partially deaf in one ear," I said. "That is why your father considers me broken. He always has."

She gasped, her hand coming to cover her mouth. "Oh, Phillip! Why did you never say so?"

"I was ordered to keep it a secret, but in truth, I do not know whether I would have said anything regardless. After the way your father has berated and demeaned me over the years, it felt safer to keep the information to myself."

"But now?"

I shrugged. "Now nothing. I only wished to tell you."

To tell anyone, really. Grace had overheard and learned of it unintentionally, but I wanted to tell someone of my own free will. My muscles relaxed, and a strange sense of contentment flooded through me. It felt good to put the secret out there, especially since Sabrina had not responded with disgust or judgment.

"Does Miss Rigby know?" my cousin asked.

I shook my head. "Your father specifically forbade me from telling the family, believing it would give them an excuse to back out of the agreement. Assumed agreement, that is. There is nothing on paper as of yet, but he gave me but a week to propose."

"So you will marry Miss Rigby?" She looked utterly disappointed when I nodded and folded her arms. "Then I had better work fast."

"Sabrina."

"Put off the proposal for as long as you can," she continued, ignoring me. "I have one more lead to follow. One last hope. Mark my words, Phillip Montfert, the both of us will be free of my father, and once we are, you can marry whomever you please." She grinned smugly before heading to the door. "And by whomever, I mean Miss Scott."

"I do not think we are on good terms at—"

"Now, if you will excuse me, I have some business to attend to."

I watched her go without another attempted word. After all, nothing I said had stopped her yet. Why did my chest always fill with trepidation any time I had a conversation with Sabrina? Admittedly, this time it was also filled with hope.

Hope I had no right to feel.

I stood, picked up Sabrina's copies of the ledger, and tossed them into the hearth.

PAYING ATTENTION TO MY uncle as he announced his plans for a future investment in an overseas textile business was difficult when my mind was so thoroughly set on thinking about Grace. It seemed the more days that passed without seeing her, the more desperate those thoughts became.

I missed her, and the desire to offer an apology for speaking to her the way I had, for unleashing my frustrations about Uncle's demands on her, nagged at me every waking moment.

Sending her payment for being my matchmaker had been more difficult than I imagined. Not because I did not believe she deserved it. She had given me more assistance than I ever hoped for, and despite my continual struggles to pull Miss Rigby into conversation, my confidence among society had grown. Much of that came down to Grace's advice, but time in her company had done the most to reassure me. I could speak to her for hours without feeling uncomfortable, thus proving myself capable to some degree.

Regardless, my hesitance to send her that banknote came from the finality of the act. Once paid, I had no excuse to ever speak with her or see her again. The loss was felt keenly in the form of a sharp pang straight through my chest, one that still had not gone away.

Pining. I was pining for a woman I could not have.

Lud, if I was not a fool.

"H-how much expense will there be in s-shipping?" Mr. Bower asked. The man had listened to my uncle with deep interest, but he was also wearing Uncle's patience thin with his questions. I did not blame Mr. Bower for asking. Investing the sort of money proposed was no small thing, and he deserved to have as much reassurance as he could.

"Not a significant expense," Uncle replied, his tone not bothering to conceal his annoyance. "Mr. Rigby has a number of contacts and knows how to negotiate with the shipping companies. We needn't worry much on that front."

Rigby, who sat next to me, nodded. "Indeed. We stand to make a great deal on this venture. It will have upfront costs, to be certain, but once manufacturing is underway, we will have no trouble recouping them."

"A-and what of the p-possible s-storms?" asked Mr. Bower. "H-how is the risk being m-minimalized."

Now both Uncle and Rigby looked perturbed. Rigby spoke. "I cannot control the weather. If you feel the risk is too much, you are welcome to leave. Might I remind you that no investment is without risk, however, and you will regret not staying onboard with us."

Mr. Bower's eyes went wide, and he shook his head. "No, no, I-I am very interested."

"Could have fooled me," Rigby muttered. "Be better if he weren't with the way he talks. Cannot get a sentence out without stumbling. Sign of unintelligence." He laughed to himself.

Did the man truly believe that? My jaw clenched. Mr. Bower suffered from a stutter, and that certainly said nothing about his intellectual capabilities. Mr. Rigby was so much like my uncle that it roiled my gut to consider aligning myself with the man in any way. What would he think were he to learn of my hearing troubles? Likely, I would be branded the same way as Mr. Bower—a buffoon with no place in a meeting such as this.

Part of me wanted to declare the truth right now. The notion was far too tempting, and I closed my eyes to prevent myself from acting brashly. Uncle might murder me if I said anything to jeopardize this.

Still, the temptation persisted.

Would a confession put an end to my courtship of Miss Rigby? Regardless of her father's opinion, would she even want to marry me if she learned the truth? Was I to keep this secret from her for the rest of our lives?

And no matter how the questions prodded, I would never have the answers.

# Chapter Twenty-Eight

## GRACE

THE ATMOSPHERE AT APSLEY COURT was solemn. My uncle had not been in the best of health since we arrived, but the confirmation that he would never get well sat heavily on all of us. The drawing room, which I had once found comfortable even amid the many suitors, conversations, and familial teasing, now felt depressing in its abundance of silence.

Rus had been absent since Rowe informed us of the family's intent to leave, and I worried about him. As heir to the title, and given his lax personality, I imagined such news would weigh on him most keenly. Rowe had also been absent more often than not, undoubtedly seeing to his father's business, as requested. He would likely stay busy the remainder of our stay in London, which I did not mind overly much. Without Lady Paxton and Annette here, I would not be able to attend many social functions, and I found that suited me.

I would not risk running into Phillip or Miss Rigby if I did not go out.

Annette, too, was not in the drawing room when I came in after breakfast. I decided grabbing a book and taking it to my chambers would be the best way to spend the gloomy day, and I had just made for the stairs when my cousin stormed through the door, surprising our poor butler so thoroughly that he fell back against the wall.

Annette lifted her skirts to take the stairs at a fast pace, her eyes trained on each step. I moved to the side to make room, hoping she would stop to speak with me, but as she hurried past, I noted the trails of tears on her cheeks and the red around her eyes.

She had been crying. My cousin did not cry. Even when I had seen her fall from trees or scrape her skin climbing on the ruins near Kenwick, she had never shed a tear.

I followed, calling out her name before she reached her bedchamber. "Annette?"

She paused long enough to look at me, then proceeded into her room. She left the door open, however, which I took as an invitation. I joined her inside, closing the door behind me. Annette sat on the edge of her bed, her hands clasped tightly together.

I sat down next to her. She trembled, and while she was not crying at present, she was near it.

"Annette, what happened?" I whispered. "Where did you go this morning?"

It had not escaped my notice that she had not returned with a chaperone.

"The lieutenant returned to Town," she said. "I met him in..." Her head lifted, and her eyes met mine, a sort of pleading swirling within them. "Where I met him is not important. Nothing untoward happened between us...mostly."

"Mostly?" I raised a brow.

Her expression turned cold. "Nothing that means anything. I simply needed to speak with him. To inform him our agreement is at an end because I am leaving Town."

I massaged my temple. "Your agreement? Whatever do you mean?"

She turned to face me, the look in her green eyes hard as stone. "You will not speak of this to anyone?"

I nodded. Having Annette's confidence meant a great deal to me, but besides that, she had kept my matchmaking scheme from Rowe. I owed her a secret.

Annette heaved a sigh. "The lieutenant and I had come to an agreement, an understanding, if you will. He was finding the amount of attention he received from debutantes a bit cumbersome to his political ambitions. He was not ready to look for a serious courtship and was desperate for something to put the women off his scent."

I recalled that day at Gunter's. The lieutenant had been surrounded by admirers, and for a time, I had assumed he enjoyed it. But then, there had been a weariness about him when he joined us and relief when he finally escaped them.

"So," I prompted. "You agreed to help him?"

"During the Morrison's ball we realized we had a similar problem," she said. "At the time, Rus, in his unfailing wisdom, thought it fun to give me a parade of suitors. I was so exhausted by it all—playing the kind hostess, the receptive lady who would not dream of turning down an admirer. I had no choice, as you know, and it grew rather burdensome to endure call after call. Dance after dance." She lifted her shoulders and let them fall. "Lieutenant Paget and I agreed to a ruse, pretending to court. The both of us were desperate for a reprieve."

I swallowed my disappointment. Annette had never claimed to have changed her mind about the lieutenant, but part of me had hoped for an attachment. None of the other callers seemed a suitable match for her. The lieutenant had complemented her wit and was not dissuaded by Annette's obvious disdain.

My cousin's chuckle drew my attention. Annette smiled at me. "Do not be so disappointed, Grace. I can see it clear as day on your face. We had an arrangement, that is all. There were never feelings involved."

"If that is true, then why..." My words trailed off as I looked over her face. She could deny it all she wanted, but something had upset her. Something to do with the lieutenant.

"Why what?" she asked, then pointed to her face. "The tears? They are not for him. I find I am emotionally overwhelmed at present. He made me angry, as he is quite known to do, and after everything with my father...well, I am a bit of a mess, I should think. Do not hold it against me."

"Of course not." I wrapped an arm around her shoulder, and we exchanged smiles. I understood all too well what she was facing. It had not been but two years since I lost my father, and oftentimes, the pang of that loss felt as fresh as the day it happened.

"How is he doing?" I asked. "Your father."

"He has been better the last two days. I think the idea of going home has brightened his spirits. Still, I cannot escape the worry. Even when I manage to put it from my mind, I see it in the eyes of my brothers. My mother. We've no hope to truly cling to, only time. I should not be so ungrateful when I at least have that."

"No one would call you ungrateful," I said. "You are mourning the time you stand to lose, and that is perfectly acceptable. You love your father very much, and he you. There is no shame in feeling sorrow for what is to come."

She nodded absently. "Mother sent word to Jack, asking him to return home. I think she fears he will not make it in time." Annette tilted her head, her smile wry. "Or he will choose to ignore it."

Jack, the youngest of the male siblings, was presently touring the continent. He and Lord Paxton had always possessed a strained relationship, one I never completely understood. Jack was rebellious and much like

Annette in his distaste for being controlled in any way. He valued his independence, and the way he chose to act on that independence often caused squabbles with his father.

I took Annette's hand and gave it a squeeze. "Jack and your father may not always get along, but I am certain he will come."

"I hope you are right." She shook her head and sighed deeply. "This Season has been far too eventful. I am quite glad to be going home. I am sorry to leave you behind, especially as I am so invested in the outcome with you and your beau."

"I do not have a beau," I said. "You know Phillip was my client. He is to marry Miss Rigby, and so, the remainder of the Season will be far less thrilling now. At least the drawing room will no longer fill with suitors."

She did not smile as I had hoped. "They were not all for me, you know. Mr. Willoughby was quite taken with you. He is not the man *I* would choose for you, of course, but he is not so bad. He seems kind and attentive if nothing else."

I scoffed. "He only spoke to me to get to you, undoubtedly."

Annette's brows furrowed. "Not at all. He looked at you with much fondness. Perhaps if you had not snubbed his attempts, he would have made his intentions more clear."

Had I? It had not been my intention. Merely an assumption the man's interests rested elsewhere. The more I thought on it, the more I wondered if she was correct.

"It seems I have been oblivious to a great many things." I heaved a sigh. "This Season has been a disaster, hasn't it?"

Annette grimaced. "Perhaps the remainder will fare better."

Optimism I did not possess. "I am sure it will be grand, and I will tell you all about it once it's over."

A day that could not come soon enough.

# Chapter Twenty-Nine

## PHILLIP

Apsley had left London. I tucked his letter into my pocket at the sound of footsteps on the stairs, his advice and subtle offer of assistance burning into my thoughts. I did not have the time nor the capacity to deal with the hope his words fostered.

Uncle descended the last few steps, his expression stern and unyielding, so opposite of what it should be for what I was about to do.

I had always assumed that proposing to a woman would be a nerve-racking affair, but having Uncle accompany me to Miss Rigby's home made the entire situation a hundred times worse. He still did not trust me not to humiliate him, it seemed.

That, and he was eager for the marriage contract to be drawn up and signed, thus sealing his prospective investment partner and my fate. Not that he cared a wink for the latter or the state in which this courtship—a term I applied rather generously—had left my heart. Miss Rigby was a lovely lady, but the notion of marrying her?

Something within me was repulsed by the idea, and I suspected it had everything to do with my matchmaker. Miss Rigby simply was not Miss Scott.

"You will request a private audience with her straightaway," said Uncle once we were in the carriage. "No tomfoolery today. A few minutes of idle chatter to settle in, and then you make the request. We have a purpose, and Rigby is expecting us. I want to see this swiftly resolved."

"Yes, sir."

"Enough of that dejected tone, boy," Uncle growled. "You stand to gain a great deal from this arrangement. Your future—"

"Remains insecure." I lifted my brows in challenge. We both knew that even if I married Miss Rigby, obeyed all of his demands, he could still change his will. Admittedly, to do so would put him at odds with Mr. Rigby given his daughter would suffer the consequences, but that was no guarantee of security for either of us.

Uncle scoffed. "Just do as you're told, and I'll have no reason to change anything."

Not today, perhaps. What of tomorrow? Or a year from now? I was tired of living this way—of walking on eggshells, always worried one wrong word or failure would land me and my mother in a workhouse.

And yet, what was the alternative?

I had none.

Apsley's letter seemed to almost burn against my rib cage, a reminder that I did have a choice. I had *something*.

I rubbed my pocket as if it would quell the hope the piece of paper was stoking. Dangerous hope that I must ignore. Perhaps if I read it again, I would realize my mistake—realize I had misunderstood his offer. No man in his right mind would butt into another's romantic affairs, attempt to interfere at a cost to himself financially.

Unless, of course, that man was a true friend. And he was, for even after I had confessed my deafness to him via letter, he had not rejected me.

I silently swore and retrieved the note from inside my pocket, fully aware Uncle watched me intently.

"What is that?" he asked before I had even unfolded the paper.

"A note from Apsley," I replied. "I hadn't a chance to finish reading it and thought to utilize our drive to do so. He has left London. His father is ill."

Uncle spit a string of curses. "Poor news, indeed. I had hoped to convince Lord Paxton to join our endeavor." He lifted his chin and har-rumphed. "But I suppose it bodes well that Apsley informed you of his departure. Speaks to your connection, even if the rest is inconvenient."

I wanted to remark on his lack of empathy. My friend was about to lose his father, and Uncle wallowed over the loss of investment gain? It made me sick, but it would do no good to voice my opinion.

With a deep breath, I turned my focus to the letter. I hated reading it with Uncle sitting across from me, but I needed to put my mind at ease. I needed to reassure myself that I was doing the only thing I could. Surely, I had misread before?

But, no. The words were exactly as I remembered.

*I know it is with great impertinence that I say this, but I must inform you of my cousin's despondency. I do not know what has happened between the two of you, nor shall I request the details, but it is clear you are both hurting. I suspect your impending marriage to Miss Rigby is the cause, and as I know of the circumstances surrounding the match, I request that you reconsider.*

*I have experienced the pain associated with love, specifically with losing it. Perhaps not by my own choices, but it was agony nonetheless. I've no wish to see my cousin or friend experience the same, not if there is a chance for their happiness. Am I wrong to believe the two of you have developed more than a fleeting tendre for one another? If so, you may ignore all that follows.*

*However, if I am correct in my assumptions, I pray you will consider the rest with an open mind and not take offense to it. You intend to marry Miss Rigby because your uncle demands it of you, holding your inheritance over your head. We have discussed the estate left to you by your father at length over these last two months. I understand the state of that asset and what it would require to restore it. I cannot offer you the capital to execute those repairs with any sort of swiftness at present, but I shall do all I can to help you find your footing.*

*Until then, know that you and Grace (and your mother, of course) will always be welcome at Kenwick Castle. My father cares for his niece, as I care for my cousin, and we would never allow her to face destitution, nor would we allow a good man who also loves her to suffer.*

*All of this is to say: you have a choice, Phillip. Whatever your uncle threatens or does, there are others who will support you. I leave the decision in your capable hands.*

*Sincerely, your friend, RA*

*P.S. Should you find yourself at Kenwick Castle, I shan't be responsible for the mental abuse you will likely suffer from living with so many females, but I should hope that not a great deterrent in the grand scheme of love and happiness.*

I refolded the paper and tucked it away, wondering what Apsley had thought of my hearing difficulties. The issue was left unaddressed, but it had not stopped him from offering his help. But then, why should I be surprised? Not once had I ever heard him disparage Grace for her weak leg. He was not the sort to disparage anyone for such a struggle.

What of his family? I had met most of them, and they were genial enough, certainly. Taking kindly to an extra burden upon the household, though, was another matter entirely. Would Lord and Lady Paxton accept my presence among them were I to marry Grace? Would they begrudge me the financial assistance that Russell Apsley offered?

I could not say for certain, and given Lord Paxton's condition, it seemed rather selfish to ask it of them. It also rankled my pride to even consider accepting so much help. I might never repay them.

*But I would have Grace.*

The thought caused a thick lump to settle in my throat and my eyes to sting.

We arrived at the Rigby's townhouse, and my body felt sluggish as I pulled myself from the carriage. Never had so much dread weighed on me. The butler welcomed us inside after my uncle provided his calling card, and we were led to the drawing room. Mrs. Rigby and her daughter stood in greeting, and pleasantries were exchanged. Tea arrived shortly after, and my mind wandered as Uncle and Mrs. Rigby spoke of the weather and the upcoming events that remained for the Season.

It wandered to darkened corridors and garden walks. To a future filled with children and laughter. And love. It felt like a dream beyond my reach, yet I floundered in desperation to grasp even a portion of it.

A throat cleared, and I met Uncle's gaze. One of his bushy gray brows lifted in expectation. It was time.

"Before we depart," I said, "might I request a moment of privacy with Miss Rigby?"

"Of course," said Mrs. Rigby, her tone resigned more than pleased. She had never been accepting of my courtship of her daughter, but I suspected Mr. Rigby had made his wishes clear on the matter.

She and Uncle vacated the room, closing the door behind them, and for the first time since my arrival, I met Miss Rigby's gaze. She must know my purpose in the request, yet her expression gave nothing away of her feelings on the matter. How did I even begin to ask for her hand? Would she know by the reluctance in my voice that I did not wish for it? How was it fair to her to begin our future this way?

I drew a breath, hoping it would keep my tone even, at the very least. "Miss Rigby, I imagine it is no surprise why I asked to speak with you."

"It is not, sir," she said gently, the corner of her mouth lifting slightly. "My father told me what to expect of today."

I nodded. "Then I must ask...I wish to..."

No, wished was not the proper word at all. If I was going to propose, then the least Miss Rigby deserved was my honesty. But still, the words would not come, as if held back, tethered by a rope deep within me.

*I would have Grace.*

*I would have Grace.*

*I want Grace.*

More importantly, I *could* have her. Apsley would help me, and I would find a way to restore my estate and repay him. My future may not look the most promising for disobeying Uncle, but Grace and I could weather it. We could spend our lives building our future together. I could not say whether the challenge was one she would accept, or if she would even forgive me after the way we had left things, but I had to try. I needed to try.

I had to get out of this drawing room immediately. The ride to Kenwick Castle could not be more than a few days. I could pack and be gone within—

"Sir?" Miss Rigby prodded. "Are you well?"

"Forgive me." The words fell out in an almost chuckle. "My sincerest apologies, Miss Rigby, but I fear I cannot offer you the proposal you expected nor one you deserve."

That little smile at the corner of her mouth grew. "I had hoped not."

My brows drew together. "You had?" It should not have been so shocking, really. Even after asking her a thousand questions, we barely knew one another. Should I be offended? I could not find it in myself to be.

"Might I be frank with you, Mr. Montfert?" She continued when I nodded. "I have long suspected your heart rests with a friend of mine. Am I wrong to assume that?"

"Not in the slightest."

This seemed to please her. "Then might I suggest you visit Apsley Court next?"

"It would do little good. I received word this morning that they have returned to their country estate. Lord Paxton has taken ill."

"Yes, I am aware. Grace told me herself not two days ago. She also mentioned that she and her guardian would remain in Town until the Season concluded. He is finishing business for the viscount, you see."

She was still in London? My heart pounded. "You are quite certain?"

"Quite," Miss Rigby responded with a laugh.

I had never felt so relieved, but it was short-lived. The smile faded from my face. I had forgotten one very important thing. "I cannot go to Grace. My uncle...he told me if I did not propose to you, he would marry you himself. You and I may hold no affection for one another, but I cannot subject you to him out of selfishness."

"You forget, sir, that I possess the ability to say no. My father would be furious, perhaps, but he cannot force me to marry your uncle."

Her response did little to ease my concerns. Women had been forced into such arrangements before. How could I know for certain Miss Rigby would not?

"My mother has her sights set on someone else for me," she added, noting my reluctance. "She will advocate on my behalf."

"Is it someone better than my uncle?" I would be hard-pressed to find someone worse, but somehow I would not put it past Mrs. Rigby to have her daughter married to the most dishonorable man in England if it meant wealth or title.

"I believe so," she answered, her voice a bit guarded. "Someone of your acquaintance, in fact."

I lifted a brow, but she said nothing. I would get no more from her on the matter, which left me to make my decision. Another moment's consideration was all I required. "If you are certain—"

"I am certain. Go, Mr. Montfert. Claim the happiness you deserve."

Scooping up her hand, I brought it to my lips and left a quick kiss on her glove. "Thank you, Miss Rigby."

My feet carried me across the room in a few swift strides. The door opened before I reached it, and both Uncle and Mrs. Rigby glanced between me and Miss Rigby. I slipped past them, but before I could make my escape, Uncle grabbed my arm and yanked me back.

"Where are you going?" he ground out.

"To propose to the woman I wish to marry."

Uncle's expression turned hard. "You are not at liberty to propose to someone else. Rigby and I have a deal."

"Then you had best go speak with him and make a different deal."

"I warned you what would happen—"

Mrs. Rigby's voice broke his threat, but as she was on my left, I struggled to understand her, though it was clear she was not pleased about the situation. I ripped out of Uncle's grasp and turned to face her properly.

"I beg your pardon, ma'am, but since I am hard of hearing in my left ear, I must ask that you repeat yourself."

The woman blinked at me. Uncle's eyes seemed to bulge out of his head in growing rage. Twice now, I had defied him today.

"You are deaf?" Mrs. Rigby demanded, her nose scrunched in disdain.

"Partially, yes."

The woman turned her glare on my uncle. "And you failed to mention this? How dare you trick my daughter into marrying this...this broken man! He could pass the trait on to their children. All of society would shun them!"

Where her words might have once stung, I found I cared very little. Uncle shouted back at her, and while the two of them bickered over whether such a thing could be kept silent, I descended the stairs and rushed out the door. Uncle would remain to smooth things over—or attempt to smooth them over—with Mr. Rigby. That gave me little time to inform my mother of what had happened. Since the decision would alter her life insurmountably, she deserved to hear it from me.

I could only hope good news would soon follow the bad.

# Chapter Thirty

## PHILLIP

I FOUND MOTHER IN the drawing room upon my return. Despite the short distance between our townhome and the Rigbys', my chest heaved from running. I hadn't any idea how much time I would have and could not afford to waste a second of it.

I sat down next to Mother, and she pressed a hand to her chest. "Good heavens, Phillip. Why are you so winded?"

"Never mind that. We must talk."

Mother set aside the embroidery she was working on, offering me her full attention. I had been so eager to tell her my decision—to tell her all about Grace—but as I looked into her eyes, worry and guilt caught up with me. What if I had made a mistake?

But no, I had not. Deep down, I knew this was the proper course. Neither of us deserved to live under Uncle's tyranny any longer. He expected much of me, but he had never treated my mother as anything more than a burden. I was done living this way.

"Phillip, what is it?" Her hand settled over mine, her face marred with concern.

"Uncle wished me to propose today." I continued when she nodded. "I nearly did, but then...well, my heart belongs to another, and I simply cannot marry the woman Uncle expects."

Mother's jaw went slack. "Your heart...you must tell me what you mean immediately. How can you go and fall in love without me knowing?"

I chuckled at the indignation in her tone. "I am sorry for keeping so much from you. When Uncle told me of his expectations, and after a week of stumbling through society, I needed help to make a match. Russell Apsley recommended a matchmaker to me—his cousin, Grace

Scott. And"—my shoulders lifted and fell, but I smiled—"I can hardly be blamed for falling for her. She is lovely and kind and intelligent. And so, so much more. She is everything. All my hope for the future."

Mother's eyes glazed over, and she sniffed softly. "Then let us not waste another moment. I must meet her at once."

She started to stand, but I held out a hand to stop her. "It is not that simple. I may have made a blunder of things and must make amends with her first, but beyond that, you understand what this means, do you not? I have defied Uncle. Severely. He will not take this lightly and has already threatened to disinherit me. You know as well as I do he will not hesitate to act on the threat, especially when I propose to Grace. According to Sabrina, her family is in his black books as it is."

I reached for her face and cupped her cheek with my hand. "Mother, he will kick us out. We will have nothing."

She smiled at me in that tender way that always brought me a sense of peace. "My darling, we will not have nothing. We will have one another. We will have love. That is far more precious than any fortune, and I can think of nothing I want more than to see you happy. If Miss Scott can provide the life you deserve, then the devil with what your uncle threatens."

"Mother!" I scolded, though my amusement was clear.

"What? I was not raised a lady, I might remind you. If you think since we have lived a life of comfort these last twenty years that my tongue has forgotten all of its vulgarity, then I assure you it is not so. I curse your uncle quite regularly from the privacy of my bedchamber."

I laughed, and her smile grew. It had been years since I had seen her smile like this.

"We will come about," she said, giving my hand a squeeze. "You, me, and Miss Scott."

I nodded, my confidence in my decision swelling. "We shall. I have a plan, but it will take some time to work out all the details. We've been offered a place to stay, but I must speak to Grace before I can proceed with anything else. And I do not know how long Uncle will give us to leave."

"Not long, I'd imagine." Sabrina's voice drew my attention. Despite the topic of conversation, she was grinning broadly. "But he will not have a say in the matter. Before you run off to see your lady, you and I have a matter to discuss. Well, *we* have a matter to discuss." She gestured next to her, and with clear hesitation in his expression, a man appeared at her side.

Mr. Barton, the man having private business meetings with Uncle.

SABRINA, MR. BARTON, AND I ventured to the library. I had instructed Mother to go to her chambers and begin packing in case whatever news Sabrina intended to give me did not, in fact, keep Uncle from forcing us to leave. With the way she grinned, her expression one of pure delight, she seemed rather confident, but I would not allow myself the same optimism until I had heard everything she had to say.

My cousin closed the door and, to my surprise, slid a chair in front of it. The furniture was not heavy enough to be much of a deterrent, and I could not help but chuckle. "Is our need for privacy so important?"

She glared at me. "It is. Once you see the evidence Mr. Barton has brought me, you will understand."

My amusement faded, giving way to hope. *Dare I allow it?*

Sabrina gestured for us to follow her to the table in the corner, and we all sat down. Mr. Barton put a stack of papers and a wrapped parcel before me, and Sabrina slapped a familiar red ledger down with a *smack*.

"What are you doing with this?" I asked, panic lacing my voice. "If he finds out you have it—"

"It shan't matter. By the time he realizes it is missing, the magistrate will have ordered him off to gaol to await trial."

Confident, then, was an understatement.

"You said this contained only numbers," I reminded.

"It does," said Sabrina. "And while those numbers mean nothing to us, Mr. Barton is familiar with every transaction it details. Every. Single. One. Both the legal and illegal."

My heart pounded. If Barton truly knew what those records meant and we could prove they were fraudulent, Uncle would stand trial.

"Everything I have here"—Mr. Barton tapped his finger on the stack of papers—"will show how your uncle has swindled people out of money and has been doing so for the last six years. In addition, I am in possession of the old engravings he used to forge banknotes. That is how it is done, you see. Your Uncle has fake notes created and then the signatures are forged. He's hired a calligrapher specifically for this. The man has been perfecting the practice for years."

"Banknote fraud?" I shook my head. "But why would he take such a risk? I have looked over the other ledgers. Many of our investments are quite profitable, and my uncle has never been a spendthrift."

"Does it surprise you that his only motivation is greed?" Sabrina asked incredulously. "It is all the man requires to take a risk. Clearly, it was worth it to him, and given how much he has gotten away with, I see no reason to think he will stop. His most recent scheme is to cheat Mrs. Ellis out of money. Her husband invested with Father for years, so he continues to make investments on her behalf, all the while claiming them to fail and require more funds. Really, though, he is putting the money straight into his pocket, and Mrs. Ellis is none-the-wiser for it. Her mind is going, you know. She forgets things. Why, just yesterday she came here believing it was May."

My brows furrowed. "It is nearly May."

"May, eighteen hundred fourteen. She asked if I had heard any news of Napoleon."

Ah. Sabrina was not wrong about the woman. Mrs. Ellis did seem frequently confused, though that had done nothing to alter her kind disposition. That Uncle would see such a woman as someone he could manipulate for gain ignited my ire.

"So, what now?" I asked. "Are you certain we have enough evidence?"

"Yes," Sabrina said firmly. "Between what we have physically, and Mr. Barton's testimony, my father will go to trial. We can also track down the calligrapher. I suspect he would turn on Father in exchange for a sentence that does not include hanging."

I met Mr. Barton's gaze, studying him closely for perhaps the first time. He was older than me, likely in his late thirties, but his expression looked worn and tired, like a man nearing the age of fifty.

"You've been working for my uncle, fulfilling his demands and executing his schemes for years," I started slowly. "Why come forward now? If Uncle is convicted, there is a good chance you will be arrested as well."

The man laughed lightly. "I did not come forward on my own, but I was convinced in the proper direction." He looked at Sabrina and smiled, diluting any venom the accusation might have carried. "I might never have done so without her support. What you say is true, however. I could easily be arrested. I am not proud of what I have done. None of this was illegal when Mr. Perry first hired me on. I was sent to find a calligrapher without being given the reason. Then an engraver willing to forge what we needed. Paper to match whatever the bank was using. Once I realized what it was all for, I attempted to back out. Mr. Perry threatened me. Threatened my family. I saw no way out of it. Who would believe me over someone as wealthy as him?"

I leaned forward, catching his attention again. "You realize that, by testifying and admitting your involvement, you might well be hanged?"

Mr. Barton nodded with a solemn frown. "I know, but I cannot go on like this. The threats against my family wear on me, never mind the guilt. If something is not done, how many more will lose their security or livelihoods? I do not wish to be a part of it any longer."

"His threats...do you have a record of them, or were they all verbal?"

"I have letters. Kept them in case. Not sure how useful they are or if the courts would even consider them."

I nodded absently. "They might if Sabrina and I testify on your behalf. We have both heard Uncle threaten you ourselves, though I did not understand the extent of it at the time. I cannot promise it will disabuse the courts of punishing you, but I will advocate as best I'm able."

"You have my gratitude," said Mr. Barton. "But I am willing to face the consequences. I just want my freedom from the man. My family's freedom."

I understood that far too well.

"We move forward then," I said.

Sabrina's hand fell on my shoulder. "We can move forward, but you must consider one more thing, Phillip."

The fearful look in her eyes gave me pause. "What is it?"

Mr. Barton clasped his hands in front of him. "While I doubt the courts will demand a forfeiture of all assets, they will likely request restitution on behalf of those who were harmed by Mr. Perry's scheme. Six years' worth of fraudulent income will be a heavy tax on any estate."

Bile rose into my throat, and I swallowed. "I hadn't considered that, and as heir..."

"As heir, you would be responsible for paying off the debts." Sabrina tilted her head, her expression ridden with sympathy. "And you would be the one to bear the social consequences. The shunning from Society."

"And that is not the worst of it," said Barton. "All assets will fall to you, into your care, but they will never legally be yours so long as Mr. Perry lives and breathes. Once his sentence is served, he has every right to return and reclaim what is his. Every right to then disinherit you."

I stood, rubbing a hand over my face, and walked over to the empty hearth. The air in the library held a heaviness that threatened to suffocate me. We could hold off on turning in the evidence until Uncle had removed me from his will, but that would only serve to throw the responsibility onto someone else. Someone who was likely young and too naïve to understand how to wade through such a swamp.

I could not, in good conscience, do it.

"The responsibility to manage it all falls to me then," I said, my voice almost a whisper. "And after working to maintain the estate and pay off whatever sum the court decides upon, I then stand to still lose everything?"

The situation was almost laughable.

Sabrina rushed to my side. "It is unfair, I know. You should not have to suffer the repercussions. None of this is your fault."

*But I will have Grace.*

The lift of my lips seemed to surprise Sabrina, which drew laughter from me. Indeed, it poured out in a way that likely made her question my sanity.

"Do you not see the irony in it?" I asked. "No matter what choice I made today, I would have been financially ruined. At least I had the mind to reject your father's demands. At least now I face everything with someone I love. The situation is not ideal, no, but it never was to begin with." My smile grew into a grin. "I can marry Grace."

Assuming she would have me, of course.

Sabrina returned my smile. "Well, then, let's call for the Runners and the magistrate so you can propose to your lady."

It was fortuitous that Uncle spent nigh on three hours smoothing things over with Mr. Rigby. At least, I assumed he remained there. Regardless, the man would not leave me alone for long. A scolding, severe and fuming, awaited me upon his return.

I paced the study, stopping occasionally to peer out the window. Mother was still upstairs. Whether she had finished her packing, I did not know, but I had sent one of the servants with word to keep her in her chamber, in addition to having my valet pack my things. Both had looked at me quizzically when receiving the instruction, and my odd request was sure to create gossip below stairs. But it hardly mattered. If all went as planned, Mother and I would not be going anywhere.

Mr. Barton had accompanied Sabrina to see the magistrate. Before an arrest would be made, enough evidence must be presented. Thanks to Mr. Barton, we had it in spades, but still, it would take time for the magistrate to look over everything and make a decision.

Time that Uncle could, in truth, use to change his will.

No matter what, I would eventually end up penniless, but I much preferred time to work out a path for my future rather than having a rug pulled from beneath me *today*. Besides, if Uncle faced trial, it would alleviate my lingering concerns for Miss Rigby. She had stated her mother would advocate for her to marry someone else, even if my uncle asked for her hand, but I was not entirely convinced.

When he wanted something, Uncle could be very persuasive.

And, of course, there were the people who would be harmed if Uncle were permitted to continue his schemes. The events of today would affect so many lives. So many futures.

*Please let them return soon.* I sent the silent prayer heavenward. Waiting was a torturous endeavor. There was only so much to occupy my mind with, and having already sent a note and a fresh bouquet to Grace—perhaps a little too soon given I did not know how the remainder of the day would fare—I had nothing else to entertain me but endless scenarios, many of which were unappealing. What if all the hope I had garnered since leaving the Rigbys this morning was misplaced? What if the magistrate found our evidence lacking?

Doubt had a way of disturbing the mind when it was left without something to give it focus and purpose.

The front door opened, but any relief I might have felt faded in an instant at the heightened, angry tone of Uncle's voice. From here, I hadn't any idea what he said, but it was not difficult to determine his mood as he stormed up the stairs.

He entered the study, his face red with both fury and the exertion of climbing the stairs at such a pace. Fear coiled in my chest, and I fought the urge to shrink back against the wall as he stomped toward me.

"Insolent boy!" Uncle grabbed my arm and wrenched me forward, but I resisted. His fingers slipped over my coat, and he nearly stumbled over.

I resisted. Never had I done such a thing. My stature dwarfed his, but that had never mattered because I had always obeyed. Always allowed him to drag me about. Demand. Control.

Not anymore.

With my feet rooted in place, he could not so much as budge me.

Uncle, seeming to come to this conclusion, glared up at me and poked his finger hard into my chest. "You dare disobey me? I told you what would happen if you did not marry that chit."

I swallowed. Had he proposed to Miss Rigby? Had her father forced her to accept? His next words quieted those concerns. "Rigby is furious, as is his wife. The whole of Town will know of your insufferable ailment by next week. Nothing I said would convince them otherwise, not even my proposition of marriage. You've ruined everything! But never again."

He gestured toward the door where a man with neatly combed, mousey hair stood. Mr. Grenville, Uncle's solicitor. I hadn't even noticed him before now.

"Come, Grenville!" Uncle waved him inside, and the man obeyed, his expression contorted with hesitancy and the grip on his brief-bag so tight his knuckles had turned white. I did not blame him. I had no desire to be in this room either.

I stood in place as Uncle led the man to the writing desk near one of the tall windows. There was no sense in asking why his solicitor was here, and I had already accepted that my future would bear the burden of financial difficulty, no matter today's outcome.

But still, I silently pleaded for Sabrina to return. No one else deserved to deal with the ramifications of Uncle's crimes any more than I did.

As if I had summoned her, a flash of dark hair drew my attention to the doorway. Sabrina stepped inside, her dark eyes filled with rage as they settled on the man who had sired her. She shifted out of the way to allow four men to pass. One was Mr. Barton, who remained next to Sabrina. Among the others was an older gentleman with a bald patch at the top of his head, and two younger men.

The older gentleman spoke first, pulling Uncle from his discussion with Mr. Grenville. "Victor Perry?"

"Yes, who are you?" Uncle's brows furrowed as he looked between the man and the two men to either side of him. I could only assume they were Bow Street Runners, recruited to assist in the arrest. Perhaps I should have advised Sabrina to bring an army of them. Uncle was unlikely to go quietly.

The older gentleman retrieved a paper from his pocket and unfolded it, reading it aloud. "Victor Perry, you are hereby arrested on numerous counts of fraud, the charge being brought forth this twenty-seventh of May, eighteen hundred seventeen, by the following individuals: Sabrina Stafford, Duchess of Rochester, William Samuel Barton, and Phillip Montfert."

Uncle's gaze shot to me. He looked nearly unhinged, a fury in him I had not witnessed even after refusing to marry Miss Rigby.

The older man continued, detailing the most egregious of Uncle's charges before finishing with, "You are hereby remanded to Newgate Prison to await trial."

A calculating look swept over Uncle's face, mere seconds of consideration before he stormed to the bookcase nearest the desk. In a rage, he threw books from the shelves, his fingers moving along the spines with increasing panic, an emotion reflected in his expression.

"You will not find it," said Sabrina with a calm I envied. "I discovered your hiding place in the false compartment days ago."

Uncle spun around, books scattered at his feet. His eyes darted from her to the Runners, and the color drained from his face as if he realized the severity of the situation. "My ledger."

"The red one?" Sabrina asked innocently. "Oh, yes. The magistrate found it particularly informative. He was also highly interested in some engravings that looked very much like the ones commissioned by the Bank of England. But do not worry. The magistrate has sent Runners to collect your calligrapher. I am sure he will clear all of this up."

Uncle's eyes rounded. "This is a mistake. They've lied! You have no evidence of any of this!" His voice quivered with doubt, and a frantic panic settled onto his expression as the runners stepped forward. "Traitors, all of you! This will never stand, and once I am released, I will see all three of you ruined!" He turned toward me, and his features twisted into a snarl as if he held me particularly responsible. I could not fault him for the assumption as I had the most to gain from his arrest.

Or he would see it that way. In truth, Mr. Barton stood to gain the most—freedom for him and his family.

A Runner rounded the desk, and Uncle shot forward, shoving his solicitor out of the way. He raced for the door, but it was blocked by the second Runner. Uncle retreated a few steps, then rounded on his heels and marched straight toward me.

I froze, my eyes catching on the glint of his pocket watch as he retrieved it from his coat. He gripped the time piece firmly and swung the chain. My arm lifted, a defensive mechanism so deeply instilled in me it required no thought. The chain whipped around my arm, and I felt the sting there first, and then across my cheek.

"Phillip!" Sabrina screamed.

I staggered back, pressing a hand to my face, already feeling the skin welt beneath my fingers. Uncle raised his arm to strike again but halted when he realized the chain was missing. One moment of confused distraction allowed the Runners to subdue him, each taking an arm. He fought against them as they dragged him from the room, his muffled demands filling the stairwell.

The older gentleman's attention swept to me. "You will likely receive a summons to testify in court, Mr. Montfert."

"Of course," I said.

He bowed with impressive stoicism. "Thank you for your time. Have a pleasant afternoon."

Job completed, he turned and left. Mr. Grenville excused himself as well, his eyes wide. The poor fellow. I was eager to leave myself.

He paused at the door, however. "Forgive me, sir, but I should like to inform you that I intend to go out of town for a time, immediately, and will be unavailable for...adjusting any sort of documentation pertaining to the estate for the foreseeable future." He gave me a significant look, and I understood his meaning. By law, Uncle still held the right to change his will while in prison.

*If* his man of business could meet with him. A shame Mr. Grenville planned to go out of Town.

"Thank you, sir," I said.

He nodded once, then disappeared into the corridor.

"Phillip, are you all right?" Sabrina crossed the room to me and placed a hand on my arm, her eyes full of concern.

I smiled softly at her. "I will be well. It is over now, and this is not the first time he has struck me in such a way."

"Well, at least he cannot ever do it again." She stooped over and retrieved the gold chain resting on the floor and offered it to me.

I inspected it closely, noting one of the links had snapped when Uncle hit me. The break was likely what had sent the piece whipping across my face, and I would have a mark for some time because of it.

I slipped the chain into my pocket and found Sabrina watching me in confusion. "A reminder," I said, patting my coat. "I fear I might question whether all of this was real, and this...this will reassure me I did not imagine it."

"That welt on your face is evidence enough. I would cast the chain into the first fire I saw if I were you. A reminder of my father helps no one."

Perhaps she was right, but for now, I would hold onto it.

# Chapter Thirty-One

## GRACE

Rus claimed every flower had a meaning, that the colors and species were a language all their own. As I stared down at the three red roses that had arrived yesterday morning, I could not help but wonder what they might say.

The curiosity was made worse considering the note attached to them: *Forgive me*. Such a curt and simple phrase, and yet one that held so much feeling.

At first, I had thought the flowers came from Mr. Willoughby, who had called on me with more frequency after seeing him at a dinner party several nights ago, or perhaps from Mr. Cosgrove, a school friend Rowe had introduced to me. I found both men jovial and kind and certainly more receptive when shown unguarded interest from me. I had even allowed myself to consider a future with them, not because I was immediately drawn to the men in that way, but because Phillip's words had left an impression.

*You allow your leg to hold you back.*

Yes. I had allowed it, despite my proclaiming otherwise. I had seen every eligible male acquaintance with the assumption they would become a friend at most. Never a suitor. Never a potential companion or husband. That assumption had prevented me from truly pursuing anyone or showing interest. I hadn't seen a purpose in it, believing it would only cause disappointment. I had been afraid.

*You allow your leg to hold you back.*

Not any longer. I would choose optimism from now on. I would choose to believe that, one day, I would marry. I would find love. My weak leg would not stop me. I could still help others find their matches until then, but the two endeavors need not be mutually exclusive.

My fingers ran over the note, the edges already worn from how often I did so. *Forgive me.* Those words could only have come from Phillip given our last exchange. In my mind, there was nothing to forgive. Phillip had spoken in earnest, and while the delivery was made in frustration, I had needed to hear it. My only regret was the criticism I had dealt to provoke his rebuttal.

Forgive him? It was I who should be asking for grace, not him. But did the flowers say more than his plea? Was there a deeper meaning, and was I a fool to dare hope for such a thing?

Drat it all. Why did Rus have to leave?

"You are scowling at those flowers quite fiercely," said Rowe, entering the drawing room with an amused smile. "Whatever have they done to deserve your ire?"

"They have secrets, I am quite certain, and the man who could decipher them is gone."

"Ah," Rowe nodded in understanding. "Well, most men, including me, haven't the faintest idea what certain flowers mean. There is a good chance whoever sent that bouquet simply believed you would like them." He paused, his eyes narrowing. "Who sent them?"

My lips pinched. I had yet to tell Rowe of my matchmaking endeavors over the last few months, but I was tired of keeping it from him. Besides, how was I to explain the flowers otherwise?

"They are from Phillip Montfert," I said.

Rowe's brows rose. A fair response since he had overheard the man speaking of his proposal to Miss Rigby. A proposal that—to my knowledge after scouring the papers day in and day out for the announcement—had not taken place.

Yet.

Had his uncle not given him but a week? That time had passed. What was Phillip waiting for?

"You are scowling again, Grace."

I heaved a sigh and gestured to the chairs in the center of the drawing room. "Perhaps we ought to sit down for this discussion."

Rowe's expression pinched with concern, but he nodded and followed me to the forest green sofa. We took our seats, and I drew in a breath, uncertain where to begin. From the beginning, I supposed. "I have been meeting with Phillip Montfert in secret since we came to Town."

"What?" Rowe sputtered. I had never seen him look more horrified. Perhaps that was not the best beginning.

"Not for anything untoward," I said quickly. "Before we left Kenwick, I decided I would spend the Season matchmaking. Do you remember? I had mentioned it."

"Yes. Of course, I remember, but I had hoped you would forget the notion or it would simply be a game to pass the time." He eyed me warily. "Grace, tell me what you've been doing. The whole of it."

I winced. "When Rus first met Mr. Montfert, he mentioned that his uncle demanded he find a wife this Season. One that met his ridiculous list of qualities. Phillip—"

"Phillip?" My cousin's brows were high on his head again.

"Mr. Montfert," I corrected. "He was struggling to make any progress, and Rus offered to set up a meeting between us. I agreed to help him make a match that would satisfy his uncle's requirements."

Rowe swore. "I might kill my brother. To put your reputation at risk this way. He hasn't the faintest idea of the pressure that comes with being a woman's guardian or running an estate. It is a heavy burden to have so many people relying on you, which he might understand if he took any of his responsibilities seriously."

I grabbed Rowe's hand, and he looked at me, his anger deflating a little.

"I do not disagree with you about Rus, but he was careful about the entire thing. We all were. I always had a chaperone. Well, almost always"—I continued quickly when Rowe's face contorted with exasperation— "You needn't worry after my reputation. It is safe, and I haven't met with Phi—Mr. Montfert in well over a week. We argued at the Davenport's dinner party. The flowers are an apology."

Rowe rubbed a hand slowly over his face with a groan. "Why, Grace? Do you have any idea how fortunate you are that no rumors are circulating about the two of you? And you did it all without telling me." At this, a flash of hurt lit his eyes.

"I did not want you to stop me," I admitted. "Can you honestly say you would not have?"

"Of course, I would have. It was reckless, and I am responsible for you."

I smiled lightly. "Which is why I did any of this in the first place. You are so focused on taking care of me—taking care of Amelia and my mother—that you think so little about your happiness. It is an honorable thing, Rowe, and I appreciate your care more than you know, but I did not wish to stand in the way of your future either. I did not believe I would ever marry because of my leg, and I did not want to be a burden on you for the rest of my life. Becoming a matchmaker was the solution to finding my independence. To finding financial security that would give you freedom, too."

Rowe shook his head. "You are not, nor have you ever been, a burden on me, Grace. I am so sorry if I did or said anything—"

"You did not." I squeezed his hand. "And I understand my folly in all of this. I had resigned myself to spinsterhood because of my ailment, but that resignation is gone."

My cousin smiled wryly. "And all it required for you to come to your senses was a reputation-risking scheme. I trust you will discontinue such behavior?"

I hummed thoughtfully. "You may trust that I will not keep things from you anymore."

Rowe scoffed, but he fought a smile. "If that is the best I can hope for, I suppose I will accept it." He nodded toward the flowers. "What of Mr. Montfert? I sense there is more you've not told me."

"Well, I found him a match. His uncle approves of Miss Rigby."

"But?" The way he looked at me suggested I would not get out of a confession.

I shrugged. "But I went and fell in love with my client. I'm quite certain he cares for me, too. None of which matters, mind you. His uncle would not approve of me after what happened between Sabrina and Lord Emerson. He blames Amelia for that, and me by extension. Never mind that I do not meet his list of qualifications."

Tears pooled in my eyes, and Rowe shifted closer. His arm wrapped around my shoulder, and he pulled me close as those tears broke free. "I am sorry, Grace."

Despite my sobs, I was not sorry. No matter how it pained my heart, I could never regret having met Phillip. Even in heartache, he had given more than he would ever know. Perhaps one day I would have the strength to thank him for it.

I TOSSED THE MORNING paper aside with a grunt, and Rowe lifted his brow, taking a sip of his coffee. Ten days had passed since the Davenport's dinner party, and still, the papers said nothing of Phillip Montfert or Harriet Rigby. The situation was perplexing, and my curiosity had grown to an unbearable monster. I could pretend my interest came down to seeing my client's success, but lying to myself was pointless. It took everything in me not to march to his townhouse and demand answers.

As his matchmaker, did I not have *some* right to know what was going on?

"I think we ought to take a walk through Hyde today," announced Rowe.

"Why?"

"Because you never leave this house unless we are invited to some party or another, and even then you feign a headache more often than not."

I scoffed. "I did not feign anything. If you must know, my megrims were very real."

"And had nothing to do with avoiding a certain gentleman, I presume? Or his supposed fiancé?"

Supposed? Hah! What an understatement that was. Why was there nothing in the papers? Did Mr. Perry wish to keep the engagement a secret or had there been no proposal at all?

I was going to go mad.

"His uncle gave him a week to propose," I said, needing some sense of reassurance. "Surely there would be something about it in the columns?"

Rowe shrugged, and I glared at him. He smiled playfully in response. "What would you have me say, Grace? Certainly, Mr. Perry would put it in the papers if a match had been made. I cannot imagine Mrs. Rigby foregoing an announcement for her daughter, either. Even a scandalous one. She is too proud to disregard a chance for such fame."

"Fame? Really, Rowe, you make it sound as though an announcement of marriage, even by scandal, will raise her status."

Rowe set his empty glass down on his breakfast tray and gestured for a footman to take it. "No, I daresay Mrs. Rigby already fancies herself high as nobility, title or not. She is rather self-important."

I could not disagree with him there.

In another bout of frustration, I reached for the paper, letting my gaze trail the engagement columns once more. There were three there today, but none of them said Montfert or Rigby.

"If you are merely going to stare at the same page, perhaps you might allow me to have a look?" asked Rowe.

"No." I folded the paper again, lifting my chin. "I shan't let you look. I am convinced the moment you do, a certain pair of names will appear no matter how many times I have checked." It was ridiculous, I knew, but I had gained a sort of possessiveness over the morning paper. Rowe had not touched a single copy in days due to my hoarding.

Which he had not once complained about.

Rowe sighed, rose from his seat, and offered his hand to me. "Come. Let us take a walk to the park. We should both feel better with a bit of fresh air, I think."

"Very well, then. Allow me to gather my things, but let us keep to a slow pace. I've no desire to agitate my leg."

Half an hour later, we walked in the sunshine toward Hyde Park. The streets were particularly crowded with the fair weather, and countless carriages drove down Rotten Row. Bonnets and top hats filled my view like a sea of colorful, moving blossoms, with larger ones created by those carrying bright parasols. Men and women alike stood conversing along the footpaths, and the titter of gossips brought a smile to my face.

I had missed the park more than I realized, especially this time of day when it was so full of people. No matter which way I looked, I spotted potential romance. It was nearly as enjoyable as reading a novel, and I made a game of creating stories in my mind for the couples we passed.

Hmm. Perhaps it was more distraction than a game. Regardless, it eased something within me, dulling a residual ache.

Only when Rowe stopped suddenly did my thoughts pull back to the present. "Mrs. Rigby. Miss Rigby." He released my arm and dipped a bow. "What a pleasure to see you both."

Miss Rigby. She looked lovely as ever, her brown hair perfectly coiffed, her eyes sparkling with quiet reserve. She would make Phillip a handsome wife, and yet, I could not say for certain she *was* to be his wife. She did not radiate the joy of a woman recently engaged, but then, would she? In all her time with Phillip, had he captured any part of her heart as he so easily had mine? And if not, *why*? Why did she not see the wonderful man he was? My mind could not fathom it.

Shaking away my thoughts, I curtsied. "Yes, a pleasure."

The women returned the greeting, though nothing of Mrs. Rigby's expression said she was at all pleased to see us. Miss Rigby, as always, smiled politely.

Mrs. Rigby's eyes narrowed on Rowe. "Which one are you?"

I fought a bout of laughter, and even Rowe's lips twitched. The woman was certainly blunt about having no desire to waste her time.

"Rowe Apsley, ma'am. The spare, as most would call me."

I scoffed quietly. That was hardly true. No one called Rowe *the spare*. At least no one who cared about him. I supposed it would make sense for Mrs. Rigby to view him that way.

The woman's frown deepened, though how it was possible, I did not know. "The rumors are true, then? Lord Paxton and his heir have left Town."

"I am afraid so, ma'am. Miss Scott and I will join them soon."

"You are leaving?" Miss Rigby's question caught me by surprise, but more so the disappointment in her voice. We had become friends but not close enough to warrant the kind of sadness she exuded in both tone and expression.

The question that had been lurking inside me for over a week teetered on the edge of my tongue. No, I could not ask. It was too much.

I swallowed it instead.

"Yes," I said. "Once Mr. Apsley has concluded business on his father's behalf, we will depart."

"Which is fast approaching," Rowe added. "I've but a letter to deliver to Lieutenant Paget, then we may leave."

My eyes darted to Rowe, my brows drawn tight. Lieutenant Paget? What should Rowe need to deliver a letter to him for? Or Lord Paxton, rather. The two men had often had private discussions even while the viscount remained bedridden, but what was so important to require a letter? And one Rowe must deliver himself. Curious.

Rowe ignored my prodding stare, shifting uncomfortably. "I hope you enjoy the remainder of the Season."

That sounded far too much like a goodbye for my tastes. I could not leave the Rigbys. Not without an answer. Was I brave enough to ask?

"Why are you not engaged?" The words slipped out, and I bit my tongue. Brave, indeed. I was no such thing, merely a wreck of curiosity and emotion.

Miss Rigby smiled, far brighter than I had ever seen. "Has he not come to see you yet?"

"Come to see me?"

Miss Rigby nodded, still smiling. "He has been busy, I imagine, but do not lose hope, Miss Scott."

Hope. That dangerous word. But what did she mean he had been busy?

I did not have to ponder the question long, for Mrs. Rigby was eager to share her knowledge of the subject. "It has been all over the papers!

Have you not seen it? Mr. Perry has been carted off to Newgate, and can you imagine it? His nephew and daughter raised the charges! Despicable men, the both of them. To think my daughter was nearly pulled into the scandal by marriage. The entire family is ruined."

I looked to Rowe, hoping he would provide more clarity, but he merely shrugged as if to say 'you do not allow me to look at the papers'.

"And there is more," Mrs. Rigby continued, so lost in her jubilance at spreading gossip she seemed to forget herself. "Can you believe that Mr. Montfert has been hiding that he is deaf? Deaf, and wished to marry my daughter! Absolutely not. Mr. Rigby and I put a stop to his courtship as soon as we learned of it."

"*After* Mr. Montfert had ended it," added Miss Rigby, who then gave me a very pointed look.

A look that I would analyze later. Right now, my stomach swirled so violently that I might lose my breakfast. Phillip had wanted to keep his ailment a secret for perfectly understandable reasons. Many of the *ton* would look down upon him. I may have chided him for it, but I would never reveal his struggles. That was not my place, no matter how I felt about the matter.

But so few knew Phillip's secret. Would he blame me for word getting out? Would he believe I betrayed his confidence?

*What if that is why he has not come?*

My heart beat quicker. No, no, I needed to stop this. Phillip did not deserve to have his name bandied about.

"Are you certain he is deaf?" I asked, pressing a smile into place with great effort as I faced the matron. "Where did you hear such a rumor?"

"Why, he told me himself," answered Mrs. Rigby.

"He...he told you?"

"Yes, right in my foyer. Admitted the whole of it." The rest of her words were muffled by my thoughts. Phillip had told Mrs. Rigby of his hearing impairment. Surely he must know the woman would judge him for it, and worse, spread it about Town to anyone who would listen as she did now.

But why? Why would he do it after being so set against it? I wondered if my words had struck him as deeply as his had struck me. I had not ceased pondering them. Did he do the same? Phillip had always listened to me and took time to consider the topics of our discussion. Our argument had been heated, but why should it surprise me that, once his emotions had tempered, he would consider my words, just as I had considered his?

More importantly, what did all of it mean?

*Forgive me*, his note had pleaded.

*After he ended the courtship*, Miss Rigby had said.

Phillip had made the decision not to propose to her. And he had told Mrs. Rigby his long-kept secret—a secret I had berated him for hiding.

"Oh, Phillip," I whispered, my words drowned out by Mrs. Rigby's persistent chatter. "What have we done to one another?"

# Chapter Thirty-Two

## GRACE

Choosing what to wear when breaking the rules of proprietary and visiting a bachelor at his home unchaperoned was much harder than I anticipated. Even in preparation for my first ball, I had not meticulously plotted every accessory, right down to my shoes. I scoffed, staring at my current ensemble of choice resting on the bed, complete with brown walking boots. He would not even see them, but here I was.

Meticulously plotting.

Perhaps much of it came to my anticipation and nerves. If I drew this out long enough, I would need to wait until tomorrow before I went to see Phillip, thus giving me more time to think. More time to determine what I would say.

A lady did not simply walk up to a gentleman and declare her feelings, after all.

What should I say instead? An apology was certainly warranted. I owed Phillip that much. He needed to know that I regretted ever pressuring him to reveal his secret. Much of the *ton* would surely judge him for it, and considering the news already filling the papers...

I had spent all of last evening pouring over the details after meeting the Rigbys in Hyde Park. Having previously focused on the engagement columns, I had completely overlooked everything else. Phillip's uncle had been charged with banknote fraud, and just this morning a mountain of evidence saw to him being sentenced for transportation. *Seven years* to New South Wales. The courts also demanded an investigation into all of Mr. Perry's finances. Into everything Phillip was meant to inherit.

Despite what Mrs. Rigby claimed, Phillip had no involvement in the crimes committed by his uncle. I had been there when he overheard

Mr. Perry's conversation with his man of business. And besides, Phillip was too good—too considerate of others—to take advantage of people that way. Unlike Mr. Perry, who I knew to be a beastly, unfeeling man. Controlling as he was, I doubted anyone in his family had known of his criminal behavior.

Until now.

How had Phillip gotten so much evidence? The papers spoke of a third person bringing up charges. A Mr. Barton. Who was he, and why had he been involved at all?

These questions and more raged within me, but they paled in comparison to my sympathy. With his family's name in tatters, what would Phillip do? The courts could seize many of his assets. Indeed, this would hardly be different from Mr. Perry disinheriting him. Everything he had done, including hiring me as his matchmaker, was to ensure he and his mother did not end up destitute.

Now, he might face the prospect anyway.

I wanted to scream on his behalf. The unfairness of it all stoked my internal fire. I wanted to shout his innocence from the rooftops. Why should Phillip be punished, even indirectly, for a wrong he did not commit? Society would shun him, and Mrs. Rigby spreading rumors of his hearing difficulties would do nothing to help matters.

How I hated that the world would turn against him. There was little I could do but offer my comfort and sympathy. Would he even want it after everything? Were we friends, or did the inkling of hope that grew after discovering he had not proposed to Miss Rigby have merit?

After another quarter hour of debate, I settled on a lavender gown with white lace trim on the sleeves and hem. My maid helped me dress and styled my hair with curling tongs, allowing short strands to frame my face. I still hadn't any idea what I would say when I saw him, but I had to go.

Every moment I remained was a moment I could stand by his side. He was not alone; he had his mother and Sabrina, but I wanted to be next to him too. And I wanted him to know that I did not think either of us was broken. A long list of his attributes, compiled by me within a matchmaker's notebook over the last several weeks, was evidence of just how much I admired him. He needed to see it.

Once I had ripped the page from my notebook and tucked it into my pocket, I descended the stairs, tugging on my gloves. I needed a quick escape. Rowe would never approve of—

"Stop right there."

Drat. I turned slowly to see my cousin coming down the stairs at a leisurely pace, a wide grin pulling his lips. He stopped in front of me, and his auburn brows lifted. "Where are you going, Grace?"

I opened my mouth to respond, but he held up a hand. "I know where, so rather than lie to me—which you promised not to do again—allow me to dissuade you of the notion."

"You cannot dissuade me. I need to see him, and it cannot wait. Come with me if you must, but I have to go." I spun around and reached for the door handle.

"He's not there, Grace."

My fingers froze on the brass knob. "How can you know that?"

Rowe stepped up behind me and placed his hands on my shoulders. Gently, he turned me around to fully face him. "Because I've spent the last hour speaking with him in the study."

"Speaking...he is here?" I glanced over his shoulder, and just as I did so, a familiar figure appeared from the corridor leading from the study. Philip rested his arms on the banister, staring down at me with a hesitant smile.

"Phillip." His name came out as little more than a whisper, and while I doubted he had heard me from such a distance, his smile grew as if he had read the movement of my lips. He took the stairs, each tap of his boots a much slower beat than the pounding of my heart. Too slow, for by the time he reached the bottom, I had abandoned my self-control, rounded Rowe, and met him there.

"Good morning, Grace," he said softly. His dark blue waistcoat made the softer shade of his eyes pop in the morning light pouring from the window, but it also highlighted the dark circles beneath them and the long, red welt along his cheek, too. The poor man likely had not slept well with all the news, and if I had to guess, the welt had come from an angry uncle.

But Phillip was here. *Why* was he here?

I had questions and so much I wished to say—so much sympathy to offer and forgiveness to beg of him. Neither of which came out of my mouth first. "I love you."

He gaped in surprise, and Rowe chuckled from behind me. His amusement sent heat flooding my cheeks. "Forgive me, I...that should not have—"

Phillip scooped up my hand, grinning so wildly my heart stuttered, and brought my gloved fingers to his lips. "It is a good morning, indeed, to be greeted with such sentiments as I have only dreamed of hearing."

His words brought out more of my blush. "Perhaps I do read too many romance novels."

Phillip shook his head, still holding my hand, though he had lowered it to his chest, gently pressing it against him. "Just the right amount for a matchmaker, I should think."

"Not a very good matchmaker," I said. "I failed to help you make a match."

He studied me, blue eyes roaming my face. "I must disagree."

Oh, dear. I had forgotten one very important accessory—a fan.

Rowe cleared his throat and waited until I had turned to look at him to speak. "Grace, Mr. Montfert has requested a private audience with you." He gestured to the open parlor door to his left, a glint of mischief in his eyes.

I whirled around to meet Phillip's gaze. Was this truly happening? Moments ago, I had been prepared to walk to his townhouse and demand to see him, fearful he would turn me away. Fearful he would resent me for pushing him to tell the world his secret.

But Phillip looked at me now with such tender pleading and hopefulness, I could no longer doubt his regard nor his intentions for being here.

"Of course," I said, my voice raspy with emotion. "If you will come with me, Mr. Montfert."

He followed me into the parlor and closed the door, effectively leaving us entirely alone. I faced him, my hands fidgeting with nerves. Where did we begin? Where did *I* begin? I had already blurted my affection for him; the rest should be easy.

It did not feel easy.

"Rowe and I saw Miss Rigby and her mother yesterday," I said when Phillip remained silent. "Mrs. Rigby had a great deal to say."

Phillip chuckled. "I imagine she did. She began a relentless campaign to smear my name the moment I refused to propose. Ironic, given she did not want me courting her daughter from the start."

I took a step closer to him. "You mean she began the moment you told her about being deaf?"

"Yes. She was not particularly happy to learn a broken man was courting her daughter. Claimed I would have passed on my ailments to our posterity and they all would be shunned by society. Yet more irony that she has been rather quick to encourage people to shun *me*."

"This is my fault. I never should have scolded you for keeping it hidden. You had every reason to hide your struggles. You were right about all of it. I am a hypocrite." I averted my gaze, and Phillip came forward until he stood directly in front of me, close enough I could feel his warmth and smell the citrusy scent of his soap.

Phillip tucked his knuckles under my chin and lifted until my eyes met his. "I am tired of hiding. Tired of worrying what others will think of me." His thumb brushed over my cheek, creating a flurry of goosepimples on my arms. "Anyone who would judge me poorly for an ailment beyond my control is not someone worth having in my life anyway."

A smile touched my lips. "I said that."

He smiled back at me. "You did, and I shall never forget it. I have learned so much from you, Grace."

"And I from you. Neither of us is broken, merely different." I retrieved the paper from my pocket and offered it to him.

Phillip's hand fell away from my cheek, his brows puckered in confusion as he unfolded and read. That confusion shifted the longer he did so. His eyes glazed over, and he swallowed hard, making his Adam's apple bob. "This is the list you made about me?"

"It is. I've been adding to it since the day we met. You will note that nothing there suggests any imperfection, but do not allow that to go to your head. I simply wanted you to know how I see you. How I have *always* seen you."

Phillip averted his gaze, his lashes fluttering as if to hold in his emotion. After a moment, he looked at me. "Did you receive my flowers?"

"Yes, and I have gone mad trying to riddle out what they mean. They do mean something, do they not? Rus told me he taught you about flowers the day following the ball."

"He did, and I am grateful to have committed some of his tutelage to memory. Red roses represent love—passionate love if your cousin is to be believed. Regardless, that is what I meant them to convey. I have missed your company this last week with a kind of desperation no poet can describe. I have longed for you, Grace. Longed for your voice, your touch, your presence. I dream of holding you, of kissing you. It is you who gave me the courage to reveal my malady to the world. You who I willingly risked everything for by standing up to my uncle for perhaps the first time in my life. You pushed me to think about my own happiness, and I have come to realize that much of it revolves around you. I may not have a physical list of qualities that I admire about you, but they are written on my heart. My mind.

"But I must also be honest. My name is in near ruin, and my finances stand to take a rather large beating. Can I assume you have read the papers and know of what I speak?" He continued when I nodded. "That is what kept me from coming to you sooner. I spent the last two days fighting for Mr. Barton, the man who helped us provide evidence. I did not believe he deserved punishment for doing my Uncle's bidding under threat of his family. The magistrate eventually agreed. As for the rest, I cannot say what the courts will decide, but it will likely be a burden upon my uncle's estate and assets. As heir, it shall be my responsibility to manage the whole of it while he is serving time for his actions. Once he returns, I may still lose everything should he decide to change his will. What I want to ask of you will not be easy or fair, but—"

"Ask it. Please, ask it."

Tears pricked at my eyes, and when several escaped, Phillip brushed them away. "My dearest, darling Grace, did you mean what you said? Do you truly love me?"

"I love you, and I am more than willing to face whatever hardships await us. So long as I have you, I have everything I need." My gaze fell. "Also, I am sorry for being the worst matchmaker in the history of matchmakers."

He laughed, wrapping an arm around my waist. He pulled me against him, and my hands came up to rest on his chest. With a smile that had turned into a smirk, he leaned close to my ear and whispered. "You are the best matchmaker I have ever hired."

"I am the only matchmaker you have ever hired, Phillip Montfert," I rebutted with indignation. "And certainly the last."

I felt his deep chuckle beneath my palm, but he did not pull away. Instead, his cheek pressed against mine, his breath caressing my skin as he placed a soft kiss on my neck. "The very last. You taught me what love truly is not by finding my perfect match, but by *being* my perfect match. I cannot imagine my life without you in it, Grace. I love you with my entire soul. All the broken pieces. All the inexperienced parts. I love you as I am and as the man I hope to one day become. Say you will marry me. Say you will help me reach the future happiness I have finally allowed myself to envision."

"Yes!" I pulled him back, my impatience nearly unbearable. "Yes."

Phillip grinned as if reading my thoughts. He leaned forward and captured my lips with his. My body seemed to scream as I returned the gesture. Returned all the longing and desire his kisses contained. This feeling was far better than any novel had described—powerful and all-encompassing. I would never view the idea of love the same again. How could I when experience brought with it a level of understanding I had never imagined?

My fingers wove into his hair, and Phillip tightened his hold on me, his kisses deepening. In his arms, I felt entirely whole. My leg would never fully heal, but his love had mended me in ways I hadn't realized I needed.

Phillip chased my lips when I pulled away. I chuckled and placed a hand on either side of his face to hold him back. My thumb brushed over the angry welt on his cheek. He seemed to sense my question and sighed. "Must we allow it to interrupt?"

"Tell me quickly. What happened?"

He laughed, and his arm loosened around me, nearly making me regret my request. Phillip dug about in his pocket for a moment and retrieved a golden chain from within. He held it up, and I took it for closer inspection.

"The chain from my uncle's pocket watch," he said when I looked at him in confusion. "It broke when he left one final mark before being escorted to Newgate."

I had suspected Mr. Perry was the culprit, and anger rekindled in me anew. "That man is despicable."

"Agreed."

"Why do you carry it?" I asked. "The chain."

He shrugged. "I have broken free of the chains that have kept me bound for so long. It is a physical reminder that he cannot control me anymore. A good reminder despite the pain of the past. And a reminder that not all broken things need to be fixed to have value. We simply need to look at them differently. Appreciate them for what they are."

He gave me a pointed look, and I chuckled. "I see."

"Good." He took the chain and returned it to his pocket. "Because I was not quite finished with our other activity."

His lips met mine, briefly, for the door opened, and Rowe poked his head inside. "Oh, you are still...I will give you one—maybe two—more minutes. Shall that be enough?"

"No, but I suspect no amount will be," I said, grinning.

Rowe glared at me in annoyance. Someday he might understand. He held up his fingers. "Two minutes."

The door closed again, and no sooner than I looked at Phillip, did he kiss me. Sweetly. Softly. With a promise that two minutes was only the beginning.

# Epilogue
## Five Years Later...

## PHILLIP

THE POUTING FACE THAT stared up at me nearly changed my mind, but as any good father strived to do, I held my ground. "It is time for bed. There will be no more tarts tonight."

"Just one tart," Rose begged, shifting on her bed. "Please, Papa." She drew out her plea, extending the vowels for so long that the word could likely create a bridge to cross The Channel.

"Not tonight, but if you promise to go to bed, I will sneak you one at breakfast."

"But breakfast is so far away," Lily moaned as if all two years of her life had consisted of such torturous waiting.

Ever the negotiator and guardian of her younger sister, Rose folded her arms. "Two tarts for each of us, or no deal."

I chuckled, and so did the girls' nurse, who stood across the room. She had attempted to get them to bed, but they had insisted on me coming to bid them goodnight. Insisted, I wagered, because I had a reputation of being somewhat for a pushover when it came to them. I loved them dearly, and they knew it well.

I pulled my lips to one side and hummed as if considering the offer with great thought. "If you go to sleep without giving Nurse a fuss, and are on your best behavior in the morning, I will concede to two tarts at breakfast."

"Each," Rose reminded, not one to be tricked.

"Two tarts each," I corrected, then leaned forward to place a kiss on her forehead. She snuggled down under her covers, and I tucked them around her before moving to Lily's bed to do the same. She giggled when I left an exaggerated kiss on each of her cheeks. The sound filled my heart to near capacity with warmth and contentment. These small memories were precious, and the more of them I made, the less space the painful ones of the past had to occupy.

Someday, they might disappear completely.

I left my girls in Nurse's capable hands and followed the corridor to my bedchamber. Soft humming echoed from inside, and I peeked into the room to see Grace standing near the window, her hand resting on her bulging stomach as she stared out at the stars. Her brown hair cascaded over her shoulders, all pins removed, and she swayed slightly to the tune of the song.

It was a sight I might never grow used to, or at the very least, would never cease to appreciate. Years spent with this woman had not dampened my love for her. No, it had only grown, just as our family continued to do.

Happiness consumed me, and though there were times when the shadows of life still found us both, we fought through them together.

I patted my coat pocket, needing another reminder that the letter resting there was real. Today, another of those shadows would vanish, and tomorrow, I would need to send word to Sabrina. She lived with her husband in Gloucestershire now, along with Mr. Barton, who they had hired directly following their marriage. Both of them would welcome the relief I had already experienced.

"Well, how many tarts did you promise this time?"

Grace's question brought a smile to my lips. I entered the room and closed the door behind me. "Only two, if you must know."

"Only," she said, grinning. "It will be three by the end of the week."

I saw no reason to argue against that probability. If I did not up the ante to three, my mother would. She doted on them as much as I did, if not more.

I sat down at the head of our bed and began removing my boots. Grace waddled over to me and gave my shoulder a gentle swat, her customary sign that I was to move over. I shifted to make room, my smile growing as she slumped onto the mattress with a sigh.

"What is that for?" she asked.

"Hmm?"

"You are smiling so wide it is concerning. Are you scheming something?"

I removed my other boot, and after tossing it aside, I wrapped my arm around her shoulder. "Not at all. Simply counting my blessings."

"Because I swatted you?" Her confusion was far too adorable.

"Because you think about me. Instead of sitting on my left, you nudged me to make room on my right, knowing I would hear you better on this side."

Her nose scrunched. "Should I confess that I did not think about it all? I simply did it."

My arm tightened around her, pulling her against me. "An even greater blessing. You know me so well, and care so much, that it does not require conscious consideration."

I doubt she realized how often she placed herself intentionally on my right side. Anytime we attended parties or balls, it was the same. Grace watched for moments where she could allay my social unease, and did so in a delicate manner that never drew attention to my hearing difficulties. I no longer hid the malady like some embarrassing secret, but I found comfort in her love and care as she made my needs a priority.

"How are you feeling?" I asked, reaching for her legs and lifting them onto my lap. She squealed in surprise but relaxed against my chest as I gently ran my fingers along her weak leg. We had found that gently massaging the muscle relieved some of her pain, especially when she was so near her confinement. The extra weight of a child often took its toll on her.

She sighed, resting her head on my shoulder. "As well as can be expected. Have you heard news of the house?"

By house, she meant the ruins left to me by my father, though it was not in that state anymore. After our marriage, Grace had insisted that we use her dowry to make repairs. If Uncle returned and disinherited me, we would at least have a place of our own that he had no claim over since I'd not used a penny of *his* money to fix the estate. Instead, I'd spent the last five years investing her dowry strategically, and it had paid off.

"Repairs have begun," I said. "It may be livable by next spring, even."

"That is splendid news. It is a relief to have something to fall back on, is it not?"

"Indeed." Though, we no longer needed it.

The first two years of our marriage had been a whirlwind in many respects. It had taken months to fully sort out the extent of Uncle's crimes. The courts had then determined restitutions, and I had immediately begun repaying those I could. Uncle's holdings were severely diminished, and with my name so tied to his, it had been difficult to find business partners willing to look past that connection. In time, my reputation was restored, but our finances were still recovering from all the loss.

I retrieved the letter from my pocket, and Grace eyed it curiously. "What do you have there?"

"News."

"The good kind or the bad kind?" she asked.

"Some of both, I suppose. It comes from New South Wales. It seems Uncle took ill about a month ago. The sickness claimed him."

Grace, the wonderful, sweet woman, had heart enough to appear genuinely sad. "Oh, Phillip."

"I will not mourn him," I said quietly. "He might have taken me in after my father's death, but it was only to serve his own purposes, not out of kindness. Perhaps I should feel guilty for feeling so relieved, but I cannot seem to do so. Even with him across the sea, I have felt the burden of his expectations, knowing one day he might return. But now...now I can truly move forward."

"You will not hear me chide you for any of it." She slid a hand around my neck and pulled me down until my lips met hers. "No one would blame you for feeling as you do. Certainly not me. Not your mother, nor our girls." She patted her swollen belly. "Not this little fellow."

"Fellow?" I asked. "You are so sure it is a boy."

She nodded once. "A boy. He wiggles around far more than Rose or Lily ever did."

"He is practicing his dancing, I think. I have it on good authority that a single dance can make a lady fall madly in love with a man. Perhaps we ought to assist him."

Grace passed me an incredulous look. "I am too inflated for dancing, Phillip."

I settled her legs back on the floor with a grin, then stood, holding out my hands to help her up. Grace rolled her eyes but placed her hands in mine. I gently tugged her to her feet.

"One moment," I said, crossing the room to the hearth. I refolded the letter and placed it next to the vase sitting on the mantle. Within the glass rested three dried roses. They had lost their vibrant red color years ago, but they served as a constant reminder of our love, just as the gold chain that wrapped around their stems served to remind me of how much my life had changed. Now, the letter was yet another physical representation that the future was mine to mold and shape.

My family was safe and secure, in every sense, at last.

I reclaimed Grace's hands and began our dance. I stepped around her while she remained in place, exaggerating my movements until she laughed, her eyes bright with the reflection of firelight.

"I think we will need to hire a dance instructor for the children rather than rely on you to teach them," she teased.

"My dancing skills worked out fine for me," I said, stopping in front of her. "They landed me the perfect partner."

"I believe your matchmaker may have had something to do with that."

"True." I wrapped my arm around her waist and pulled her as close to me as her protruding stomach would allow. "Perhaps I ought to thank her again."

"You certainly should," she whispered. "A few kisses will suffice."

A payment of gratitude I never hesitated to deliver.

MAY, 1817

# EDWARD

EDWARD STARED DOWN AT the note delivered to him by Rowe Apsley moments ago, his brows drawn in confusion. He broke the seal, curiosity tugging at him so thoroughly that he read without leaving the foyer.

*May 25th, 1817*

*Lieutenant Paget,*

*By now you are likely aware that I have left Town to return to my country estate. I am forwarding you my direction along with this letter of invitation to join me at your earliest convenience as a guest at Kenwick Castle. We still have much to discuss of your political aspirations, in addition to your quest for justice. I remain, as ever, a silent partner who wishes to see you find success.*

*As for the funds we previously discussed, I have a proposition that I believe you will find, at the very least, of great interest and intrigue. For the sake of persuading you to visit, I will not detail it here but shall await word of your arrival with as much enthusiasm as a sickly old man can muster.*

*Until then, I remain your friend and humble patron,*

*Lord Paxton.*

Edward smiled to himself. An invitation to Kenwick Castle was precisely what his dismal mood needed, and if he could trust Lord Paxton—and in all honesty, he *did* trust the man—then the journey would prove worthwhile on several fronts.

And if his visit happened to provide an opportunity to vex a certain red-headed lady? Well, then all the better.

Thanks for reading Matching Mr. Montfert! I hope you enjoyed the story and are looking forward to Edward and Annette's book as much as I am. You can order the next book in the series here: https://www.b klnk.com/B0F4MMVP4P

# My Books

## HISTORICAL ROMANCE

### The Time Pearls

In Time With the Duke
The Future with the Marquess
Courting A Modern Lady

### Apsley Family

Saving Miss Scott
Matching Mr. Montfert
Evading the Lieutenant

### Standalones

An Unfortunate Alliance

# My Books

## ROMANTIC COMEDY

**I Heart New York**

You Wish
If the Suit Fits
White Picket Defense
Saved By Mistle Tow

# Author's Notes

Under the strain of funding the war with France, in addition to the burden of importing grain after several seasons of crop failure, the Bank of England was desperate to maintain its bullion reserves. A restriction was enacted by the Bank that allowed them to forgo payments of gold and silver in exchange for banknotes. After several raids on provincial banks, the public began to lose faith in the Bank, thus threatening complete economic collapse. In 1797, The Restriction Act was passed in order to preserve the dwindling reserves by suspending specie payments for a limited time frame. It also authorized the use of notes as *de facto* currency. By limiting the time frame for restriction, faith in the banking system was restored and banknotes became a common way to exchange larger sums for payments.

However, the increased circulation of banknotes also paved the way for increased forgeries. It became a huge problem in England, especially in 1816/1817, where records show a large number of convictions for banknote fraud. Records also indicate that many of these forgeries were very credible and were difficult to distinguish from the real thing. The Bank of England did attempt to implement ways to prevent the rising fraud by changing the mark on the engravings every month, which is why Mr. Perry requests new engravings in this story—in an attempt to keep up with the Bank and their constant changes.

The courts took any accusation very seriously, and the punishment for being found in possession of or handling one was the same for producing a false note. Both could be sentenced to hanging or transportation, especially as the system operated under a *guilty until proven innocent* clause.

Mr. Perry was sent to Newgate to await trial. In reality, he would have been there for far longer than a few days, but in an effort to preserve the pacing of this book (and keep him from changing his will, which he would have found difficult to do after transportation), I gave him a speedy trial. Common convictions were either hanging or transportation to New South Wales for seven years. I chose the latter since he was a man of wealth and some influence and it fit the narrative far better in this instance, but I suspect given the length of his criminal activity and the extent, he would have stood a real chance of facing death. The calligrapher, who's fate I did not mention, likely would have been hanged to prevent him from using his skills in such a way again.

Despite the implemented time frame, the Restriction Act was renewed annually until May of 1821, at which time specie payments were restored in full.

I'm not an expert on any of this, but I tried to write this story with as much accuracy as I could while also taking a few liberties.

# Acknowledgments

This was one of the fastest books I've ever written, and I have several people I wish to thank for helping me get it into shape so quickly.

First, I'd like to thank my sweet mother for being so willing to answer my questions at the start of this book. I wanted to make sure I made Phillip as authentic as possible with his hearing difficulties. My mother has suffered from partial deafness since birth, and her insight was vital in getting Phillip's character right. I hope I did him justice, Mom!

A big thank you to my critique partners, Justena and Miranda, for being so willing to give me feedback. An especially big thank you to Justena for reading through this thing a second time just to ease my anxiety. You are a gem, and I am so grateful to have such an amazing friend!

I'd like to thank my beta readers—Leigh Walker, Beba Andric, and Molly Stratford—for helping me tweak this into something a little less messy. And a thank you to Janice Green for catching my mistake on page one and saving me from total embarrassment.

I'd also like to thank my family for being so patient with me as I whipped this book out. It required so much of my time to write within six weeks, and they were such troopers through it all. And I'd like to thank my Heavenly Father for helping me through the doubt and struggles. I questioned myself so much throughout this process, and I'm so grateful to have had the inspiration to put this story together.

Lastly, thank you to all my readers, whether new or old. Your support and encouragement mean the world to me.

# About the Author

Brooke Losee lives with her husband and three children in central Utah where she enjoys fishing, gardening, and gathering as many rocks as her pockets can hold. Brooke obtained a BS in Geology from Southern Utah University but has always had a passion for all things books.

Brooke began her journey to authorhood in 2020 with the notion of publishing one novel. That book turned into a series of seven, and the Pandora's box of ideas was unleashed. Her works range from fantasy to historical, all featuring a sweet and clean romance.

To follow her writing journey and keep informed about upcoming stories visit http://www.brookejlosee.com.

www.ingramcontent.com/pod-product-compliance
Lightning Source LLC
Chambersburg PA
CBHW061807190726
48289CB00007B/2109